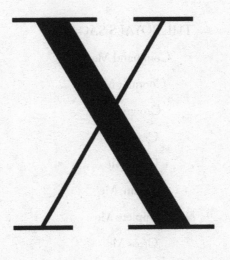

ALSO BY GENEVA LEE

THE RIVALS SAGA

Blacklist

Backlash

Bombshell

THE ROYALS SAGA

Command Me

Conquer Me

Crown Me

Crave Me

Covet Me

Capture Me

Complete Me

Cross Me

Claim Me

Consume Me

Breathe Me

Break Me

Find more at:

GenevaLee.com

THE ROYALS SAGA

X

GENEVA LEE

ESTATE

ESTATE
PUBLISHING • ENTERTAINMENT

www.GenevaLee.com
First published, 2021.
Cover design © Date Book Designs.
Image © Volodymyr/Adobe Stock.

In memory of Norman Lee,
Who filled my childhood with art and creativity and stories
of far-off places and books. You didn't just give me my
name, you gave me the world.

CHAPTER ONE

The club is for graduates of Oxford and Cambridge. As I am neither, I shouldn't be here. My education came with bloodstains and fatigues. Still, I find myself at another insufferable party, pretending that I have anything left in common with these people. It's insulting how doors open for money or titles. I have both.

I have titles—as in multiple titles.

I have a name that will open any door in this country.

I don't want any of it, and it is impossible to forget that here, among the crowded sycophants eager to play at being my friend.

"Hiding?" Jonathan asks, slipping onto the terrace next to me. He pulls out a pack of clove cigarettes and offers me one.

I shake my head. "No on both counts."

"In that case, the party is in there, mate. I know you're a little rusty on the etiquette." He flicks open a lighter and lights his smoke.

Jonathan Thompson's presence is as cloying as the smell now drifting toward me. I can't help but remind him that I'm not a spoiled university brat intent on networking. "Why are you graduating now? You're old as shit."

Jonathan was my sister's friend before the accident. Younger than me, but old enough that he should have left university behind by now.

"I took two gap years after the accident," he says breezily, taking a drag from his cigarette.

"How nice for you," I say tightly. Without thinking, I reach for the pack of smokes and take one. I need to do something destructive that doesn't involve Jonathan's face.

I hate the casual air he has about the accident that took my sister from our world. But he wasn't in the car that night. He'd stayed at the club instead. He's just another person who mourns her.

He isn't responsible for what happened to her—I am.

"I think of her every day," Jonathan says in a quiet voice.

I study him and see what others don't—the bravado and the charm are a mask. He might truly mean what he says about thinking of Sarah. He might be fucked up over what happened. I don't care.

Caring costs too much, and its price can't be paid with money.

"Brimstone tonight?" he asks.

I nod. I don't have anything better to do than find a warm place for my cock, and I've become a fixture at the club. The noise, the packed cluster of bodies, the flames—

it's as close to hell as I can find in London, and hell is where I belong.

"Don't invite Pepper," I say. The blonde has been like a shadow since I returned home and just as difficult to lose.

"I never do." He shrugs like it's a lost cause. Reaching over, he lights my cigarette. I'd forgotten I took one. "There. I better get back."

I turn and watch him go, wondering if this is the rest of my life. It's a fitting punishment to be dragged to another bar and another club to be photographed and fawned over. I may have been sent from London, but I've never really escaped.

Seven years ago, I made a mistake. I've been paying for it for the last six. Now everyone wants to pretend I've atoned, that we can go back to our previously assigned lives.

I need a distraction.

But while my father has been detached enough to not care where I go at night, I somehow know there is one place that will catch his attention.

There is a door in London that leads to the only club I am interested in visiting.

It would open for me now. But I was dragged away from there with blood on my hands, and I've chosen to leave that door closed.

I don't know how much longer I'll be able to ignore how the darkness there calls me.

It would take a miracle to keep me away.

A woman darts into the hall, her eyes behind her like

she's attempting to escape. When no one follows, she sinks against the wall and pulls at her black dress. It's too tight for her, which is exactly how clothing should be on a woman like this. The fabric puckers over her breasts, and I want to set them free—take them in my mouth.

I can almost hear how she'll moan.

She startles, finally realizing I'm here. Her hand flies to that perfect chest, and she gasps—the most perfect little sound in the world, and I haven't even touched her. Yet. I want to make her do it again. I want to see what other sounds I can draw from her.

The silence between us stretches as she stares at me fixedly, no doubt trying to grasp who she'd discovered. Then her eyebrows knit together in concentration.

"I don't think you're supposed to smoke here," she says loftily—a pretense to appear in control of the situation. She seems like the type who likes to play it safe. Her body, which keeps angling towards me as though intent on betraying her, appears to have other ideas. I resist the urge to curl my finger and beckon her closer.

I don't need to see if she'll come. I know she will.

"My apologies." I try to bite back a smirk and fail. There are other things I'm not supposed to do here, and I find myself considering doing them all to her. "Are you going to report me for conduct unbecoming?"

I step back onto the terrace to appease her and hope she'll follow.

She's flustered by the gesture, her lashes fluttering. "I wouldn't want you to get into trouble."

"We wouldn't want that." Wicked thoughts pour

through me and carve a smile across my face. I want to get her into trouble.

Her cheeks flush pink like she knows what I'm thinking—or maybe she's thinking the same. Except that this girl doesn't know what to think. I can tell from how she keeps looking me over. She'd like me to take her to bed. I already know that. But I'm not interested in sex. I want to fuck her. I want to own her. I want to do things to her that will turn more of her soft white skin red.

Her teeth sink into her lower lip, and I glimpse what her face will look like while she's riding my cock. I arch an eyebrow. It's half invitation and half question.

Does she know what her body is asking for?

"I think that I should warn you of the dangers of smoking," she says quickly.

I've gotten to her. Good. It will make this more interesting.

"Poppet, you would not be the first." I flick the cigarette into the rubbish bin without looking at it. I want to tell her that I don't smoke. I want to reassure her almost as much as I want to touch her. There's no reason I should care what she thinks of me. So why do I?

"Have we met before?"

It's the last thing I expect her to say, and then I realize what's caught my attention about her. This woman didn't seek me out. She isn't lingering to try her hand at scoring a prince. She has no idea who I am.

I'm just a man in a room that she can't seem to walk away from, and suddenly, I don't want her to walk away.

"I think I would remember you. It's more likely that

my reputation has preceded me," I say, falling back on charm, but the truth of the moment burns through me. She's drawn to me. Whatever she's glimpsed is what's keeping her here, not my family or my title.

No one sees past those things. Even I see it in the mirror each morning.

"A ladies' man then?" she asks, looking neither surprised nor excited by that prospect.

"Something like that," I say, wondering what she wants me to be. "What's an American girl doing in this snobby old place?"

Her answering smile is forced. I've struck a nerve. "I'm a British citizen, actually. Although I grew up in the States. Mom's American. She met my dad when he was studying at Berkeley."

Is that why she doesn't know who you are?

"And a California girl, too. I can't imagine why you'd trade the beach for rainy old London."

"I like the fog." Her voice is soft, and my head turns on the sound, instinctively straining to catch every word.

I want to ask her if she likes the dark? But I already know the answer. She's full of light. There's no place for her in my world.

She holds out her hand, and I stare at it for a moment. "I'm Clara Bishop, by the way."

"It's nice to meet you, Clara Bishop." I take it and lift it to my lips, wanting to taste her—just once. But the moment my mouth touches her skin, I feel it. It's electric, a lightning bolt to my groin that splinters up and finds purchase in my chest.

But it doesn't satisfy me. My eyes land on her lips, wondering if that would, at the same moment that a familiar, and unwelcome, blonde comes around the corner.

Clara pulls her hand away, but I don't think. Catching her arm, I yank her to me. I'm pleased with how her body melts into mine as I angle my face to hers. I need to kiss her. My whole being tells me that this woman belongs in my arms, and I coil them possessively around her waist. There's a moment of hesitation before she submits, her mouth parting to my tongue. I flick it across her teeth, and she welcomes me deeper. This isn't a dance. It's not a game. It's real.

Her legs buckle, and I catch her, keeping her upright —keeping her with me.

It's where she belongs. Just like my hand belongs on the small of her back. The shift that nearly brought her to her knees realigns my world for one moment, and I see something when I look at her—a feeling I lost a long time ago.

It's a curious mix of hope and desire, something like a future: purpose.

I release her so suddenly she stumbles, and I steady her.

The feeling pounds through me. It claws at my skin and burns in my veins. I want to kiss her again. I want to carry her away.

I want it so much that I don't.

She searched my face, her own a question I can't answer. "Why?"

"My motives are less than chivalrous," I say, taking

my hand from her and instantly missing the contact. "That woman is a particularly horrible mistake of mine."

"You kissed me to avoid your ex-girlfriend?"

"I would not call her my ex, but my apologies all the same." *Keep it civil*, I command myself. Pepper's appearance was an excuse to do what I already wanted, but even I couldn't understand it.

I enjoy control. I demand it—of myself, of others. I just lost it entirely.

Her wide eyes are watching me now, and they are the most delicate shade of gray—the color of heavy morning fog. I think I could get lost in her eyes and be happy. I take a step toward her, then think better of it and move toward the terrace.

"Congratulations on your matriculation."

"Did you graduate as well?" she asks softly.

She really has no idea who I am, and I laugh before I can cover my mouth with my hand. This puzzle of a woman with her oddly affecting attitude wants to know who I am. "I took a rather different career path. Are we playing twenty questions?"

"Will you tell me who you are?" Clara asks.

I wink, playing the role I've been dealt. "I think the point, poppet, is to figure that out."

"You took a different career path? But you're here—" she gestures around us "—at a prestigious club, so you're either a well-dressed waiter, or you come from money?" Her eyes narrow. I've annoyed her, and it makes me want to do it again. I want to see how she'll respond.

"That wasn't a yes or no question."

"If you don't want to play..." She looks behind her at the party she abandoned, and I don't want her to go back to those people.

"I merely want to play by the rules, unless you'd rather I ask the questions," I suggest.

Her throat slides, and I imagine all the small nuances of her body. If this is how she reacts to a conversation...

Fuck.

"Do you come from money?" she asks.

"You could say that." She's going to play.

"Yes or no."

"Yes," I say, leaning to catch a lock of her hair. It's as soft as her lips, and it has my cock thinking about how delicate other parts of her must be. "Is it my turn yet?"

"I haven't asked all twenty questions," she whispers.

"Don't spend them all at once." I tuck the hair behind her ear. "It's best to leave some anticipation."

"You already know who I am."

"But there are lots of things I'd like to know about you." I resist the urge to kiss her neck barely. Instead, my words whisper across her skin, and I see her shiver. "And I'm dying to hear you say yes."

"What if the answer is no?"

"Trust me, it isn't." I can't keep myself from tasting her again, and I brush a kiss across her jaw.

She pushes at her dress, but it does nothing to hide the tight pop of her nipples against the fabric or the flush lingering on her cheeks.

"Last question," I say, "and then let's see if you can guess."

She hesitates, and I live in a lifetime in that moment, wondering if she'll figure it out.

"Who are you?" she asks.

I shake my head and mouth yes or no, but inside me, my heart rockets into my throat. It was a cheat—a last-ditch effort to find out.

And somehow, it was the right question. I'm not certain I know the answer to it.

"I should be getting back," she says.

I rake my eyes over her, wondering briefly if I could be whoever she hopes I am. "I hope to see you again, Clara Bishop."

I don't wait for her to leave. Turning to the balcony, I wonder what the fuck just happened. I want to ask her. I want to know what she felt. When I look behind me, she's gone. Her scent, vanilla and rose, hangs in the air like her final question—equally intangible—but it's her kiss that lingers.

And I want more.

CHAPTER TWO

Mud clings to my limbs as I drag my body through grime and blood. The gnarled wreckage of a helicopter smokes in the distance. I need to reach my friends, and then I see her lying in the muck. Struggling towards her, there's a blinding flash of light.

Headlights.

I'm on a street in London. Pain sears through my side and I look down to discover half of me is missing; a rib is visible. I choke against bile as my eyes spot her again, her body twisted on the concrete. I don't feel anything as I crawl toward her and gather her body in my arms, trying to find a pulse. Someone yells, but I can only stare at her. It's not my sister. It's someone else.

It's her.

A hand grabs my shoulder, and I jolt up, swinging defensively. My fist whizzes past a worried face, clipping his glasses.

"Alex, calm down." Edward jumps back before I can take another shot at him.

I blink, damask wall coverings swim into view, erasing battlefields and bloody pavement, and I relax into the chair. Shoving a hand through my hair, I check my watch. Six in the morning. Brilliant.

"You okay?" Edward asks carefully. He's been walking on eggshells since I arrived in London. I can't blame him. We're practically strangers. When I left, he was a kid. Now he's an adult with problems of his own.

"Fine," I bark, my throat dry.

"You were..." he hesitates as if weighing what to say.

"Screaming," I finish for him. In my first few months in Afghanistan, I'd gotten shit for my nightmares from those bunked around me. After that, they'd seen enough horrors that I wasn't the only one calling out in the night. No one talked shit anymore. Then again, no one talked about it at all. "It's nothing. Bad dream."

"You're still sleeping out here?" My brother takes a seat across from mine. He's still in silk, striped pajamas, and his hair is tangled from sleep, but he doesn't act tired.

"Bed's too comfortable." A bed is for someone soft and welcoming. Someone like her: the girl I kissed. Clara. I think of her lips and almost need to adjust myself. Then, the dream returns to me, and I remember that it was her in the street.

But why?

"Too comfortable?" Edward asks, taking me from my thoughts of Clara. He raises an eyebrow, but he doesn't press me to talk about it. He can connect the dots—draw a line from where I've been and what I'm telling him now. It's a Royal family tradition to not pry. If something can be left unsaid—if a door can be closed to an unsavory truth—it's best not to speak or question or reopen that door. There's a lot that goes unsaid behind these walls, and I'm not the only one not talking.

"Why are you here anyway?" I ask him.

"You were screaming," he reminds me, his mouth quirking up like this is obvious. His bedroom is down the corridor.

"Not here." I gesture to the parlor that's become my unofficial bedroom. "Buckingham."

"Dear old dad wanted me here before I took up residence elsewhere." His words carry the load of a heavier burden. "When I finished at St. Andrews, he insisted I come straight home and learn my bit."

"Which is?" I ask. Currently, my father is avoiding me with such devotion, I assume he honed the ability purposefully during my time at the front. We've barely spoken more than five times in the few months I've been home. There has been no mention of my duties other than a revolving schedule of sodding appearances I am expected to make. He doesn't ask me about the dreams or why I sleep in a chair at night or anything. It suits me fine given that I hate the man and I hate being his heir.

"Behave. Smile" Edward forces one like he's offering me a sample.

"Pretend," I add for him.

"Pretend?" he repeats with practiced confusion.

I've been waiting for him to tell me, but it seems

obvious he won't. He's spent a few weekends at home while he was finishing his final term. There'd been a trip to the country with *friends*. I've spent enough time with my little brother to know that he's keeping a secret.

"I know," I say with meaning.

"I'm not sure—" he starts.

"Look, I get it. If you don't want to tell me, I understand. You...you barely know me, but I see you with him." I don't want Edward to think he has to hide who he is from me like he does our father.

"Him?" He's still playing dumb, clinging to the lie as my mind clings to the dream.

"David." I decide that he can avoid uncomfortable topics as is the family way, but I can't. Secrets will bury us all alive if we let them.

"No one knows," he says quietly. He sinks into his chair like he's deflating.

"I assume David does."

"He's aware," Edward says dryly.

"And he's also in the closet?"

Edward's eyes flash, and I realize I've misstepped. "Sorry. Is that not PC?"

"I guess it is. I just never really think about it," he admits, "and I suppose he is, and he isn't."

"What the hell does that mean?"

"I think he'd be fine with being open about it if..."

"If you were." There it is—the double-edged sword of loving a Royal. I'd seen glimpses of it as a child before my mother died. The woman I knew and loved transformed into someone else when the camera came out. She fell silent. She took his arm. She became a different woman—his wife. His queen.

But never his equal.

It isn't done. Edward knows it. I know it.

Why the fuck would he drag someone into this life—even secretly?

"Do you love him?" I ask, wondering how far he's let it go.

"Yes," he murmurs.

"Shit."

"I guess I have your blessing." His tone remains flat, colored by hopelessness.

"Love complicates things." Especially for us.

"I think being gay is complicated enough," Edward says. "Why not add love into the mix?"

"Does he know? Father?"

Edward laughs. It's completely joyless. It rings through him as hollow as a bell. "Of course. Why do you think I'm under his roof? Wonder where he'll send me to fix me."

"Don't be afraid of him."

"I'm not. I just...not all of us got to leave."

I clench my jaw holding back an angry retort. He doesn't know why I was sent away. He's no idea how real that danger truly is, and if I tell him, he'll never have the courage to be true to himself. Instead, I stick to the facts. "War isn't a vacation."

"I'm sorry. That was a terrible thing to say." He hangs his head a little, but I wave it off.

"I don't think either of us had a grand time for the last

seven years. Although, you did graduate university, which makes you far grander than me," I remind him.

"Come off it. You're a war hero," he says. "The party tonight is for both of us."

It isn't, but I don't correct him. I'm being trotted out like a prize stallion for his graduation party, not as a guest of honor. My father's only intention is to put me out to stud as soon as I've made a suitable match—a girl he will pick out for me, no doubt—and only after the wedding. Propriety must be considered. Then he'll outlive me and hand the throne to my child. He's stubborn enough to do it and witless enough to not realize that I don't want the crown. I won't marry. I won't further the bloodline.

"You've had your own education," Edward says kindly, mistaking my silence for something else.

"Yes, I suppose my degree is in blood and suffering. I learned how the world works on a battlefield. Fear drives us. It makes men seek power. It makes men do terrible things. It controls all of us."

"They didn't teach us that at St. Andrews."

"Don't worry, I'll keep it out of my toast this evening," I promise him.

"I don't know," he says thoughtfully. "I wouldn't mind seeing his face if you let that slip."

I can't help but smirk. "Consider it a graduation present."

. . .

"WHOSE GRADUATION IS THIS?" My father storms into the breakfast room and drops a stack of magazines. A tabloid nearly knocks over a teapot.

"Edward's, I thought." I don't bother to look at the cover. He wants me to, which is enough of a reason not to do it.

"This is not at one of your disco clubs," he roars.

I bite back a smile at the thought of an actual disco club in London. "You're being cryptic."

His eyes narrow, and it's like staring into my own. It's the only feature we share: blue eyes. Although, his have gotten watery and mine brighter. It's ironic given that I've never seen the man cry.

"I've overlooked your late-night debauchery because it's been kept to appropriate venues. Everyone expects you to be a bit pent-up. No one thinks anything of those stories," he says in a sharp voice. "But that is the bloody Oxford-Cambridge Club. Who is this woman?"

My eyes shift to the paper automatically, no longer interested in our skirmish, and land on her. There are two pictures. The first is one of her exiting a flat, utterly unaware that she's been photographed. She's in shorts and trainers, and she's more beautiful than I remember— more beautiful than she is in the dreams she haunts. The other shot makes my balls ache. Someone snapped a photo of our kiss. I have a good idea who, and I'll be sure to make Pepper pay. For now, I'm lost to the memory captured and smeared across a gossip rag. Her body pressed to mine. How her lips parted so eagerly despite her surprise. She'd folded into the kiss, submitting so naturally that I'd nearly picked her up and carried her off like a prize.

Why hadn't I?

"Who is she?"

I barely process the question, still reliving the moment. "Clara Bishop."

I've tried not to think of that name. Knowing it makes it hard to stay away. I've considered seeking her out, but something about her is dangerous. I can feel it.

"I know who she is," he barks, breaking through my thoughts and bringing back to our confrontation. "Everyone knows who she is, but what is she to you?"

"What?" I can't follow what he's asking me. Because my father, who is neither perceptive nor empathetic, is not reading my mind. He doesn't know that I'm wondering why even this picture has this effect on me.

"Is it her graduation? Is she your lover? How did you meet?" He bombards me with so many questions I feel as though I'm at a press conference.

"She's a girl I met." I try to sound casual, but I feel anything but. Clara is not just a girl I met. She's a mystery. She's the star of my nightmares. She's featuring in my waking fantasies. I don't know her at all. I tell him so.

"You can't go around kissing girls at exclusive clubs, especially Americans. The press assumes you're in love with her."

"Love?" I repeat. "They have a lot to learn about me. It was Jonathan's graduation—a party you made me attend."

He ignores me. "What kind of message do you think this sends? People are speculating if it's serious."

"It's not," I say flatly. I walked away from her. I left her behind. I'd forced myself to leave her alone—to not seek her out. It's more difficult to do with my father dragging her into the mix.

"There are reporters camped out at her flat. I hope you made things very clear for her and that she's not the attention-seeking..." he trailed away, staring at me as I abandoned my breakfast and headed toward the quarters I used primarily as a closet. "Where are you going?"

"I won't let them bother her. They have no business disturbing her privacy."

"And you're going to do what?" he demands. "Go tell them that? You've been away too long. I don't have time to teach you your place, but allow me a moment to refresh your memory. The press doesn't care what we say. They care what sells papers. Drawing attention to her will only sell more papers."

"I should apologize," I begin.

"You should have kept your cock in your pants in the first place. There's a party starting in a few hours. You aren't going anywhere," he informs me. "And after, you won't seek her out. She's an unsuitable match in every way."

"Not this again," I grumble.

"Who you are seen with matters and an American? You won't see her again," he says with the air of someone rarely told no.

It's why I say it now.

"No." I continue past him toward my room and the waiting tuxedo. "Maybe I'll fall in love with her instead."

I won't, but seeing the look on his face makes me almost consider it.

GARDEN PARTIES CAUSE me to miss the war where no one wore ridiculous hats or conversed in subtle barbs. There's less courtesy among Edward's pack of friends than in a mess hall, and the civility here is far less palatable.

And then there's my brother playing his role: charming, debonair, studiously ignoring his boyfriend who's sitting at a table alone while Edward flirts with a redhead.

If this is what my future holds—tea parties and false flattery—I wish I'd never come back. At least it would be easier to have never gone. I would be numb to this life now, conditioned to accept this as normal. But I don't fit in here.

I don't want to fit.

I'm about to quietly excuse myself from the festivities when Pepper Lockwood catches me. She's smart enough to have brought her mother, so I won't tell her off for what she did to Clara. That's the limit of her intelligence, as far as I can tell, because it was stupid for her to piss me off. I know she took the photo, and I know she sold it. What I can't fathom is why.

The Lockwoods blend into the scene well, their flowery blue dresses another floral addition to the landscape of partygoers. It's amusing to see Pepper like this—

her make-up toned down, along with her sex appeal. At the clubs, she prefers to wriggle on a hook like a piece of meat, waiting to catch something. I've never bit. Here, the intent is different. Both Lockwood women are on the hunt for husbands by the look of it.

"Alexander," Mrs. Lockwood's voice is coated with sugar as she takes my arm. "I can't believe how much you've changed. You're a man now."

Thank god, she was here to inform me.

"But you haven't aged a day," I say. It's not polite flattery. Thanks to modern plastic surgery, she hasn't aged a day. "You could pass for sisters."

Pepper looks less flattered by this proclamation. It's all the more enjoyable because it's true.

"Still a lady's man." Mrs. Lockwood flashes a mouthful of brilliant white teeth. "Unless the rumors are true..."

"Most rumors about me are true." It's easier to be what they want me to be. No one's interested in anything else.

"But you're not seeing an American, surely!" Her hand flutters to her chest like this caused her actual pain.

I wish I was seeing that American right now, but since Pepper got me into this mess, I don't dare bait her mother. Whatever I say could easily wind up as tomorrow's headline.

"No," I scoff, gently pulling my arm free and shoving my hands into my pockets before either can try to hook me again. "Of course not. It was a prank someone played on me."

"Well, it's not funny at all," she says seriously.

I level my gaze at Pepper. "No, it isn't."

"You'll have to be more careful of who you kiss," she says innocently.

"I think I'll be more careful of my friends," I tell her. Forcing a smile for Mrs. Lockwood, I cock my head toward the shrubbery. "You must excuse me. I have to find my brother."

What I want to find is a moment alone, but it's not in the cards. Some press secretary or attaché grabs me and hauls me toward the tent where my father and brother wait. Edward's smile is thin-lipped. I glance over to the table and see David's is nonexistent.

My father doesn't even bother feigning happiness that we're here. That doesn't stop him from taking a Champagne flute and lifting it.

"Thank you for coming today to celebrate my sons. No father could not be prouder of them." His voice booms over the crowd, which falls into rapt silence.

I don't miss what he actually said. Judging from the way Edward flinches, he didn't either, but we both hide it well.

"Edward has continued our long relationship with my university and graduated a year early," he continues.

"Nerd," I whisper to him.

"Wanker," he says under his breath.

Father frowns but quickly goes on. "And Alexander has served his country and the world in the fight against terrorism. He's seen first hand the sacrifice made by our men and women in uniform—two very different educations, but important nonetheless in reminding us all of our duties and responsibilities. I am certain both my sons understand the important roles they play in the world now. So please join me in raising your glass to them."

It takes effort to lift mine. It feels as heavy as the yoke he's hung around my shoulders with his poison-laced speech. I don't drink. Instead, I wait my turn.

"I warned Edward that I would speak today," I begin when the crowd quiets. "His concern over what I might say is warranted given that I missed the last seven years of his life and thus might recall some more embarrassing moments. That's not what I think of when I look at my brother, though. Mostly, I'm surprised—surprised to find a man where I left a boy. A graduate where I left a student. The only thing that hasn't changed is that he is still my brother, so it's good that's the most important thing of all. Without family, we're nothing. Please raise a glass to my brother, who is my better in every way—save eyesight."

Edward's smile lights his face. He pushes his glasses up as if to emphasize the truth of this final statement. Rather than taking a drink, he turns to hug me. It's an odd sensation. We aren't usually the type of family that embraces. But I find that I don't hate it as much as I might have expected.

"Thank you," he whispers.

"I couldn't let him get the last word in," I admit, earning me a laugh.

A crowd gathers around us for their turns at offering well wishes. When I finally manage to sneak away, my father catches me almost immediately.

"I'd like to introduce you to someone. Her daughter—"

"Not now," I cut him off. "I've had as much as I can take for today."

"I thought after that speech there was hope. You played the situation well, but you haven't learned anything," he says with disgust, staring at me like I am an unwanted weed.

"I thought I learned about sacrifice," I say, calling him on his bullshit. "Giving up seven years of my life wasn't enough? Send me back."

"Why? You don't even see the truth," he hisses. "You didn't go there as a sacrifice. Other men sacrifice themselves for King and country."

"And why did I go?" I spit back.

"Punishment," he says coldly.

I don't ask him for what. That list is too long. Turning, I stride away, uninterested in more of his recrimination and unwilling to flatter one more simpering mother. When I reach the hedge, I loosen my bowtie and unbutton my collar. But I still can't breathe.

I need away from this—away from these fake people playing their given roles. I need someone real—and there she is again, plucking at my subconscious. Clara is real. I'd felt her. I'd held her. I want to tell myself no. I want to stay away, if only because I have no desire to drag her into the battle between my father and me. Because if he finds out, I've seen her, he won't let it rest.

But I belong to no man. No country. Not yet. I can only answer to myself, and somewhere in London, I've left Clara Bishop to hide out in her flat while I sipped champagne at a garden party.

I can think of a number of ways to make it up to her, and she's going to enjoy every minute.

"Fuck." It's like I have no choice. Pulling out my mobile, I call Norris and issue one command. "Find her."

"Are you certain?" He doesn't ask me who I'm referring to because he doesn't have to. He's seen the papers. He expected this call.

"Yes," I say for once being completely honest. "Find her. I need to see her."

I've never been more certain of anything.

CHAPTER THREE

The club's music filters into the private room, and I know she's finally here. When had I sent Norris to collect her? An hour ago? A lifetime ago? All I know is that it feels as though an eternity has passed, and now she's arrived. I turn from the orgiastic dancing below to find Clara standing behind me. A smile creeps over my face as I take in her jeans and t-shirt. I've caught her off guard. This isn't a girl who bothers with bars and clubs. She was home, but doing what? I want to ask her. I want to know everything about her. All I know now is that she's just as pretty like this as she was in that tight, black dress. She didn't change to impress me, and for some reason, warmth spreads through my chest at the thought. Before I can process what that means, her eyes narrow, and her chin lifts. She's mistaken my grin, assuming that I'm mocking her appearance.

What she doesn't know is that it only makes me want her more.

She saunters toward me like a queen and stumbles. My arms shoot out to catch her, but she corrects herself before I do.

"I'm fine," she says, stepping to the side like it will be that easy to get rid of me. "Should I curtsy or something?"

"Please don't." I can't help grinning. She looks so defiant that my palm itches as I imagine putting her over my knee. I almost hope I can't tame her. Almost.

"I wouldn't want to offend you, Your Highness," she tacks on the title like a jab, but it doesn't strike.

I want this moment to last. It's foreplay. I know she feels it as well: this tension building between us. There's only one outlet for it. As eager as I am to claim her, I want to enjoy this. "Can I get you something to drink?"

"Yes." But she frowns as though surprised by her own answer.

"What is your poison, Miss Bishop?" I ask her slowly. I want to tell her she's mine. That the only thing I want to taste in this room is her. I want her on my lips. On my tongue. No poison is sweeter than a beautiful woman.

"I just graduated university, so I'm not picky," she says, her voice slightly strained.

"Used to the old plonk then?" I ask, flashing her a smile. "Sadly, Brimstone tends toward—"

"Real booze?" she says with a snort of laughter.

"Exactly."

"Then I'll take what you give me."

I suck in a breath, wanting that to be true. I've imagined exactly what I would give her for days. I've pictured her on her knees with those wide eyes staring up at me, her mouth full of my cock. I've wondered what shade of red that pretty skin will turn under my palm. I have so much to give her, but I'll start with a drink.

Clara peers down at the club, riveted to the scene. Brimstone has that effect on people. The club, decorated to look like the pit of hell, is hot enough to be the real thing. The owner is an old friend if a man like him can be called that. He doesn't seem to mind me making use of the upper room. Another night I might have found a girl downstairs and invited her up. No one here holds a candle to Clara.

"Can they see us?" she asks as I hand her a Scotch.

I shake my head. "It's like those mirrors on police procedurals. To them, it reflects back the club."

She takes a long sip, and my attention focuses on her lips. I watch her throat glide as she swallows. Her long neck is elegant, and she carries herself with artless ease. Clara Bishop is the definition of a good girl. I can already see that. It makes me want to play with her. I want to free her from herself and see what she's like when she'd come undone.

"You must come here often," she says.

"I've been told to go to hell a number of times," I say tightly. "I decided to take the advice."

"Ahhh," she says, a nervous giggle slipping from her. "Brimstone."

"My natural habitat."

"I doubt that." Her words soothe me, and her hands begin to reach as though she wants to touch me. The

desire in the movement is different from the energy crackling between us. I don't have a name for it. It's nothing
I've felt before, but it radiates off her like sunlight on a
warm day.

"I owe you an apology," I say, moving next to her and
brushing my shoulder against hers. Her response is what I
hope. Her lips part, her nipples harden under her shirt
until they poke against the thin cotton shirt. She's as
attuned to my body as I am to hers.

"No harm done," she says, adding, "Your Highness."

I can't help laughing at her stubborn adherence to
decorum. We're past the point of her acting like I'm above
her. Although I'm increasingly interested in having her
under me. "Alexander, please. Norris informed me that
no less than *two dozen* members of the press are camped
in front of your flat."

"Alexander," she says, my name tripping over her
tongue like it's new vocabulary. "Once they see how
boring my life is, they'll go away."

"They'll make your life hell until then." I need to
remember that I'm no good for her. This interest I feel
shouldn't go farther than this room, not while we have the
media's attention. I know all too well how relentless they
could be when pursuing a story. I won't do that to her.

"Is that why you went to Iraq?" Her eyes flash like the
question escaped without her permission.

I want to tell her it was Iraq and Afghanistan. I want
to tell her why I went. I want to share the blood and pain
and hatred I'd felt. But I don't do any of those things.

"Back to our game? I suppose I advised you to save a few." There's a sparkle in her eyes. I don't understand, but I like it. I like it too much.

"Yes," I answer her. It's simpler than the truth. "Yes, it was."

"I'm sorry. That's none of my business. It's only..."

"Only?" I press.

"I wish you hadn't gone," she murmurs, and a chain that weighs my heart loosens at her words.

I can't look at her. I don't know what to say. This woman who doesn't know me—this woman I don't know—makes me wish I'd never left, too. There's a lost life in her words. One I might have had if I hadn't been sent away. I'd have gone off to university. Oxford, perhaps? I'd meet her in a class. I'd take her to a proper bed and fuck her senseless, and then maybe breakfast. Maybe more.

It's the life I didn't have. The life I will never have.

"I can handle it. It's very kind of you to be concerned," she says when I don't speak. Turning, she puts her glass down like she's decided to go.

"Clara," I say her name automatically before she can walk from this room and out of my life.

"Yes." She swallows, and there's that sparkle in her eyes from before. It glints like a beacon to me.

"As much as it pains me to say this—and believe me, it pains me—for once, those leeches did me a favor. I tried to find you at the party, but no one knew who you were." I need her to know that she's different, even if I don't understand why or how. "I've thought about you a lot."

She stares at me, her breath catching, and it's all I can do not to kiss her.

"Since last weekend?" She's surprised, but I don't understand why. Can't she feel how much I want her? Hadn't she felt the electricity in that kiss? It had lingered long after the party ended like a beacon calling me back to her.

"Is that so hard to believe?" I move closer until I feel the heat of her skin. She smells like rose petals and promises I won't keep.

I circle her trying to decide how far I can take this—how long I can get away with making her mine. Maybe we can see each other again if we're careful. Maybe this relationship isn't doomed to me talking her out of her knickers here and fucking her against the wall. I smile as I imagine how she'll moan. Pausing behind her, I lean in so that my lips brush her earlobe. "If you knew what was good for you, you would run."

"Am I in danger?" I hear the effort it takes her to ask the question.

"People around me tend to get hurt," I whisper. I can see the freckles that dust her shoulders and start up the back of her neck.

"Will you hurt me?"

I get the strangest feeling she wants me to say yes. The darker fantasies I've allowed myself to imagine flash like a slideshow. Riding crops and ropes. Metal and creamy skin. Slender wrists bound.

"You've been reading the tabloids," I force myself to

say, knowing that whatever this attraction is between us, I'm alone in those dark desires. "Don't believe everything you read, Clara. I have never done anything to a woman that she hasn't asked for...*begged* for."

She spins around, words on her lip, but they fall away. I've dazzled her, but what she doesn't know is that she has the same effect on me. All I can think of is her lips. I want to brush my hand down her cheek. I want to slip my hand around her waist.

She takes a deep breath. "Do you like that? Do you like women to beg?"

I laugh to disguise the growl threatening to rumble from me as she says *beg*. Fuck, I want her to beg. "I enjoy making women ask for more. I enjoy making them whimper and cry out and call my name, and I'd very much enjoy making you beg."

"I'm not really the begging type," she says weakly.

"You could be," I say. "I can see it in your eyes: the desire to be commanded and taken. You'll enjoy it when I fuck you."

"*Yes, please.*" Her voice is so quiet I wonder if I've imagined it.

I trace her collar bone, wishing it was my mouth on her. I won't be satisfied until I've tasted every inch of her skin. My arm circles her, drawing her against me until she can feel the promise of my cock against her soft belly. I know she'll love it when I fuck her. I know she won't be able to get enough.

But I won't be able to either. "You should go."

She sways as I let her go. "I probably should."

Clara studies me for a moment like I'm a puzzle she can't piece together. I want to take her hands and guide them to all my parts. I want her to put me back together. I want to be the man she hopes to see now.

But that's impossible. "You asked if I would hurt you, Clara. I can't lie and say that I won't. I want nothing more than to strip you bare and pin you to that wall. Hold you there until you beg for my cock, and when I finally give it to you, you'll beg me never to stop."

Despite my intentions, I step toward her. I'm trying to give her a choice, but even I don't know what it is. I'm warning her away. I'm asking her to stay. I tell myself that I don't know what I want, but it's a lie.

I don't want Clara to walk out that door.

I run a hand through my hair, shaking the thought from my head. It's unfair to do this to her—to drag her into my life when I can't be what she needs. "But if I do that, it will only ruin you."

"This isn't an old novel," she retorts, but I hear the way her words break like I'm breaking her. "I'm not a hapless virgin."

I don't think. I need her to see that I want her, but that I'm giving her up because... I grab her and pull her against me. "I've thought about your lips all day. I've pictured you on your knees with that pretty little mouth wrapped around my cock, sucking me off. If I had you now, I would want more. Once wouldn't be enough. But enough is something a man like me can never have."

"Because I'm not royalty?" she asks, her lashes fluttering like I've overwhelmed her with my mood swings. The feeling is mutual.

"I think they'd be more pissed that you're American, but really no one cares about that," I say darkly. I try to smile, but it can't ease the situation I've created. How had I expected this to end? "Because nothing beautiful can survive around me. Do you understand that? They'll destroy you, and if they don't, eventually I will."

"Maybe I can take care of myself." She twists in my grip, but I hold her. I'm not ready to let her go. Not yet.

"Maybe you can," I admit. "But don't tempt me into risking it. I can't be held responsible."

I drop my hold on her, hoping she'll leave before I change my mind. Instead, her hand shoots out, and she grabs my shirt. The growl I've been holding back escapes as our lips meet, and I feel Clara shiver. Her body feels so fucking amazing in my arms. I want to explore it, and I slip a tongue into her mouth in invitation. When she accepts, I slide my hands down and lift her off her feet. I thrust my tongue into her mouth, giving her a preview of what's to come. She has no idea all the places I plan to explore. She's strong, but there's a natural submissiveness to her. I feel it in how her legs wrap around my waist and how her body molds to mine like she can fit herself into my life. I want it to be true. If only so I could take her now. Clara's hips rock against me, and I know she wants release. Her movements are urgent, as raw and vulnerable as she is. Even as I continue to taste her mouth, I know the truth.

She may not be a virgin, but she might as well be.

She's never been fucked by a man like me. She has no idea what to expect, and as much as I want to show her exactly how good it feels to be owned, she might not be ready. My hand reaches for her ponytail, and I pull until her mouth breaks free of mine.

"This is your last chance," I warn. I can feel her slipping under my control. She's going to be mine. And then pain flickers through her eyes.

"No," she whispers.

I don't want to let her go. I want to kiss her until her no becomes a yes. I'd seen it there. What changed? Lowering her to her feet, I spot the tremble of her legs, but I don't trust myself to steady her.

"You're a smart girl." I pause, wanting to ask her why. Instead, I kiss her forehead. One final taste. "Norris will see you home safely, and I'll have my people work on getting rid of those reporters."

"Thank you." The regret I feel coats her words.

"Goodbye, Clara Bishop." I stop myself from telling her I don't want her to go.

She backs away from me as though she can't trust me not to follow her. When she reaches the door, there's nothing left to say except one thing. "Goodbye."

The glass panel closes behind her, and I force myself to stay here. In this room. In this spot. It's more difficult than I'd imagined. Maybe that's because this is the second time we've walked away from each other. Maybe because this time she said no. I respect that. At least, I want to. I've almost fooled myself into thinking I could let her go. I'm out the door and on my way down the stairs before I realize I can't.

I can't explain it—to myself or her. But I'll make her understand.

Clara Bishop belongs to me.

CHAPTER FOUR

Pushing my way through the crowd, I make my way through Brimstone. But I'm caught in an endless, circular hell, glimpsing Clara and Norris but never quite reaching them. Around me, mobiles come out, but I don't give a fuck if I've been recognized. I can only think of getting to her before she leaves again.

And then I make a decision.

If I do, I won't let her go again. If I don't, it's a sign. I'm playing a stupid game with myself, but I'm a man who's willing to gamble. I've never believed in destiny, but since I met Clara, I'm starting to have a little faith.

Spotting Norris's salt and pepper hair in the crush of club-goers isn't difficult, given that he's got twenty years on everyone else. Forcing my way to him, I discover he's alone.

"Where is she?" I demand, the noise carrying away my words. He gets the point and gestures toward the main entrance. I can't hear him, but I know what he's saying.

She ran.

Smart girl. Stupid girl. I don't know how to feel. She listened to my warning and took action. I just wish she hadn't run outside where a swarm of paparazzi has been camped out all night.

I don't think. I follow. There's no time for apologies when I push people to the side or shove between couples. Norris catches up and helps to clear the path.

When we reach the door, the bouncer's attention is on the scene unfolding on the street. I hear the reporters before I see them.

"Miss Bishop! Smile, love!"

"Miss Bishop, how long have you been involved with the Prince?"

"Miss Bishop, is it true that the King has condemned your relationship?"

"Were you secretly married in Oxford?"

I open my mouth to redirect their attention to me—to give Clara a chance to run. I didn't reach her first—they did—and it's all the reminder I need that I won't drag her into this. I won't let her endure the mud-slinging and invasions of privacy. Clara wasn't cursed with this life; I was. It's not her burden to bear. But before I get one word out, she steps in front of the lot of them.

"I'm sorry to inform you all that I have no relationship with Prince Alexander. Someone has made a dreadful mistake. I do not know the Prince. I am not in love with him. And I highly doubt the King gives two figs about me."

Something inside me snaps into place as I watch her,

but there's no time to consider what it is. The paparazzi surround her within seconds, followed by onlookers eager to get a glimpse. Clara disappears from view, and my heart vanishes along with her. In its spot, anger blisters and bursts from me. "Enough!"

Questions die on lips. People back away. No one here will dare question my authority, nor will they keep me from her. I take a step and pause, waiting for self-preservation to kick in. When it does, a path clears for me, and I see her on the ground, her hands covering her head protectively.

I've done this. I'm the one that asked her to come. I'm the reason she wound up on those bloody tabloids. Moving to her, I kneel and guide her hands gently away from her beautiful face.

"Are you okay, Clara?" I say only loudly enough for her to hear.

She nods, her eyes flickering to the crowd and their cameras. None of them exist to me. I can only think of her. I need to get her away. I need to help her.

Taking her hand, I lift her to her feet as a new onslaught of questions finally starts. Even my authority has a time limit.

"Alexander, is this your girlfriend?"

"Alexander, is it true that your father doesn't approve of your relationship with a commoner?"

Clara cringes, and I bite back a rebuke. I won't lower myself to speak to this scum that knocked her to the ground. But how can't they see the truth? There is nothing common about this woman. Placing a hand on the small of her back, I claim her for them to see. She can reject me. But I will not allow them to see her as less than me. A few months ago, I was covered in dirt in the desert. I might have been born with a title, but it doesn't make me better than her. If anything, I'm so much less.

Norris rushes to the car and opens the door. His eyes meet mine as she climbs inside, and I see the question there. I don't even have to consider it. Getting in next to her, I slam the door to the cameras and questions. Clara stares at the ground, and I worry for a moment that she's in shock. There will be time for apologies later. Now I need to know she's okay. Instinct kicks in, and I wrap an arm around her. Drawing her to me, I inhale sharply when she buries her face against my shoulder. I want to believe I can comfort her, but this is new to me. Instead, I rely on caring for her like I was taught in that club—in that world, I was denied. Clara isn't my submissive. Not yet. But right now, she needs time to process what happened. So I become her anchor, waiting for her to return to me.

She feels delicate in my arms, and I know she needs my protection. One wrong move, though, and I could crush her. Silence hangs between us as we make our way through London. My time with her is running out. I have a choice to make.

"Clara." I love the way her name tastes on my lips. "Are you okay? I'm sorry you had to go through that. I should have known better than to kiss you." I screwed up when I kissed her. I'm doing the same now—holding her, being seen with her. I don't need to complicate this anymore.

Lifting my arm from her shoulder, I run a hand through my hair and wonder what to do next. Clara sits up, breaking contact between our bodies. I allow it, but I don't like it. Touching her seems to soothe some of the ragged need I feel whenever she's near.

"I'm fine. Things got out of hand. I'm afraid you're more experienced with this sort of thing than I am," she says, meeting my eyes.

"Unfortunately, you're right." I hold her gaze until her ass wiggles against the seatback. "I know I should be sorry that I kissed you, but I'm not. In fact, I'd like to do it again."

"I'm not stopping you," she whispers.

I force myself to look away from her. But I can't pretend she's not here. I can't ignore her perfect body pressed to mine in the suddenly too small backseat. Her presence—my desire—doesn't change the facts. "You said no."

She blinks as if just remembering this herself. "I didn't mean it."

"What mixed signals you give me, Miss Bishop. That's a risqué thing to do with a man like me."

"And what kind of man is that?" she demands.

"A man who takes what he wants." I let her digest my words. Clara doesn't back down, though.

"You haven't taken me."

She has to fucking defy me, which is possibly even

sexier than the brief glimpses of submission I've caught when kissing her.

Bringing a strong woman to her knees—knowing you're the only one who can tame her—is a rush beyond comparison.

"We met under unusual circumstances." My hand reaches for her knee, and before I can rethink the gesture, a subtle tremble rolls through her. I wouldn't have felt it if I wasn't touching her. I should be a gentleman and stop myself. Instead, I find myself hoping to elicit another reaction.

"You weren't looking to pick anyone up?" She pretends to ignore my hand, but pink creeps over her cheeks. I want to see that rosy glow coloring the rest of her fair skin. It takes effort to focus on what she's saying. "Not your usual scene?"

I try to hold back a smile. Meeting her was the last thing I expected that day. "I rarely find such exciting company at the Oxford and Cambridge Club."

"Why were you there?" she asks.

"My friend Jonathan received his degree. He conned me into coming," I say.

"I have a hard time imagining you being conned by anyone."

"Then you must not know Jonathan."

"Wait," she says, "do you mean Jonathan Thompson?"

"The one and the only. Do you know him...well?" I'm trying to be delicate, but I want to know.

"By reputation only," she says quickly, and I relax.

"Jonathan claims he bedded every girl in his class," I say. "I'm glad to see you had higher standards."

I'm not certain why it matters. Clara's life before me is not my concern. In point of fact, her life isn't my concern now. But the thought of Jonathan touching her bothers me more than I'd like to admit to her or myself.

"Says his good friend."

"Some people you should keep close." I hope she hears the warning in my words. I have no interest in discussing Jonathan with her—only in keeping her away from him.

Clara turns her attention to the streets and the buildings outside her window. Are we near where she lives? Is she counting the moments until she can be well shot of me? I couldn't blame her, but instead, she stays close to me, keeping our bodies in contact.

"Where are we going?" She looks at a building as we pass, and I realize it's where she lives: a simple brick building in East London.

It's not the usual choice for a girl with a trust fund. Then again, the file Norris brought me on her noted she took a job at a non-profit. Nothing about this girl lines up with her bank account.

"There are reporters following us. Norris will lose them before I take you home." Without thinking, my hand moves from her knee up to grip her thigh.

I can't stop myself from touching her. I want to comfort her. I want to kiss her. She draws me to her bright light like I'm a suicidal moth. I'm not a creature meant for her. I belong to the dark, but even knowing that, I don't pull away from her.

"Clara," I murmur, knowing I can't avoid this. I have a duty to her, and no matter what happens, I will see to it.

"Hmm."

"I need you to know that no matter what happens next—if you get out of this car and never speak to me again—I will see to your protection." I mean it. Part of me hopes she'll take me up on the offer. I do my best to ignore what the rest of me wants.

Her eyes close against me. "Why?"

"Because you are the only person who wished I'd never left." I try to sound casual. I'm not sure why this means so much to me.

"I'm glad you came back," she says softly, peeking up at me.

The boundary I'd tried to set crumbles as her words slam into me. I don't want to consider why, but I can't deny the shift.

"I want you." The line crossed, I make up my mind. I know she wants me as well, but I'm not certain it would matter if she didn't. Clara's body has been mine since the moment we first touched. I'm afraid I won't be satisfied with only that now. "But not tonight."

Her eyes fill with accusation, but it only fuels my desire. "Is that what you do? Toy with girls until they drop to their knees for you?"

We both know I could take her now. I shift in my seat, trying to adjust myself.

"Do you need me to beg for it?" she asks.

I caress my fingers against the rough fabric of her jeans, wanting to make her squirm more. "Need? No. Want?" I swallow. I know exactly what I want from her. "I want to hear you beg for me. Beg for my cock. Beg for me to fuck you, and you will, poppet. But. Not. Tonight."

"Why?" There's a frantic edge to the question.

"Because your entire building will be surrounded by the morning, and I'm not interested in sex, Clara. I want to explore you. I want to rip those clothes off of you and take you to bed. I'm going to fuck you until it hurts, and I want to hear you beg me to do it." I stop and let myself imagine her spread beneath me. The vision only reinforces what I already know. "And I need more than a few hours for that."

She stares at me, and then finally, her tongue darts over her lips as though she can taste my promises.

"I get what I want." I silently dare her to question this.

"When?"

"Tomorrow." I won't be able to wait a moment longer than that.

"And the reporters?" she asks hopelessly.

"I'll deal with them." It's the least I can do. I've won a gamble I didn't know I'd placed. Clara Bishop has agreed to see me again. In truth, she's agreeing to more than that. We both know where this leads. I search her face for doubt and find none. She wants this as much as I do. The realization makes me even harder than I already am—a feat I wouldn't have thought possible. "Norris will pick you up at eleven."

Her lashes flutter shyly as she eyes her apartment building. Teeth sink into her lower lip as if she's holding back. I want to unravel all her secrets.

"Then I'll see you tomorrow night," she murmurs.

"Oh, no. Eleven in the morning." I take her face in my hands. I want to be clear about this. "I told you I need time, poppet."

It's a promise laced with warning. I will take her slowly. I will claim every inch of her. Whatever is sparking between us, I can't contain it. But I don't just need to fuck her. I need to taste her. I need to touch her. I want to now, but holding back will make tomorrow even more delicious.

My lips brush over hers, and she parts her lips with a soft sigh. I'm barely able to resist the offer. If I start now, I won't be able to stop. "Until then."

Norris helps her from the car and rushes her inside before a wandering reporter catches up with us. I want to follow and see her safely to the door. I want to lock her there, protecting her from the attention I've brought to her life.

But even as I fight the urge, I know the truth. The safest thing I could do is keep my distance from her. Now that she's no longer next to me, I wonder if I could walk away now.

I know three things:

I should call this off now.

I won't be able to shield her from the press or my family indefinitely.

I have no control over my attraction to this woman.

The last trumps the others, and I can only hope that after a night with her, I'll let go of my preoccupation.

Norris gets back in the car without a word, and we drive in silence. After a few minutes, he clears his throat. "Home?"

"I suppose," I say ruefully, my thoughts lingering behind with Clara. "I need to get my own place."

"Perhaps, you should speak to your father," Norris advises me. His eyes survey me in the mirror.

"I don't want anything from him. I'll get a flat."

Norris resumes his practiced silence, but the absence of his guidance is deafening.

"Out with it," I order him.

"You think it will be this easy?"

"The flat?" I clarify.

"Amongst other concerns." He's choosing his words with the caution of a man familiar with my family's poor temper.

"If we're talking about Clara, let's use her name," I say flatly. "You think it's a bad idea?"

"I think a woman like that deserves more than a hotel suite."

I already know that. "I can't give her more. It would expose her."

"Alexander, she's already exposed." He turns the car onto a side street and I watch the lights of London flash past the window while I absorb what he's saying.

"All the more reason to keep this private." I don't leave room for him to question this. I know Norris is right.

Clara deserves more than a man like me can give her. "Can you see to that?"

"Of course," he says in a clipped tone. He doesn't approve, but I don't try to fool myself.

I'm a selfish man. I'm going to hurt her. I won't be able to protect her, because I pose more danger to Clara than any reporter or tabloid headline. She's not the type of girl who fucks a man like me for thrills. She's not the type of girl a man like me beds for fun. I'm going to take so much more than her body—and the worst part is that I don't care if I hurt her. Not if it means I can have her, even if it's just for one day.

CHAPTER FIVE

I play it safe and book my favorite suite at my favorite hotel. Then, I have a fresh suit delivered. The last thing I want is to return to the palace and the sham of a life being forced on me. It's easy to sleep. Tomorrow Clara won't merely exist in my dreams. She'll be in my arms.

When Norris phones to say he's on the way the following morning, I head down to meet her. It's best to do it like this before I can talk myself out of it. Because as much as I want to take her to bed, I know this is a mistake. Even with all my precautions, we might get caught. The lift doors slide open, revealing her and erasing my doubts. She's wearing a long, blue dress that covers too much of her body while also clinging to her perfect curves. She's a walking wet dream, and I wonder what I'll find when I strip away the veneer of propriety she's worn since we met. I've seen glimpses of something primal and responsive when I touched her before. She submitted naturally to my kiss.

And then she said no.

Clara Bishop is a mystery I want to solve if only to make her unravel.

With my mouth.

With my hands.

With my cock.

I know she wants that, too, because she stares at me with wide, innocent eyes that dare me to show her a world she's never known.

"Clara." Holding out my hand, I wait for her to cross a line she hasn't strayed past. She's not the type to sleep with a man she barely knows. Maybe that's why I want to fuck her so badly. I have to stop myself from licking my lips, and when she takes my hand, I want to drag her into the lift so I can do just that.

Instead, she follows me to it with a trust I don't deserve. The moment the doors shut behind her—the moment I finally have her to myself—she whips around like a wild animal who's fallen into a trap.

"Is something wrong?" Have I misread the situation? A moment ago, she seemed so willing, as certain of this as I am. Now, she's staring at those doors like she made a terrible mistake.

"I should have said thank you to Norris. It was rude of me."

Her horror steals a smile from me because it's the last thing I expect her to say, and somehow it proves that she's as civilized as I imagined. But Clara is different than the false friends I've known my whole life. She seems genuinely upset with herself.

Norris is my friend more than most who boast about it publicly. It means something that she sees him—that she remembers his name. Still, I'm not about to let her obsess over it, not when we're finally alone.

"I'm sure the salary I pay him makes up for any perceived impoliteness on your part."

"It was still rude." She frowns before determination sets in. "Please give him my apologies for my behavior as well as my thanks."

I make a note to do just that. For some reason, I want Norris to like her. Probably, since he'll be shuttling her around. I don't think one day with Clara is going to get her out of my system.

Her frown fades into that artless vulnerability that drew me to her that day at the club. She's overthinking things like she did when she told me no at Brimstone. "I thought perhaps you'd come to your senses."

I don't mean to say it. Somehow I keep warning her, but like last time, it only pulls her closer. In the enclosed space, the scent of roses dances across the air. "Have you come to yours?"

"You're not the dangerous one." I take a step toward her, wanting to breathe her in deeper, but she's the one that inhales sharply.

"Maybe I'm a wolf in sheep's clothing."

I think I want that as much as I want her to be the innocent lamb. I want to see every side that she hides from the world. "I guess I'll have to strip you and find out."

"Where are we?" she asks, looking around the lift for clues. It's a charmingly naive question.

Where does she think we are? I thought I'd been clear about my intentions to fuck her until she could barely stand. Or maybe she knows where we are but is clinging to modesty I'll have to spend the next few hours destroying.

"The Westminster Royal," I tell her.

"Swanky hotel." She sounds impressed, which pleases me. Partially because I rather like the suite, but mostly because I want to rip her knickers off.

"They appreciate their guests' privacy, which is something I appreciate."

"Do you check-in under a false identity and leave under the cover of night?" There's laughter in her question that she doesn't let loose, so I laugh instead.

"It's not quite so clandestine as that. Although most of the staff only knows me as Mr. X."

"Does that make me Mrs. X for the day?" She claps a hand over her mouth, her eyes widening as she realizes what she said.

She doesn't expect my reaction. I don't either.

"I rather like the sound of that." Too much, and I'm not sure why. I study her for a moment as if I might find the answer written across her face. Instead, I only see her nerves coupled with want, and for some reason, I need to reassure her, which is why I say the last thing I should. "Mrs. X. She sounds rather wicked."

Her tongue darts over her lips, and I'm reminded of one of the many fantasies I've entertained about what she might do with that perfect mouth.

"Are you okay with that? With this arrangement, I mean." I check myself before she gets the wrong idea and ignore that I seem to be getting the wrong idea myself.

This can only end one way.

With a number of mind-blowing orgasms over the course of a few days, a week, maybe longer. But whatever lines we cross, there's one firm boundary I'll make sure we both respect.

"I hadn't expected..."

"A hotel?" I want to explain that it's for the best. It's harder to get attached to a temporary bed. A hotel offers an anonymity of heart that keeps things from getting complicated. It's why I didn't go home with her last night. It's why I didn't see her to the door. We're here for one reason. A hotel is a reminder of what that is.

It's also protection against the paparazzi that are still stalking her flat. I don't want her to have to fend them off. That's my burden, and one she doesn't need to bear.

"Yes." She doesn't meet my eyes, and I realize she's trembling.

I don't know if I've upset her or scared her or if it's just nerves, but I need to. Taking her chin in my hands, I direct her gaze to mine and nearly lose myself in the gray ocean of her eyes. "I wanted to be certain that no one found out about this."

Clara wrenches away from me, turning toward the

doors like she's hoping they'll open. What then? What did I say?

"What is it?" I press closer, afraid that the lift will reach its destinations and I'll finally lose her. "Why are you looking like I've got you in a corner?"

"I have a little self-respect, you know." She glares at me, and I try to keep my eyes on her face even as her nipples bead under her dress. Is she responding because she's angry? Because that's...fucking hot. My cock notices, too, and I shift my feet, trying to give it room in my slacks. "If you're worried about being seen with me, perhaps it's best that you let me off."

"I can't." I'm suddenly glad I chose this hotel and its private lift.

She crosses her arms, covering the proof of her arousal. "Try."

"This lift only goes to the Presidential Suite. I can't let you off until we reach it, but..." I press the red button she'd eyed a moment ago, calling her bluff. The lift shudders to a stop and she stumbles against me. "I think you've misunderstood me, and I'm not interested in taking a woman to bed who thinks I'm a liar."

"Then explain it to me."

"With pleasure." If I have to spend the rest of the afternoon convincing her in this lift, then she'll find I can be quite persuasive. "I was under the impression you wanted the paparazzi to leave you alone."

I pause and let this sink in. Clara shrugs her thin shoulders, unwilling to concede that she had wanted that only yesterday. Now I know one more thing: my girl is stubborn.

"I wanted to respect your desire for privacy," I push. "By now, you'll have done your research on me."

She nods. Clara might not have known who I was when we first met, but that won't be the case anymore. I have no doubt that we've both done our research. But while my intel is based on fact, I imagine what she's read about me is a little more colorful.

"Reporters love to take photos of me with women and speculate on our relationships. Old friends become new flames. Waitresses become flings."

"So you didn't sleep with all those women?" she asks.

I bite back a smile. There's no need to lie. "Not all of them."

"Lovely."

"I believe you told me that you weren't a hapless virgin." She wants to run, but I won't let her. I back her against the wall and cage her between my arms. I won't force her to do something she doesn't want to do, but I will make her listen. "I assume we can be open about our sex lives."

"We can."

"Good, because I want you to be open with me, Clara. I'll have you either way, but you'll enjoy it more if you aren't busy thinking I'm a dick."

Her smile is a bit grudging but bright.

"A smile. Now that's lovely. I wonder if I'll see that after you come when you're still full of me." She needs to remember why we're here. She needs to remember why she came. It will be easier to remind her once she's actually come. "So are we agreed?"

"To share our sex lives?" she asks.

We might as well get this out of the way. "I need to know the women I sleep with are discreet. That they use good...judgment."

She rolls her eyes, and I know it probably sounds ridiculous. "I've been with one guy. My college boyfriend. And I'm on The Pill."

So I was right about her sexual history. Mine is a bit more diversified.

"What about you?" she presses.

"More than one." I don't need to tell her how many. She won't like it. "I'm always cautious, and I can assure you that I'm clean."

This earns me another frown. It's cute, but I prefer the smile. "And that's important because?"

"I felt it should be addressed before I took you to bed, and because I don't think I can wait until we reach the suite." I can't keep my hands off her for another minute. Pushing her against the lift's mirrored wall, I show her exactly what she's agreed to as I tug down the straps of her dress. A primal sensation rises inside me and escapes from my throat when I catch sight of delicate lace caging her full tits. "Your breasts are more perfect than I'd imagined."

She slumps against the wall a little, but true to form, she dares to ask me, "Should we do this in the elevator?"

I brush my index finger over her lips, thinking of all the things I'd like to do to her in this lift. "Oh poppet, I know what's worrying you. You're worried that I'll get my quick fuck in the elevator."

"I don't want you to get bored with me before you even get me to the room." Her voice is small, shrinking to hide from me.

"That won't be a problem." I trace her collarbone. I'm ready to kiss her—to taste her skin. To taste every inch of her. She obviously needs to be reminded of that. "Your body was made to fuck, Clara. Has anyone ever told you that?"

She barely manages to shake her head.

"It is," I say. Men at Oxford University must be bloody stupid. They should have been bowing down to this woman, not sticking their noses in books. "I find it very inspiring. I don't know if there are enough flat surfaces to ride you on in the suite. But if it would make you feel better—" I continue to work her skirt up until it's bunched at her hips. With my other hand, I slide a finger past the waist of her knickers lower and lower until I find what I seek. "—we can wait and go upstairs."

Her eyes slam shut as I circle her engorged clit. "We should..."

I take it as a compliment that she can't finish the sentence.

"Perhaps I can offer a better solution." I love listening to her little noises, but there's something I want to do more. "I need to taste your sweet cunt, Clara. I've been thinking about it for days. Will you let me do that?"

There's a moan mixed with permission, and I don't wait for her to change her mind. I need to taste her. I need her on my tongue. My fingers close over the band of her thong and rend it cleanly. It snaps with ease, as delicate and easily broken as I hope she will be.

I drop to my knees and brush my hands down her thighs. "Spread wider," I order, groaning silently when she acquiesces. "Beautiful."

My hands move up, parting her so I can study her. Her skin there is silky and as soft as the delicate pink petals of a rosebud. I push a finger inside her, then another, enjoying the slick arousal I discover.

"Are you always this wet?" Fuck, I hope so.

I watch from between her legs as she shakes her head.

"Do I do this to you?" Is that too much to hope for? Because I'll gladly do this to her over and over.

She nods, but it's not enough. I want to hear her admit it. I want her to hand over that part of herself. "Say it, Clara."

"Yes."

"Yes, what? What do I do to you?"

"You make me wet." She moans, and my control nearly slips. I won't take her here. There will be time for that later. I might want to destroy the last shreds of her modesty, but one matter at a time.

"Good girl," I murmur. She deserves a reward, and I need to taste her. Leaning in, I find the rose-scent of her skin mingles sweetly on that delicate pink flesh as I draw my tongue over the swollen pink bud. Her hands splay against the wall as I lick her with slow deliberation. In this moment, she belongs to me.

I need her to remember that, though. Her breath is

already quickening, her hips are bucking toward me. "Not until I say, poppet."

Her whimper pushes me over the edge. I've been holding back, but I want to earn another moan, another little cry, another yes, please. I want to own Clara Bishop's pleasure. I'm sure she'll find I'm a generous master. But I need to prove it.

"Come," I command before covering her with my mouth again. Her taste floods my tongue as pleasure rolls through her. I pause for a split second before continuing. She unravels again, and now my cock is becoming painfully aware of the situation. But even though aftershocks rock through her, I continue to nibble her clit like it's my own private, fucking feast.

She comes twice. But that was with my mouth and hands. It feels like a challenge to take her over the edge again, especially with nothing more than my lips and tongue, but I'm game. I drag the orgasm from her, and her resistance makes it the most powerful.

"Now you're ready for me to fuck you." And God, am I ready to fuck her.

"Yes," she whispers.

There's no doubt. No hesitation. She's given herself to me. I can't keep the pleased smile from my face.

CHAPTER SIX

I step from the lift, shucking my suit jacket from my shoulders, and toss it on the sofa. It's sad how comfortable I feel here, but it's one of the few places where I can relax without running into a curtsying staffer. There's enough room to spread, although my private quarters dwarf it. Still, it has one perk that Buckingham will never have: she's here. I considered carrying her inside, but the gesture felt too romantic. My feelings for Clara are mixed up enough.

A rose flush settles onto her cheeks as she stares out the window, her eyes wide. It's been so long since I bothered to look out over London that I can't imagine what's caught her attention. Maybe it's the dreamy distance in her eyes, but I'm almost jealous. I've never seen this city as anything other than a burden—a price I'll one day pay for false power. Watching her, I want to see it as she does.

Moving behind her, I peek over her shoulder, already

distracted by the press of her soft body against mine. "Enjoying the view?"

"I am. You?"

"Very much. The city isn't bad either." It isn't, actually. From here, it pulses with life, mirroring how I feel. The Eye can keep spinning, and the tourists can snap their photos. I'll take a stolen afternoon away from the world.

My lips find her neck, and I want to taste her again. My teeth graze her as I consider the possibilities, and then I give in with one small nip to her shoulder. She melts against me, and I note her response to the suggestion of pain. Clara Bishop doesn't share my sexual tastes, but she keeps showing signs she might. The thought is enough to make me want her again. This whole city will be mine someday, but I only want her. Drawing her skirt up, I push the wadded fabric against her stomach and move her closer to the glass, exposing her bare cunt to the world below. She shivers like she realizes what I'm doing— showing her off like a trophy. Not that I would ever allow anyone to see her like this. For the time being, she belongs to me.

"I'm going to fuck you in front of this window," I promise her, stroking my hand along her until I feel her growing slick against my fingers. "I'm going to show the whole city that I take what I want."

Clara sucks back a gasp, widening her stance a little to grant me access.

"I'm going to make you come in front of the busiest street in London." I'm playing a long game with her clit, drawing her closer and closer and then pulling her back down before she can spill over. I want to make her come, but I enjoy the little noises she makes too much to do it yet.

"Please," she whimpers, pushing against my hand. Her hips move in welcome, and I have to force myself not to send her over. Clara might not be a virgin, but she's never been with a man like me. I can feel how tight she is —which is reason enough to go slowly—despite the raw temptation.

"Soon," I whisper. "But not yet. I need to see how far I can take you. How much that beautiful cunt of yours can handle."

Her ass grinds into my groin before she says the one thing I can't resist. "I can handle anything you give me."

I don't think. She's in my arms. I kick open the bedroom door and drop her on the mattress.

There's too much clothing. I want her naked and spread in front of me. I want to lick every inch of her skin. I want to see the prize I've won.

"Take that off," I demand.

I suspect Clara is the type that waits until night to fuck—the girl who wants the lights off—because there's just a delicious second of hesitation before she does as I command. She pushes up and lifts her dress over her head. The sight of Clara on her knees in that delicate lace bra and nothing else will be with me the rest of my life, burned into my brain.

"I almost wish I hadn't destroyed those panties." Not that I want anything covering her, but now I wish I could rip them off again. "I'll have to get you a new pair so I can fuck you in that sweet lace."

She bites her lip, and I can't wait any longer. "Spread your legs."

Clara does as she's told, watching me as I begin to undress. I've seen enough of her stubborn streak to assume she's not always this obedient. Maybe it would get tiring to have her resisting me if we spent time together outside the bedroom, but knowing she would...I like that more than I care to admit. Because that means she's giving me control—no matter what she said before. That means there's hope that she might be exactly what I need.

Confusion clouds her eyes for a moment when I don't take off my undershirt. Later, I'll tell her it's the price of admission. I don't owe her more explanation than that, but I'll make up for any disappointment she feels now in other ways. Sliding my belt free, I consider what she would do if I looped it around her slender wrists. Or what she would do if I turned her over and...

Clara stares at me as if she can guess what I'm thinking, and there's a flash of fear.

One thing at a time.

Dropping it to the floor, I distract her with what I do have to offer now. Pushing my boxers to my ankles, I wait for the reaction I know to expect.

Apprehension. That's the inexperience looking at me.

Excitement. That's the woman looking back at me.

Pure lust. That's simply Clara.

It radiates off her. It's impossible that she could be so innocent and so wonton at the same time.

I stroke my hand over my shaft, considering how first to take her. I can think of quite a few ways I'd like to fuck her, but I'm still a gentleman: her needs come first. Literally. "Since I'm not certain your tight little cunt can handle me, I think it's best if we try a more...traditional style."

She giggles, and she looks as surprised by her reaction as I am.

"Are you laughing at me?" I smirk. "Don't be naughty, or I'll have to take you over my knee." Another test, but this time the apprehension tightens through her, so I plaster another smile on my face and push the desire to feel my palm against her backside deep inside me.

I could consider how far she'll let me go all afternoon, but I'm tired of waiting. Grabbing a rubber from the nightstand, I sheathe myself before I drop over her. I'm nearly ready when her hand slides under the hem of my undershirt. The reaction is as instantaneous as earlier, but this time it's born of survival.

I grab her wrist and nearly crush her as I lose my balance. "No."

There's a moment of heavy silence before she begins to push at me. I can't blame her for having this reaction, but I want her to understand it can't be helped.

"Clara, stop."

She takes this order too far, freezing in place underneath my body and glaring up at me.

"This can stop now. We can stop now." I need to tell her this, and she needs to hear it. I have no interest in forcing her. "But I don't want it to, and I don't think you do either."

"I think I do!"

I'll change her mind. "Let me say one thing, and then you can decide. If you say stop, that's it."

"That's it?" She sounds like she doesn't believe me.

"I only have one rule when it comes to sex."

"Only one?"

I silence her with a single look. "I don't take off my shirt, and before you ask, I don't explain why."

"That's your only rule?" Anger gives way to incredulity, at least temporarily.

I can imagine the kind of rules Clara has in the bedroom—ones I'd willfully ignore. But I'm a knobhead, and she's an angel—so I'm likely to get my way on both counts.

"My only rule," I continue. "I don't like women to touch me there."

She takes this as well as can be expected. "You want to put me on display for all of London, but I'm not allowed to touch your abs? That hardly seems like a fair trade."

"I promise that you won't feel that way by this afternoon," I say. "I don't think you'll have any doubts about my generosity then. But you can say no now and leave. I'll understand."

"I assume others have said no to this then?"

"You know what they say about assumptions, Clara."

In fact, no woman has ever turned me down. I don't

really feel arguing this point further will get me back in her good graces.

Instead, I cheat. Slipping my hand down, I find her clit and rub my thumb across it until her eyes close. "Perhaps I could convince you?"

She's either considering or toying with me, and I don't care which so long as I'm touching her. Her breath picks up, each pant boosting my confidence.

"You don't have to tell me why," she breathes. "Just tell me one thing—do you not take it off for throwaway fucks?"

I can't process her question. It nearly breaks my brain to try. I don't even realize that I've stopped until she peeks up at me.

"Throwaway fucks?" I repeat flatly. I get the gist of what she's suggesting. I have no idea why she thinks so little of herself.

"Girls like me," she practically squeaks. "Girls you fuck and forget."

"I don't like that term." I don't like her using it. "I've had casual sex before, Clara, but always with women who understood that's what it was."

"We've never discussed it," she says, looking a bit frightened. "Look, I've never had a fling. I don't know how this goes. I'm usually a relationship girl, so help me understand. Do you keep your shirt on to keep your distance?"

I bite back a groan of frustration. It's all making sense now, and as usual, I've cocked things up. "I thought I made my intentions clear. I wasn't under the impression this was a fling."

Clara's eyes widen like a doe's, and it occurs to me that maybe I'm the one getting the wrong idea. Why settle for snogging a prince if you can shag one? Why have a little fun when you can go temporarily mental and do something out of character? Because this is out of character for her. She's made it clear, and I've been ignoring it.

"Do you want a fling?" I force myself to ask.

She stares for a moment. "I assumed..."

"There's that word again. I'm not interested in you as a throwaway fuck. Why would you think that?"

"If it walks like a duck, and it talks like a duck."

"I think this is one time where you could use fuck in that statement." I let go of the hand I'm still holding and push off her. "I don't know what to do with you, Clara Bishop. I've been thinking about fucking you since I saw you in that tiny black dress at the party. When you said no to me at the club, I thought that was it, and then you changed your mind and agreed to a date."

"This is a date?" She starts like I've thrown cold water on her. I can only hope her body doesn't have a similar reaction.

"Isn't it?"

"The Royals really are fucked up." She grins a little at me, and some weight lifts from my shoulders.

"Don't I know it?" My answering smile isn't nearly as amused. "So did you expect flowers? The cinema?"

"Usually, I expect a little more conversation on a date," she says slowly.

I try to see it through her eyes. What would a normal chap do? Pick her up and take her to dinner? Bring her those damned flowers? She deserves as much, and I've mocked her. "Maybe we should start over."

My cock disagrees with this assessment, and it takes effort to continue. Clara might deserve those things, but if she expects them, she will be disappointed. "I don't court women. There wouldn't be a point."

"But we're on a date." She sounds confused.

"Dating and courting are two different things. You and I could go to dinner or to the country, or we could stay here and fuck. That's dating to me. Courtship implies expectations. I don't do romance, and I don't do long-term. If you're looking for more, I can't give you that. What I can give you is pleasure. More pleasure than you've ever known in your life. I will spend every moment I have with you taking you to the edge and holding you as you spill over." She squirms at my words, and I realize that's what she wants. But it's not as simple as her throw-away fuck implies, and she needs to know that. "Isn't that what everyone is looking for when they go on dates? Why pretend we're after something else? You're attracted to me, and I'm attracted to you. I want to fuck you all day long, and then I'd like to see you again and fuck you again. Could you agree to that?"

She bites her lip again, and I move without thinking, my body taking control of the situation. My cock is pressing against her entrance before I realize she hasn't agreed.

"Yes."

It's enough. It's what I need to hear.

I kiss her before she can change her mind. Slipping my tongue against hers, I roll my hips until her legs fan open. One thrust and the argument would be over. She gasps, and I want to swallow her pleasure. Sucking her tongue languidly, I wonder how long I can make this last —how much more I can make her want me. I want her to forget her worries. I want to show her that my way means pleasure without the baggage of my family and title. I circle the crown of my cock against her clit until her nails clutch my shoulders. Then I slip inside her—barely.

"I want you inside me." Her voice is soft, but I hear her plea. She's not begging. Yet. That will come. But that's not the point. I push inside, her cunt clamping against me as her body arches into mine. It feels better than I ever imagined. It's never been like this before. I have to remind myself to move. Holding her to me, wanting to feel her breasts brush against my shirt, I bring us to the edge, our eyes still locked together.

She wants to look away—to close her eyes and fade into the safe and known.

But I won't let her. "Say my name."

"Alexander." She's panting now, her arms tightening around my shoulders.

"Again." I grab her hips and urge her hips against me harder and faster, meeting each movement with a thrust.

"Alexander." She comes with my name on her lips and her eyes on me like she's been waiting her whole life to be given what she needed. I wait, wanting to give her that without taking my own pleasure. But her climax clenches against my cock and pushes me over. Digging my fingers into her hips, I empty inside her, already thinking of when I will take her again.

I don't know how it's been with other men. I only know that this is the part where, in my experience, the girl stumbles off to the loo, and I don't want Clara going anywhere. Wrapping my arms around her, I draw her to the bed and hold her against my chest. With her in my arms, my racing heart settles. I don't know what to make of that, especially with her still breathing so heavily against me. I want her to feel the peace she's given me, so I kiss her forehead. She relaxes instantly, folding into me with an ease I don't deserve but finding myself wanting. Maybe I'll always want her—want to fuck her, want to hold her, want to kiss her forehead.

But a man like me doesn't get stolen kisses and a woman who still blushes when she undresses. We don't get always.

CHAPTER SEVEN

I lose myself in her. When all I want is to watch her fall over the edge again, it takes restraint to stop. Clara needs a break. Her body might be responsive, but she's never been with a man like me. I can tell by how her teeth sink into her lower lip with every thrust, how her eyes roll back with every touch—she didn't know it could feel this good. I aim to show her exactly how much she's been missing, but there's no need to rush. My self-control slips as she rolls out of bed, stretching against the wall like she's just finished a rigorous work-out session. But she arches her back a bit too much, putting her perfect, round ass on display. I want her again—the desire tears through me and escapes with a growl. She's turning me into a goddamn caveman. When I spot the sly grin flash across her face, I realize she's enjoying it.

I consider lunging for her and dragging her back between the sheets.

"I'm going to take a shower if you care to join me," she says, her eyes sliding to the undershirt.

It's a nice tactic, but I'm well-versed in strategic maneuvers. Still... "Tempting, but I'm going to order room service. Any requests?"

"I'm not picky." She pauses, and I wonder what's going on in that sexy brain of hers. "Actually, get some champagne."

"Your wish is my command." Jumping up, I mean to head toward the phone, but her eyes linger on me. No doubt she appreciates that I don't bother with pants. But I'm nothing compared to her, even if her gaze continues to follow me as I cross the room.

Not that I mind the admiration. I just want to return it.

She doesn't look like a woman; she looks like a goddess with her glowing skin and her soft hair cascading over her shoulders. The makeup she'd so carefully applied is now smudged but somehow even sexier. She looks well-fucked, and I like it. If only every afternoon could be spent seeing to her sinful body, life might be worth living. As it is, our time is limited. I intend to make the most of it. Holding out a hand, she takes it with some apprehension. But all I want is to kiss her—to feel her against me—if only to remind me that she's here and for now, she's mine. My lips meet hers, and somehow it's easier to ignore the primal urge to take her again. It doesn't make sense. My cock isn't usually so well-behaved. Instead, the taste of her kiss sends my heart racing. It seems my body is getting confused, so I pull back and avoid looking at her, instead smacking her bare ass.

It's all about perspective. We have an arrangement. "What would you say if I suggested you only wore that around me?"

"I'm not wearing anything." She sounds almost grateful for the redirection, and I catch myself wondering if she feels it, too.

So much for perspective.

I slip into the role I'm used to playing. Smirking, I charm her by being exactly what we need me to be.

The playboy prince.

The bad boy.

Exactly what they say I am. What I'll never escape.

"Exactly," I say. I really wouldn't mind if she was nude all the time. I'd rather prefer it.

"You're a bit of a fiend, aren't you?" She laughs, and now my cock takes notice.

"I'll show you just how much," I reach for her. If she runs, it will give us space. If we wind up in bed, I'll fuck her until I'm too numb to do whatever this is. It's a win-win.

She sidesteps me and backs toward the loo. "You promised me food and champagne."

It's the right move to put space between us, but the less enjoyable one. Clara is smart. She's not taking me for a ride. Well, not like other women I've known. She doesn't want to play mind games or try to make me fall in love. She's here for the sex. It's refreshing.

At least, it should be.

"Food and champagne." I focus on the task at hand, but I can't help but drink her in one last time. "But then I'm going to have my way with you."

"Promise?" The question is hopeful, small, uncertain. I want to give her my answer now. No talk necessary.

"I promise that you're going to spend the rest of the afternoon screaming my name," I tell her what she wants to hear.

A momentary haze seems to descend over her, and she trips over her own feet. I catch her, and now she's back in my arms, exactly where I want her. "You're testing my resolve, poppet."

She stares up at me, blinking rapidly as if she's processing this. Or trying too, at least. It only makes her more beguiling. Staring into her wide, gray eyes, I'm temporarily lost, drifting at sea. I force myself to take a beat.

"Standing there, biting your lip, with your hair down. I give you ten seconds to get out of here, or I'm taking you back to bed."

Her squeal tests my resolve, and when the bathroom door shuts behind her, I consider following her. I would take off my shirt and lift her against the tiled wall, make love to her under the water, and screw these feelings out of my system. If she let me after she saw the truth—saw what I really am—what I hide beneath my clothes and beneath my skin. I let the wrong woman see once—a proud, angry, fearless woman. And when her eyes filled with pity, I became her nightmare.

Clara would pity me, too. It's her nature.

"Order some goddamn food already," I say under my breath as I hear the water turn on in the bathroom.

The least I can do is feed her. But the moment I look at the menu, I realize I know very little about Clara Bishop. What if she doesn't eat gluten or has a food allergy? It would be my luck to kill a beautiful woman with a peanut. I could go into the bathroom and ask, but I don't trust myself to see her naked and wet. A man only has so much restraint.

I settle my dilemma by ordering everything and a good bottle of Champagne. They assure me it will arrive swiftly. No one in the kitchen knows who is in this room, but they know what room is calling. Unfortunately, impending room service demands clothing.

As it turns out, waiting is boring—and made harder by knowing Clara is nearby. I haven't had enough time with my new toy yet. I want to play with her, discover every little sound she makes.

She fought me earlier, and it had only turned me on. I tell myself I would have stopped. I was raised a gentleman, after all—but I can't ignore how her protest made my cock ache to fill her. It's fucking sick. I know it. She deserves better. A nice barrister or doctor who's in touch with his feminine side and never thinks about silencing her with his body. I'm building her ideal man, turning it into some perverse psychological torture when the food arrives.

The staffer is older and only barely betrays that he recognizes me as he wheels the cart inside. He's probably attended to rock stars and diplomats and god knows who else, but being the prince of England carries a caché that can't be matched.

"Sir?" he asks as though he's talking to any guest, and I motion for him to leave it by the chair. Peeling a few bills from my wallet, I tip him for his discretion. It's the strict standards that set the Westminster Royal apart.

I resume my musings on how much better Clara will be when she moves on, deciding that she might be better served as a career woman.

Clara appears in the hotel robe, which is a bit of a disappointment. Although, if she'd come without it, she might end up never getting fed. She's even more beautiful with her hair piled on top of her head. She looks at ease —comfortable.

"Did you order everything on the menu?" she asks, taking in the array of dishes that take up both the top of the cart and the shelf underneath it.

"Personally, I worked up an appetite," I shrug as if this is a normal amount of food, "but if you need to work on your own, I still want to screw you against that window."

She holds up a hand in protest. "Stop. I'm famished, but maybe after?"

That can be arranged. I like taking care of her in every way that I can. "You continue to surprise me, Clara Bishop. One minute you're running away from me, and the next—"

"You have my panties off in a lift?" she interrupts. "Be honest, this isn't the first time a girl has dropped her knickers for you."

"Well, no." I can't lie. "But you hardly dropped them. That reminds me that I need to buy you another pair."

She pretends to not care, but her eyes hood slightly. She enjoyed having them ripped off. I'll buy her another pair just so I can see that reaction again. I stashed the ruined pair in my suit jacket. It may be a tawdry souvenir, but I'll know where to find them. Then again, I might prefer she leave that sweet cunt bare. She seems to guess what I'm thinking and heads toward the room service cart with renewed purpose. Her eyebrows shoot up when she lifts the lid on the first dish and discovers hamburgers.

"I hope it's okay." I can't help but join her, suddenly hungry myself. But rather than reaching for the food, my hands find her hips. There's only one thing here that can satisfy me. "You aren't a vegan or something? I haven't mortally offended you?"

I'm about to tell her there's a salad here somewhere. Chicken. Caviar, I think. Clara twists in my arms before I can.

"It's fine," she reassures me. "I love meat."

My cock responds to her Freudian slip with petulance. Apparently, Clara is determined to turn me into a sex fiend.

"Tell me more," I tease.

"After we eat." She pulls away, and I let her go. Clara grabs a plate without bothering to check the other offerings. "I had no idea the royal family ate things like hamburgers."

"Oh yes, usually it's only crown roast and leg of lamb and mint jelly." It's meant as a joke, but it comes out bitter. There are some subjects that I can't take lightly, even if I'd like to. "Actually, my family dinners are terrible. Stiff. Too many courses. Too many forks. Someone's always picking a fight, usually me. Maybe that's why I skip so many of them."

Clara swallows hard, studying me for a moment. Her hand's frozen mid-air. Then she shakes it off. "I can relate to that."

"Ah yes. Your parents are web entrepreneurs," I say. "Lots of dinners alone?"

Her eyebrow arches into a question mark. "Checking up on me?"

"I was interested, and if I have to spend my whole life in the public eye, I might as well enjoy the perks of my position." I take a seat next to her, wondering how she'll take this. Surely, she can't have expected me not to look her up. How did she think I'd found her? She hadn't left a glass slipper.

"Translation: it's okay for you to spy on me."

I laugh off the accusation, not wanting her to know she's right. "It was not nearly so clandestine. You probably learned more about me on the internet than I did from MI5 files."

"I have an MI5 file?"

"Not really. Hence why I didn't learn much. I wanted to know how the pretty American girl wound up at a boring British graduation party."

"I'm not American. Not really."

"That did catch my attention." I take a bite and consider what that means. It feels important somehow, but I'm more interested in why she made that choice. "You chose British citizenship. You could have chosen dual citizenship. Why?"

There's a momentary pause where she weighs what to tell me. Her answer is simple but loaded. "There's nothing for me in America."

"That sounds like a story." I want to hear it. I want to know how Clara Bishop wound up at Oxford and then at that club and in my life.

"How about you?" she asks like she doesn't already know everything about me. That's the joy of having your life documented by every media outlet in the world—not a lot goes unreported.

"I'm an open book. You only have to go as far as the nearest tabloid to learn everything you need to know about me."

Her head tilts before she shakes it and returns to her meal. "I doubt that. Tabloids seem to think rumors are facts, after all."

"Yes, they do." I'm not hungry anymore. Abandoning my plate, I stand and move toward the window. She has questions, which isn't unreasonable. "What do you want to know, Clara?"

"What will you tell me?"

I smile flatly and turn to watch the London Eye spin outside the window. I know the right answer. Instead, I answer honestly. "Nothing. I'll tell you nothing you want to know. I'll crack a joke or distract you with a kiss."

Clara falls silent, and I almost look to see if she's checking the exit. It would be the smart move—and the one I don't want her to make. How is a woman supposed to react when you tell her that you'll lie to her? A smart one might run, and Clara is smart. I've seen her marks from Oxford. But she's something else, too. Something hard to place.

"You'll like me better if you believe the tabloid headlines," I add when she doesn't speak.

"Even the one that claimed you had an orgy at Brimstone last month?" she asks, breaking the tension.

"Wouldn't you rather believe that one was true?" I smile. "It promises inhuman stamina."

She smirks as though to say it had already been established. "I will admit I don't like the idea of you screwing a whole room full of women."

There's confidence in the confession, and I realize what that hard-to-place characteristic is: she's brave.

"Ahhh. The jealous type?"

"How would you feel if I screwed a room full of men?" She calls my bluff.

That image pops into my head, and I react, my fist hitting the window frame and surprising both of us. "Touché, poppet. But I should warn you I'm not good at sharing."

"No doubt that comes from never having to share much as a child."

"More than I would have liked." I don't want the distance between us anymore. I need her to see me—to understand me. "While I'm fucking you, no one else will. Do you understand?"

She stares up at me for a second before calmly placing

her dish on the table and standing to meet my eyes. "Is that an order?"

"You didn't seem to mind my orders earlier." Maybe she needs a reminder. My hand pushes between the folds of her robe to the taut plane of her stomach. "You liked being told what to do."

"In bed," she says, moving away from me. "I don't like being ordered around."

"I wouldn't dream of ordering you around outside the bedroom, Clara." What would be the point? Our relationship can't go further than that. But what she did in any bedroom did concern me. "But asking you not to sleep with other men seems to be on point, no?"

"Am I allowed to sleep with other women?" She says flatly.

"No, but that's an interesting idea." But—I could never find another like her.

"Okay, down, boy. I'm just trying to prove that you're being irrational."

"It's not irrational," I say. My hand lashes out and yanks open her robe. It's time for show and tell. "I have many things I plan to do to this body. I want to take my time with it. I need to, so I'm not interested in playing games. If you want to be with me, I expect loyalty."

This time she doesn't try to back away. There's no protest when I step closer and slip a hand between her legs. My fingers stroke along the bare flesh until she's whimpering.

"I have no issue with exclusivity, but you don't do relationships," she says in a strained voice.

"I don't court. I'm not looking for romance or marriage. I want to fuck you, Clara. I want to make you come, and I want your perfect cunt to be mine exclusively." Her eyes shudder for a moment when my thumb finds her clit. Then they reopen, blazing with determination, and I feel her hand on my cock.

"This is mine then," she says.

I bite back a smile, even as I thrust it into her warm, soft palm. "It's all yours, Clara."

I kiss her to end the argument because I don't want her to think about this. I'm offering her so little. She'll see that eventually. I'll let her go back to her life then, but for now—for however long we have—I'll make her mine. My fingers slip inside her and work until her breath comes fast and heavy, her forehead pressing to my shoulder, and as she unravels me, I almost convince myself this can be enough.

CHAPTER EIGHT

The royal family's motto should be: Keep your friends close and your enemies closer. It seems I have to endure a cadre of back-stabbing acquaintances at every social event—my life in London is a string of one demanded appearance after another.

"You don't look excited to be here," Edward says under his breath before kneeling to speak to a small child waving to him behind the cordoned-off entrance to the theatre.

That's an understatement. There's one place I'd much rather be, and it's wedged between Clara's thighs.

"Does anyone enjoy the opera?" I mutter to him as we continue down the ragged red carpet. It's seen as much action as I have, but of an entirely other variety.

Edward guffaws and shoots me a look. "Of course, I do."

"You have your reasons," I say dryly.

"My kind does love the theatre," he agrees, his mouth

pinching slightly when he catches sight of our father ahead of us.

Another reason to dread this evening.

"It's a wonder he lets me attend," Edward says. "It's so gay of me."

My brother's carefully concealed homosexuality was no secret amongst the family, but our father has made it clear it will never be public knowledge. As if he's thinking the same thing, Edward peeks over his shoulder to the parasitic group of young aristocrats that's always at these goddamn events. Judging from the frown that momentarily eclipses his smile, David is among them.

He's made the mistake of falling in love. I wasn't around to teach him that this life and commitment are mutually opposed concepts. He never saw our parents together. Our mother died when he was born, so he doesn't have the memories of the screaming matches and ultimatums. I know the picture my father paints of his marriage. I also know the truth. It's why I won't make the same mistake. Nothing—not even love—can survive this life.

"You haven't told me how you met," I said.

"You want to discuss this now?" he whispers, glancing around as though someone can hear us in the crowd of onlookers. Considering that Norris won't allow anyone within a few yards, I think we're safe.

"What else is there to talk about?" I shrug. My brother, who wasn't exiled to the desert, has an active social life, which means we haven't spent much quality time together. "Maybe we should save this conversation for inside. I'll need something to keep me awake during the performance."

Edward rolls his eyes. "It's not terribly interesting."

"Neither is the opera."

"David was in the same circles at St. Andrew's. We danced around things for a while until one of us made a move."

"He made a move," I guess.

"Is it that obvious?" Edward shoves his hands into his pockets, doing his best to look like we aren't discussing his most closely-guarded secret.

We share a number of characteristics: our mother's coloring, dark hair, blue eyes. But nothing about Edward screams domination.

"Good for David," I say with a low chuckle. It must have taken guts to gamble that he was right about Edward's interest.

"Just don't say anything," he says in a rush.

"I know it's a secret." I look toward our father, feeling the familiar bubble of hatred in my chest. "But why should it be? It's nothing to be ashamed of."

"The monarchy isn't exactly progressive. Dad needs time to get used to the idea and—"

A woman falls against me, and I catch her instinctively, wrapping my arms around her. My palms slide against black silk, and there's a flash of tumbling blonde curls as she presses herself closer. Before I can process the sudden turn, two sinuous limbs hook around my neck.

"Smile," she demands.

I do it, posing for the next picture that will appease

her—and my father. Then, I extricate myself as politely as possible. I'd rather push her away and find the nearest shower. It feels wrong to touch another woman when I've spent most of today fantasizing about Clara. But it's not just any other woman. It's Pepper.

To me, she's still my kid sister's best friend—far too young and off-limits. Even if I could process that she's a woman now, I wouldn't be interested. Maybe it's the way she manages a photo op every time we're within a mile of one another. Maybe it's that there's a snake hiding in her smile.

This wouldn't have happened if you brought Clara. Where the fuck did that come from? I've spent the equivalent of a day with the woman. The last thing either of us needs or wants is to draw attention to the relationship. Plus, there's the very real possibility that my father and his sycophants would corner her and tear her limb from limb. Pepper would probably lead the charge.

But it's the fact that she doesn't belong here that makes me wish I'd invited her. I don't belong either.

Pepper lingers, continuing to brush against my arm. The touches turn my stomach.

"I'm not the Royal you're interested in," I remind her with a smile for the cameras still following us.

She stumbles back a step but regains her footing gracefully. Her eyes narrow into slits before she shakes off my subtle threat.

"What was that about?" Edward asks as we finally reach the foyer.

"You don't want to know," I assure him.

"I doubt most men would turn Pepper down." He's searching for information. My brother reads the tabloids.

"You would," I point out.

Edward straightens his bow tie. His eyes on the door, waiting for his boyfriend to arrive. I have no idea why. They won't risk being spotted together. He echoes my earlier sentiment. "I have my reasons."

"I do, too."

"Why didn't you invite her?" Edward asks, turning the force of his mirror-like gaze on me.

"I thought tonight's show was a comedy. You would have preferred a tragedy?" That's what it would become if I'd brought Clara here amongst this viper's nest.

"No one could object to a legitimate relationship." To his credit, he sounds like he believes this. It's worse than I thought. Not only has Edward made the mistake of falling in love, but he's also made the mistake of buying that love conquers all.

"She's half-American," I remind him. "The wrong half."

"How can you be the wrong half?"

"No accent. Self-confident. Feminist." I might not have spent much time with Clara, but all these things are apparent. They account for why I find myself drawn to her. They're also one of many reasons a relationship won't work.

"So, you're just shagging her?" Edward picks at his cufflink, his eyes still on the entrance.

"Are you just fucking him?" I ask as David enters with Jonathan and Priscilla.

"I don't know what to make of that," Edward mutters. Neither do I. Why am I being so defensive where Clara is concerned?

"He looks miserable," I say. "Perhaps, you should save him?"

Edward flinches at the suggestion and turns away. "Let's find our box."

I follow as he strides away, leaving his real-life behind, abandoning the man he loves. It's fitting, I suppose. Neither of us is a white knight. We don't save the day.

That only happens in stories.

I WAKE up the next morning at the Westminster Royal with a hard and extremely frustrated cock. After an evening with family, I needed distance. The hotel is beginning to feel more like home than Buckingham.

But the bed feels empty.

I don't know what Clara and I are. I only know that I haven't been inside her for over forty-eight hours. My cock, it seems, is keeping track of our time apart.

Fisting it, I run my hands along the shaft, trying to get up the enthusiasm to do it myself. The trouble is that it's felt her beautiful cunt squeezing over it, and it's less than interested in a pathetic stand-in. Still, thinking of how she responded to my touch—how her body submitted again and again—is only making me harder.

Reaching for my mobile, I shoot off a text to her with one hand, my other still stroking myself. What else am I going to do today? My day is mercifully free of more official engagements. I'm merely a photo op waiting to be dragged to the next ball or state event or memorial day. Despite my father's insistence that I need to learn about my future responsibilities, he keeps me away from the important meetings. I'm not king yet. I'm only expected to sit and wait until someone hands me the crown. At least, I know the best way to kill time.

Clara responds almost instantly, but it's bad news: *Can't. Shopping and lunch with my mom.*

For a moment, I imagine tracking her down and slipping into a dressing room. It only makes me want to fuck her against a wall. She wouldn't be able to stay quiet—all those hot, desperate noises escaping her full lips. Everyone would know what we were doing. Fuck, the thought makes me harder. I want them to know. I want them to hear how she begs for it. I want to enjoy the shocked looks on the other shoppers' faces when I stride out, practically holding her upright because I've fucked her so hard her knees are weak.

But that will bring the press to her door. It will destroy the few shreds of privacy she has left after our disastrous meeting at Brimstone. The speculation surrounding us remains high, even though I've been careful to not be seen with her. It's for the best. The media will eat her alive—or what's left of her after my father gets through destroying her.

Still, that means I'll have to find a more discreet way to see her. Dialing Norris, I touch base.

"Are you keeping an eye on Miss Bishop?"

"I have a man tailing her." He sounds concerned,

which is one of his three resting states. "She's at a spa of some sort. Would you like me to meet her?"

"No." There's no point. I'll have to tempt her away, and no matter who has his hands on her at the spa, I'm betting I can make her a better offer. "I was only checking in."

"Very good." Norris hesitates, and I know he wants to say more. It's been off between us since I got back from the Middle East. He needs to know his opinion still matters to me. It does, but that won't always mean I take his advice.

"Out with it."

"Checking in on Miss Bishop belies a certain..."

"I'm not stalking her," I tell him.

"That's not what I'm suggesting." His voice is so dry the connection practically crackles. "I hope you're being cautious."

"I think that I am," I bite out. What does that mean? No one saw us together at the hotel. I'm not copying anyone on our text messages. I didn't take her to a family dinner. "We're being discreet."

"I'm not concerned about when people find out," he corrected me. "I'm concerned about your heart."

"My heart?" I repeat, wondering where this came from. "My heart is the only bit of me that you don't need to worry about."

Silence stretches across the line before he finally clears his throat. "We'll keep an eye on her."

"Thank you." I hang up the phone and glare out the window. Below me, millions of people are leading perfectly ordinary lives going to jobs, shopping, meeting friends for a pint. I have to justify wanting to fuck my girl-friend in private.

Girlfriend. I let the word sink in. I don't hate it as much as I thought I would. Mostly because it suggests ownership, and I want to own Clara Bishop.

I send her another text:

There's a window in this room that would benefit from having your naked body spread across it.

It takes her a moment to respond. When she does, I groan. Apparently, she's going to tease me back.

I'm already naked.

I pop off another: *Tell me more.*

What I actually want is to tell her to get knickers on and tell whoever's hands are on her to shove off. That body belongs to me.

There's no response after a few minutes, and my mind flashes to a muscular man kneading her tender, flawless skin. It seems prudent to remind her that I don't share:

As long as no one else is touching you, poppet. That's my job, and I take my job very seriously.

Her response is frustratingly brief:

Noted, X.

I like her dirty little nickname for me almost as much as I like the one I've given her. Poppet—that's what she is. She lets me play with her, lets me direct her, lets me pull her strings.

I want to see how far I can take that. I want to feel the vibration of my palm when it makes hard contact with the soft flesh of her ass. I want to tie up those slender wrists and fuck her mouth.

I want my hands on her.

But I have to wait until this bloody lunch date is over. I order room service, giving up on getting myself off. When you've had champagne, it's hard to go back to water.

The game between us progresses throughout the day. I imagine her stealing glances at her phone and trying to hide her blush. She can't. I know exactly how pink flushes her cheeks when she reads them. It's the same shade that lovely ass of hers is going to turn when I show her all the other ways I can pleasure her later.

Lose your knickers, I order her while she's shopping at Harrods. She doesn't know that I know exactly where she is, but she doesn't need to. It's all part of the fun.

Who says I have any on?

I know Clara Bishop is wearing knickers, but I get hard anyway. She's not the type to wander around London with a bare cunt. It's one of the reasons I'm going to enjoy teaching her to do just that. Because Clara Bishop is a very good girl, and I'm going to teach her how to be wicked.

I wait until I receive word she's at lunch before I unleash the next barrage of texts:

I need to have my mouth on you. I need to make you come.

I need to hear you crying my name as I fuck you.

She's had enough time with her mother. It's my turn now, and I won't wait much longer. I know exactly what table she's been seated at in Hillgrove's, and if she doesn't dine quickly, I might walk in and carry her out myself.

I'm especially tempted after her next text arrives:

But how can I scream your name with my mouth busy sucking you off?

Fuck. I need her. Now.

You won't know until you've tried.

Christ, I'm so fucking hard for you.

Finish eating and get your pretty ass over to me.

I won't wait much longer for her. She's won this game, and her prize is the rock-hard dick she'll be riding all afternoon. It's time for her to collect her winnings.

I need to see you now. The Westminster Royal.

There's no response, but I know she's on her way. I can already feel her coming.

CHAPTER NINE

When the lift opens, I don't think. I'm on her, my hands and lips vying to see which can cover more of her. Lifting her into my arms, she doesn't resist. She's so pliable, responding to me as I cradle her neck—as I crush her against the wall. I nearly take her right there. It's all I can do not to. I don't think she'll stop me—protection or no. I don't think I can stop myself, and the tiny voice in my head reminding me to care about such things is drowned out by the rush of blood pounding through me.

And then I taste salt on my lips.

It takes a moment to realize she's crying, and now that I do, I feel like a wanker. Had she been crying when she arrived? This is why I don't do relationships. I don't notice things like that.

Or care about them, I tell myself. Except I do.

"Clara." I tilt her chin up so that she has to meet my eyes. "What's wrong?"

She turns away, pushing against me like she wants to be freed. I can't understand why.

"What's going on?" Something is wrong, and I appear to be the cause of it.

"This, Mr. X!" She holds up her phone, and I catch sight of a news article.

"I'm not sure I understand what's happening here." That's a lie. What's happening is the inevitable result of pretending I can have my cake and eat it, too.

"What's happening is that you're an asshole!" She's finally caught on to that. It took her longer than most. I'd almost allowed myself to believe it might be different between us—that she might see me for who I am.

Not that I even know who that is.

But I've fucked it up. Moving to the bar, I lift a bottle of bourbon. "Drink?"

She shakes her head, her shoulders set. Clara's determined to stand her ground. I pour myself a drink.

"So TMI is reporting that I was seen with Pepper last night?" I ask.

This is true. I was, but she doesn't know the circumstances. Annoyance ticks inside me, but I can't decide if it's the results of Clara's assumptions or Pepper's fame-mongering.

"Weren't you the one that said tabloids report rumors as facts?" I continue. "Because I rather appreciated the truth of that statement. Sit down, Clara."

She folds her arms over her chest but otherwise remains still. "I'd prefer to stand."

It's such an adorable little stand-off that I'm already imagining it ending with her over my knee.

"Suit yourself." I don't bother to participate in this stand-off. Instead, I take a chair and focus on my drink, knowing it will rile her up. She needs to get this out of her system—or allow herself to get so worked up that she gives in to what she really wants from me.

"So you know her?" Clara presses.

"Of course I know her. I've known Pepper for years." If only she knew how much I wish that wasn't the case.

Her cold indifference falters for a moment when I tell her the truth. "You aren't making me feel any better."

"Are you jealous?" This makes me smile. I like the idea of Clara Bishop asserting some ownership. Probably, because she seems so hell-bent on pretending that she's comfortable with our arrangement. I know she's not.

Everything about this should bother me. Instead, I rather appreciate the possessive side of her argument. It's an interesting development.

"Who is she?"

"A friend of my sister's." Bringing Sarah into this adds a wrinkle I don't appreciate, though. I don't talk about my sister. Ever. I down the rest of my drink to cover my discomfort.

"And that's it? Wasn't she the girl at the club?" she asks.

So she had recognized her, remembered her. I owe Pepper for whatever this is between Clara and me, but I can't exactly say that which is leaving room for her to fuck with Clara's head. Pepper doesn't even know I'm seeing someone, and she's still screwing it up for me.

"She was," I admit. "You're wondering if I'm using you to get to her."

Her mouth falls open, and I know I'm right. "We're connected, Clara. Can't you feel it? At first, I thought it was just sexual." So much of it is, but that's not what has me abandoning the bourbon and going to her now. "The way your body responds to mine. How it feels when I'm inside you. But it's more than that. I know you feel it."

She swallows hard, as affected by our nearness as I am. "Why even bring it up? You don't do commitment, remember?"

"I remember." Fuck. She has me there. To be honest, I don't even know what I'm saying. What is it that I want from Clara Bishop? "I don't understand it either. I don't even know why I'm explaining myself to you—"

"Because you want exclusivity, remember? You demanded it from me! But apparently not from yourself!"

"Do you think I fucked her?" I take a step closer, pleased with how her body seems to angle toward mine despite how pissed off her suggestion makes me. Does she think I would do that? Go back on our agreement?

"If it walks like a fuck and talks like a fuck," she spits back, recalling our earlier argument.

She has trust issues. That makes two of us, and I can think of only one way to solve that problem.

"I don't lie, Clara," I murmur so that she has to listen closely. I want her to hear this next bit. "And if you accuse me of doing so, I will take you over my knee."

Her eyes widen, her mouth forming a surprised O as she backs away from me a little too slowly to be entirely believable.

"You'd like that," I say, moving toward her, eager to close the space between us. "I see it in your eyes—the hunger."

Clara's hand flies up, but it's a shaky barrier. I catch it and bring it to my lips, kissing it once and savoring how she trembles.

"I'll never lay a finger on you without your permission, but the sooner you accept the truth, Clara, the better."

"What truth?" Her question is forced because she already knows the answer.

"You want to submit to me. You want me to tell you what to do with that sweet little mouth. The way your body responds to mine. It wants to be controlled. Dominated. You want to be dominated. You're so incredibly strong, Clara." I trace the flat plane of her stomach and feel her muscles constrict. "But you need to lose control. You want to."

She shakes her head, but her words are turned inward. "No, I don't."

"You'll be safe with me." I will protect her. She has to see that. Pulling her toward me, I wrap my arms around her, hoping she can feel the truth of it. "I'll never take you further than you can handle, but I will take you to the edge. I will give you more pleasure than you ever thought possible."

Her throat slides, and I wonder if she's swallowing

back a yes or a no. I can see her fighting with herself, and every ounce of me wants to release her from that struggle —to give her the bliss she can only know under my domination.

"I'm not like that," she says in a small voice.

I refuse to allow her to turn away. Staring into her eyes, I will her to see what I'm offering her. "I don't think you understand what I'm offering you. Release. My only thought is of your pleasure. When you give yourself to me, I take that responsibility seriously, Clara."

She turns as though my gaze burns her. "What are we talking about? Ropes and safe words?"

An image of Clara bound in red rope flashes through my mind, and it's all I can do not to throw her over my shoulder and carry her into the bedroom.

Yes, I want ropes and safe words. I want to paint her ass red with my hands. I want to watch her slip into a place where all she knows is my touch.

"Small steps, Clara, but yes. A safeword is a necessity. For now, I want you to trust me. I want you to trust that I will give you pleasure."

"And you'll punish me too?" she asks. "Threaten to spank me if I misbehave?"

"Only when you don't trust me." Which won't be an issue for long, not once she gives in. I know I can show her. "Without trust, you can't give me control, Clara, and then we can't have what we both need."

"You mean what you want!" Her voice pitches up to the verge of hysterical.

"Need," I say firmly, "What you need."

"I... don't..." She shakes her head like the words are stuck.

"Yes, you do." How can I make her see this? I feel it in her. It draws me to her. As much as I want this—as much as I crave the submission of her body—I long to see her free more. "Let me show you."

She pulls away. This time shaking her head with rejection as her eyes grow wet. "I can't. I'm sorry."

And now I see what's holding her back. It's not denial or ignorance. It's fear—an unnatural fear. She isn't scared of what I'm suggesting because it's unknown. She's scared because someone made her that way.

"Someone tried to break you before," I say sadly.

She's crying now, and I want to wipe the tears away. I want to take back what I've suggested. If I had known...

"I'm not him, Clara. That's not what I want to do to you." But how can you explain that there is a difference between submission and humiliation—a difference between giving control and having it taken from you.

"You warned me," she accuses me. "You told me you would hurt me!"

"I did." But that wasn't what I meant. And in the end, even if I convince her to stay now and build the trust I've nearly destroyed, I won't keep her. She deserves more.

She hesitates for a moment, waiting for me to give her a reason to stay. "I should go."

"You probably should," I say, wishing I could let her walk out the door but knowing I can't, "but I wish you wouldn't. Go to bed with me one more time. Let me show you. Let me give you pleasure."

She's already backing away, and I feel a veil descend between us. She can't see what I'm offering, and I can't show her—not until she's ready. Not until she asks.

"I can't," she says.

"You won't." I can't let her go without delivering this final truth. I hate myself for not reaching out for her. I hate myself for not being able to lie and tell her it was all a joke. I hate myself for needing more than she'll give.

I hate myself for scaring her.

CHAPTER TEN

Clara Bishop is not a woman who can be drank away. Still, I've tried. The subtle thump of music is all that penetrates my hiding spot. Below me, hundreds of people are crammed into Brimstone, enjoying themselves or, at least, forgetting whatever troubles plague them. Lucky bastards.

"Let's go down there," Jonathan suggests, eying the crowd. I've no doubt he's spotted some potential conquest. He's dressed for the evening. A button-down, cuffed to look casual. Expensive shoes of some sort. With his blonde hair and blue eyes, he could take home more than a few conquests. I, on the other hand, need a shave, and I'm in a t-shirt and jeans. I know he expects a wild evening. What I can't figure out is why I invited him in the first place.

Maybe because only alcoholics drink alone? But I'm not really drinking. I'm not doing anything, a fact my father reminded me of this morning.

"You go." I grin, trying to sound encouraging. I really would like it if he left.

"Is this about that girl?" Jonathan asks. "You know, the best way to get over her would be to fuck someone else."

My fake smile flattens, even though he has a point. "Not interested."

"You always told me that sometimes a girl needs to get fucked out of your system," Jonathan reminds me. "You'll feel better after."

It's like he's telling me to take some medicine for a headache. "I'm not fucking coming," I growl. "Go!"

My hands close into fists as I try to keep this from getting physical. Because right now, I want to throw him out—toss him to the crowd. But why?

He didn't say anything that wasn't true.

A dark look flashes across his fair features, but he rearranges his face into an apathetic mask. "Fine."

The door slides open, and club music punctures the air as he exits. It reminds me of the night she came here to visit, and I look up, half-hoping to find myself back there. What would I say to change the direction our relationship took?

Nothing.

There is no relationship. There won't be. She was smart enough to run, and I need to be man enough to let her.

Moving to the window, I stare into the crowd, losing myself to the faces below. Maybe he's right. Maybe a night with a stranger would fix all this. I'd never let a woman get to me before. It's always the other way around. I sleep with a woman. It's good. I fuck her again. She gets ideas. It's the natural course of things. I can't blame her. But I do send a clear message by moving on to someone new. Once a girl sees she's replaceable, she understands. It's how I've always operated. I'm not looking for a fucking princess or a happily ever after. No man is.

So why can't I go down there and take some stranger to my bed? Why am I up here nursing a bourbon and wondering if she'll respond to my texts?

There's another burst of club music, and I look up, expecting Jonathan, but it's only Norris, dressed in a suit and looking a bit too James Bond for Brimstone.

He stares stoically at me as if waiting for an invitation to join me. It's been like that since I got back from the front. Before I left, he treated me like a charge—lecturing and interfering as much as he thought necessary. I don't know if he sees me as a man now or if he gave up when all his well-intentioned fathering failed, and I wound up bleeding on the roadside holding my dying sister. I've never asked.

I hold up my glass and motion for him to pour himself one.

"Are we drinking or admiring it?" He doesn't bother with the bourbon. I knew he wouldn't. Not since he's been stuck playing bodyguard and chauffeur.

"Neither." I turn my attention to the club.

"You aren't going to find her down there," Norris says softly.

"Who?" I'm tired of this conversation. I'm tired of

people seeing through me and acting like they know what's best for me. I know exactly where to find Clara Bishop. I know she starts work in the morning at Peters & Clarkwell. I know she's been shopping with her best friend. I know she doesn't want to see me. I know I shouldn't want to see her.

Norris doesn't answer me. He's been around when I've received reports from friends inside SIS. He knows I'm tracking Clara, but he's kept his thoughts to himself, and it's driving me crazy.

"I'm not looking for her," I say, my eyes glued to the swarm of club-goers.

"You don't have to," he says in a clipped tone. "You know exactly where she is. You always do. If I might, that's not exactly healthy behavior for either of you."

I know that, too. She admitted she'd had a bad relationship before. I'd had to stop myself from seeking out information on this ex of hers. But I had checked up on her. "I'm not stalking her."

Norris raises a gray brow. "Just because you're using MI5 doesn't make it right."

"I just want to know that she's safe. That the reporters are leaving her alone." I walk away from the window, away from him and the accusation. But I can't seem to get far enough.

"The reporters have been quiet," he says. "They seem more interested in Ms. Lockwood since that photo at the opera."

"I guess I owe Pepper one," I bite out. "She took the heat off Clara. It's what I wanted, you know. Clara to have a normal life. I never wanted anyone to find out about us."

The pause between us is deafening, but it's what he asks next that's loaded. "Why?"

"Because she doesn't belong in my world." It's obvious. I live in a world of glass crowns and pretty cages. No beautiful creature belongs there. "It's better to keep her away from all this."

"But it's part of who you are." Norris watches me as I continue to pace, his eyes sweeping along with me while the rest of him remains still.

"Why would that matter? She doesn't belong here." She doesn't belong in the ugliness surrounding me. I can only imagine what she'd think. I'd made the mistake of showing her a glimpse of my darkness, and she'd run. "If she knew the truth about my family, she'd disappear forever."

"Isn't that what you want?" Norris says. "Show her. Lose her."

He's calling my bluff. I know because this has already occurred to me. All I have to do to lose Clara is allow her closer. She'll see the truth. She'll run.

CHAPTER ELEVEN

I've always favored control. That seems more important now than ever before. If only I'd employed such restraint last night. Jonathan hadn't succeeded in sending me home with anyone, but he had managed to get me totally pissed. I have the headache to prove it.

Rolling over, I spot a glass of orange juice and a few pills. Apparently, my debauchery had not gone unnoticed. I ignore a flash of memory that involves me and a bottle of Scotch and one of the palace's many reception rooms. Who knows who saw me? I take the medicine gratefully, ignoring how much I might pay for them later.

My cock is stiff, painfully hard, and heavy. I stroke it absently, even though I know nothing will come of it. I have no desire to jack off, but that doesn't mean I'm not horny. I've never wanted to fuck so badly in my life.

The issue is there's only one person I'm interested in fucking, and I've promised to stay away. I did it in her best interests. Now I'm wondering if I've thought enough about my own interests.

I'm interested in the freckles that dust her shoulders and flutter down to her breasts. Breasts I need in my mouth. I recall how her body writhed, how she'd fallen undone over and over.

"Fuck," I groan as my climax covers my palm. But the pleasure is dulled like it's been filtered through a sieve. All the good bits are absent, what's left is weak and unwanted.

For one startling moment, my eyes still blurry from sleep, my head still pounding from my hangover, I wonder if I'll ever get off again properly. I'd told myself before that I'd screw her out of my system. I hadn't gotten the chance to do that.

But what if Clara Bishop is a woman you can never have enough of? That's the trouble. I can't risk more. I won't put her through this. I'm not about to lead an inno-cent into hell just to get my rocks off.

Then again, it is our secret. We'd agreed to that. If no one knows I'm still seeing her, then I can ride this out—ride her—until I'm finally sated.

I sit up, determined to find her, and clutch my head immediately. I need breakfast first. That will give me time to come up with a plan. Clara fears me. I need her to see she shouldn't. I can be different for her. I can need less if that's what it takes to have her.

When I finally exit my apartment, dressed in a t-shirt and jeans, I find the cleaning staff patiently waiting to access it. I shoot them an apologetic smile before heading towards the kitchens. I'd opted for a casual look, banking on my ability to blend in with the crowd more easily.

Edward catches me before I'm past our family wing.

"He's on a rampage," he warns me, shoving a stack of tabloids into my arms. "Hit the stands an hour ago."

"What did I do now?" No doubt someone took a picture of me at the club, stumbling drunkenly out, and sold it to pay for a few pints of their own.

My body constricts when I spot the first headline, each muscle tightening as though if I stand still long enough, the rage seeping through me will evaporate.

It doesn't.

Scanning the report, if one can even call this rubbish that, doesn't help either. I have no idea how they did it. Or who is responsible. All I know is that every personal text message I sent to Clara—every filthy, wicked thought I'd used to tempt her to my bed—is there in black and white.

"Father will be here any moment," Edward continues. "I expect"—

"I don't give a fuck what he thinks," I growl, ripping the papers in half. "I need to go."

I stalk off before he can stop me. There's only one person I owe an explanation—and I know exactly where to find her.

NORRIS ISN'T SPEAKING to me. I gathered he was upset when I gave him the address where I needed to go. He's seen the report on her. He knows where she works. He knows she's just started her job.

"Let it out," I finally bark from the back seat of the Rolls. I can avoid my father's wrath. Hell, I even revel in it a bit. But Norris doesn't usually give me the cold shoulder. He's more into the standard lecture.

"I don't see the point." His eyes stay on the road. His control makes me feel like a wild card. There's no emotion betrayed in his voice. His body remains relaxed. I assume this is a holdover from years in military and private service. I don't ask.

"But you don't think I should go to her." He'd made his feelings on this known. He didn't approve of me checking up on Clara Bishop on paper. Why would he encourage me to seek her out in person, especially after this fiasco?

"Timing is an art form few humans master. None of them are male." There's an unexpected dryness in his tone. Norris is cracking a joke. There might be hope for us yet.

"I need to see that she's okay. I got her into this mess."

"By not staying away? Will going to her improve matters?"

He has a point. I refuse to admit it. "Just drive."

This time I catch his lips twitching in the rearview mirror. Maybe he's human after all.

Peters & Clarkwell takes up one floor of a nondescript office building not far from Westminster. The benefit of this is that everyone here is busy going about their days.

Work and lunch and whatever else normal people did during the week.

I shove my hands into my jeans and stroll toward the lift, pleased that no one seems to notice my appearance. Apparently, the paparazzi hasn't caught up to where she works. Yet.

There's no use pretending that she'll remain a secret now. They'll follow her incessantly. My father will demand answers. I didn't lead her into hell gently. I'd dropped her into the inferno. She needs me to protect her now.

I'm planning to tell her—planning to explain exactly how things are going to be when the lift slides open, revealing her. Her knuckles are white on her bag's strap. Her cheeks are burning with a lovely shade of embarrass-ment. Every ounce of me wants to shove her against a wall, hike up her skirt, and show her that I'm capable of all the things I'd promised in those sodding text messages.

She stumbles when she spots me, but before I can respond, she straightens and heads straight for me. I hadn't expected that.

Clara Bishop is strong.

Good.

She needs to be.

THE BUZZING behind her reminds me more of a beehive than an office. Heads pop over cubicles. There's a woman whose tea is dripping on the floor as she holds the cup at an odd angle. Every person in the office is staring at me. I only care that she's staring, even if her glare is murderous.

It's a pity all these people are here because Clara Bishop is sexy when she's angry. I can't help thinking about the perfect body under her proper office clothes—of what I want to do to it.

"What are you doing here?" She crosses her arms over her chest, still fuming, but now that she's closer, I realize the fury stops before it reaches her eyes. I recognize the hungry, wild look she can't hide. It had been there when I took her to bed. I'd seen it as I pushed her to the edge and then over it. Her breath catches, and I can almost hear her say it. Yes, please. She'd been so polite with her desire. So eager. So pliant. I want her to say those words again.

"You've had long enough. I need to talk to you." I don't give her the chance to argue with me. I doubt she would in front of her co-workers. Instead, I take her by the arm gently—I'll save the roughness for when I get her into bed—and lead her toward the lift.

But she's not exactly following my lead. Her body is rigid, coiled tight, and I wonder if it's her anger or how long it's been since I fucked her that's bothering her.

"Couldn't you text me?" she asks dryly, sounding anything but amused.

I sigh and drop her arm as we step inside the lift. "I guess you saw that, too."

But I don't wait for her response. I can't wait. I'm on her, pressing her body against the stainless steel wall of the lift. I need to feel her body against mine. My hands pin her wrists above her head as my hips lock against her.

I know she can feel my cock pressing into the soft flesh of her abdomen. I might be going too far. She'd made her feelings clear the last time I saw her, but I hadn't imagined the connection between us. It hangs between us now, an invisible thread pulled tight between her body and mine. Surely, she feels it. She has to.

"Alexander!" Her cry is half panic, half prayer.

"Why haven't you answered my texts?" I demand.

"The whole world can read that you want to go down on me on a gossip site, and you're worried about that?" she stammers, her eyes widening. Her body stays perfectly still, resisting the tug of that connection between us. It's too controlled, but I sense something more lingering under the surface of her rebuke: concern.

Concern for me.

She has pushed me away. And she has come when I've called. She's torn between my warnings and my temptations. The truth is that she's too good for me—too kind, too normal—and we both know it. So why don't I just let her go? I think of the texts and the lying tabloids. It's been a long time since I gave a shit what any of them had to say. But I care now—I care what she thinks. I don't want her to believe them.

"I don't give a damn what they can read!" This realization explodes from me, and I back away, afraid I'll scare her. "Why do you care what they think, Clara?"

"Me?" Her hand goes to her heart—to the one part of her I will never let myself have. "You were the one who wanted to meet me in secret at a fucking hotel!"

It takes me a moment to process this. She thinks I was

hiding her because I was ashamed? As though any man wouldn't want the world to know the things he'd done to a woman like her. "I did that to protect you. You were scared of the paparazzi."

"They were reporting we were in a relationship," she says, "and I didn't know who you were at the time."

"We are in a relationship," I tell her even as my brain struggles with the concept. We are? Where did that come from? I'm surprised to discover that I do very much care about this fact—and it is a fact to me. Clara Bishop belongs to me. She did then, and she does now.

Her mouth opens, her perfect lips are wide but unmoving. She blinks as if clearing her thoughts. When she finally speaks, confusion coats her words. "We broke things off."

"You were overwhelmed, and I gave you space, but did you think I would allow you to end things like that?" I ask. "I made it clear that I hadn't had my fill of you."

"But you didn't want to be seen with me," she babbles, her eyes darting between me and the floor. "You can't pick and choose when to be in a relationship!"

"I wanted to protect you." I brush my index finger along the curve of her cheekbone, marveling at the supple softness of her skin. "I didn't want to scare you. I can do that all on my own."

Her answering laugh has a hollow ring, nearly smothered by the ding of the lift doors. "You can at that."

"So is that what's going on?" I pull her from the open lift toward a deserted alcove where we won't be seen. "A misunderstanding?"

It couldn't be that simple. Her tears tell me as much. "I wish it was."

"You're scared of me." It's my fault. Why wouldn't she be scared? After I'd warned her to run? After I'd pursued her anyway? I've been as dogged as the goddamn paparazzi and my motives are even less chivalrous. "I tried to warn you."

"Maybe I don't understand," she says to my surprise.

I grip her hip tightly, the need to touch her driving me and making it harder to think. She needs reassurances. I have no idea how to do that. Physically, I can protect her —and I will. But how do I prove she's safe with me in other ways? How do I guard her heart from the world— and from myself?

"When I told you that I was protecting you from the reporters, how did you feel?" I ask after a moment.

There's hesitation as she considers. "I guess that—" she pauses for what feels like an eternity "—I felt safe."

"Why?" If she felt that way, there's hope. She needs to understand. I need her to understand.

"Because you care." There's revelation in her voice.

There's something else, though—a hint of sadness. I wonder what she's faced. Who has let her down? Betrayed her? I decide, at that moment, that I won't allow myself to do the same.

"I do care, Clara." I hover over her, our mouths inches apart. Not so I can kiss her, but so that there's no chance she doesn't hear me. "I didn't want you to experience being trashed by the tabloids."

"So it wasn't that you didn't want to be seen with me?" she asks.

How could I have been stupid enough to not see this coming?

"Have you looked in the mirror lately? I can only assume you haven't, so let me describe what you look like right now. Clara Bishop has large, gray eyes with fluttering lashes and a button nose. That would be enough to make her pretty, but then she has these pouty lips that make me hard. Her hair is silky and soft, and no matter how much she tries to control it, there are always some locks that escape to drift down her neck or blow across her face. I can't help imagining letting it all down, watching it fall over her shoulders as she comes on my cock." I press into her as a reminder of what she does to me. "She drives me crazy, and I honestly don't care who knows it."

"But you don't do relationships, Mr. X," she says softly.

"I don't do romance," I remind her gently, "but if you'll let me, I will do pleasure."

"There's no one else then, Mr. X?" She's taunting me with the alias, calling my bluff.

"Too formal, poppet." I don't know how to assure her that we are on equal footing—that we want the same thing.

"Okay, then. There's no one else then, X?"

"I'm true to my word, Clara." And I mean it with every fiber of my being.

She trembles but this time, it's with fear. "But you want to dominate me."

Someday she won't fear it. I'll help her—guide her there. For now...

"I want to give you pleasure. When you found out I was protecting you, it made you feel safe. That's what I want to do." I brush my lips across her jaw, earning a shiver of pleasure this time. "I want to show you that I can protect you while showing you the heights of pleasure you've never known."

"I don't know." Uncertainty colors her words. She truly doesn't.

I drop my head to her shoulder and consider my options. I can't force her to understand, but I can give her time—and what she needs. Lifting my eyes to meet hers, I mean it when I promise, "You win."

"I do?" She sounds surprised.

"We'll do it your way, Clara. I want you. I want you any way I can have you."

"You agree that I'm not your submissive?" she asks slowly.

"I agree not to push you, Clara—unless you ask me to..." I leave it hanging. Clara Bishop will ask me to dominate her body—beg me to. It's as inevitable as my arrival here today. Neither of us can walk away from this. Not anymore.

Her body, which has been still against mine, strains into me with unspoken need.

"Soon, poppet." I tuck her hair behind her ear, meaning it. I can't resist kissing her neck to seal my promise. "What are your plans this evening?"

"I'm flexible." The answer is coy, and I know that I've won.

I smile at her answer, not at what I'm about to ask her. "There's a thing this evening. Would you go with me?"

"What kind of thing?"

"A ball." I press my index finger to her lips before she can refuse me. "And before you say no, it is for an excellent cause. We're raising money for endangered animals. And furthermore, I don't want to go either."

I know what I'm asking her, but I need her to understand where we stand. If she thought I was trying to hide her, I would prove her wrong—in the most public way possible. Still, she should know what she's getting into. Not that there is any way to fully prepare her.

"There's no going back after something like this," I warn her. "If you want a chance at normalcy—at privacy —you should say no. But if you want a relationship, it seems as good a place as any to start."

"What about you? Do you want normal?" she asks seriously.

I tell her the truth. "I don't even know what those words mean. I never have."

She strokes my cheek, trying to comfort me, even as I see the war in her eyes. Maybe she understands the stakes more than I think. Maybe she knows this is a mistake. I'm not even certain I'm doing the right thing.

"I can protect you from this. We can meet privately if you prefer," I offer. "If you don't want to come tonight, I understand, but please understand me when I say"—my eyes hood—"you will come tonight in other ways."

This earns me a grin. "Is that so?"

I kiss her because I'm running out of ways to convince her to be by my side.

"But they know about us," she says when we break apart. "They have the texts."

"By Monday morning, MI5 will know who hacked my account, and they'll be in jail."

"And that will be another huge story. The kind that links back to this one," she says. "An arrest won't erase that."

"No, but it will send a message, and don't worry, I've devised other ways of contacting you."

"Carrier pigeons? Smoke signals?" she teases. Clara, in a good mood, is like a rainbow on a cloudy day. It makes the storm worth it.

I can't help feeling a little cocky now. "That can be arranged."

She looks at me, and I think maybe I can be Prince Charming if she asks me. "I can't keep pretending you mean nothing to me. I don't like hiding or secrecy, but I still want my privacy. Is that something we can make work?"

"Of course." I want her life to be as normal as possible. I owe her that much if I'm going to be selfish enough to keep her.

"I'll go," she finally agrees, but almost instantly, I see doubt creep across her beautiful face. I kiss her until she can't remember why she was worried. I kiss her to forget that I am still worried.

CHAPTER TWELVE

Clara,

I know I've scared you. I have no right to ask you to be with me. There are risks, more than I've let on about, but I can't release you. I'm afraid that now, even if you tried to run, I couldn't let you go. I crave your body. The touch of your skin. The sweet silk of your thighs against my face and the taste of you on my lips. Even as I warn you away from me, know that you are mine, and I protect what is mine. Even from myself.

X

It's my fourth attempt to write her a note today, and I'm running out of time. I must have suffered a temporary bout of madness when I asked her to go to the party with me. I'd left out a few important details.

Tonight isn't simply a ball. That would be too easy. It's my father's birthday party. I'm not certain who I'm trying to send a message to: her, him, or myself. I don't want that kind of attention on her, but if we're going to do this, it's inevitable.

Which means it's time to send the sodding note. There's no way to prepare her for this. Sliding the card into a red envelope, I use my personal seal to ensure this message is only read by her. It's archaic compared to text, but I can't stomach the idea of the press twisting our words—or knowing the private details of our sex life. Clara's body belongs to me. I've made that clear. I don't want to share it with anyone, even a tabloid headline.

"Can you deliver this to Clara's flat?" I ask Norris.

He crooks a bushy eyebrow as he accepts the card. "A love letter?"

"A warning." It's a much more accurate description of the contents. I'm throwing her into the water well aware there are sharks. In my family, there are no safe spots to learn to swim. This is the closest I can come while still protecting her.

"If you don't mind me saying so," Norris pauses to clear his throat, "you could try to romance the poor girl."

"Romance? Are you getting sentimental on me?" If I'm honest, Norris has never struck me as the type.

"Old dogs know the best tricks," he advises me. "And getting a girl to fall in love with you is the oldest trick in the book, as well as the hardest."

My blood turns to ice at his words, freezing me to the spot. "I don't want her to fall in love with me."

I mean it with every ounce of my body. Falling in love with me would be the worst mistake Clara could ever make.

Norris doesn't respond, but I see the doubt in his pale, blue eyes. I try to see the situation as he does. I've gone after this woman repeatedly. I've broken my promise to stay away. I've invited her to meet my family.

"I'm not in love with her," I tell him.

"You don't have to convince me." He sounds...amused.

"But you're probably right," I continue ignoring the laughter he's obviously suppressing. "If she has to put up with my family this evening, she deserves more than a note. Do you have any suggestions?"

This is new territory for me. I've rarely done so much as buy a woman dinner in the past. It's never been requisite to getting one into bed, and I've never felt the need to have a second go with a woman once I'd had her. I suppose dating requires a bit more in the activity department. Although I doubt she'll complain about the orgasms in her future.

"Flowers, sir," he says. "Flowers are always well-received."

"Will we have time to pick some up?" I could always go to the garden and find some myself, but I can guarantee the staff will gossip. I'd rather my father not know that I'm bringing a date tonight. The element of surprise is all I have working in my favor. With any luck, he'll be too shocked to be rude.

I don't hold high hopes for this method.

"Allow me. I need to deliver this after all." Norris flashes me the card. "What kind of flowers do you want to give her?"

I recall when I was very little, and my mother helped me address valentines to my primary school class. We chose one for each student based on my whims. She would look at the list of children's names and say, "What makes you think of Annie, darling?" At the time, my answers were selfish or stupid or some mixture of the two.

My mother would like Clara. She'd tell me what flowers to give her or help me decide. I can almost hear her ask me now: what makes you think of Clara, darling?

I think of the blush that creeps over Clara's porcelain skin when I say something filthy to her, of the color of her lips after I kiss her for hours, of the way I imagine her delicate flesh would redden under my palm.

"Red roses. I'll give her red roses." Beautiful and delicate like her, but with thorns as dangerous as this arrangement.

CHAPTER THIRTEEN

Her flat isn't what I expect. Clara belongs in a tower, locked safely away from the world. Instead, she lives in East London in a pre-war flat that looks less than average. I can't help noticing the lack of security for the building. She's far too exposed here. We're lucky there's a back entrance and that Norris has found a quiet backstreet not populated by paparazzi that leads directly to it. The man deserves a raise or a knighthood. I doubt he'd accept either.

"We should put someone on her," I say to Norris. He's riding shotgun this evening since we've taken a limousine.

"Your father isn't going to like it," he mutters.

"My father never likes anything I do," I remind him.

"I'll look into it." Norris opens his car door and exits the limo.

I follow suit, and he stares at me.

"Sir?"

"I'm going to pick her up." I reach inside and pick up the bouquet I've brought for her. It's enough that he's stuck running my errands. I didn't even buy the flowers. "This is a date. I should play the part."

He pauses, weighing his options. He knows me well enough to know that I'm going inside with or without him. "I'll be right here."

Having a bodyguard at the back door isn't exactly normal as far as I know, but it's as close as I'm likely to get. I nod, relieved for the small bit of ordinary I'm allowed, and head inside.

I take the stairs two at a time despite my tuxedo. I practically grew up in formal wear, but now it feels restrictive. I'd grown used to a uniform of fatigues. Now I'm stuck in the uniform of a prince. I'm not certain it suits me anymore.

Pausing at her door, I run a hand through my hair, mussing it out of place. At least, that makes me feel more like me rather than some slicked and shined version of Prince Charming.

It's not until I knock that I realize I've never done this before. I've picked up plenty of women in bars or at parties. If I'd attended tonight's evening alone, I would have had a dozen options for potential companions for the night. But I've never knocked on a girl's door. I've never brought a woman flowers. Clara Bishop is my first date.

But she isn't the one to answer the door. I barely process the blonde who opens it because before I can say hello, I spot her.

Dressed in silver silk that dances over her perfect

body, the swell of her breasts on display, Clara is every dream I've ever had. Dark curls spill over one creamy shoulder as striking as the scarlet red of her lips against her fair skin. Looking at her, I suddenly understand the answer to every question that's ever been asked.

Her.

The blonde breaks the silence. Moving to allow me entry, she says, "It's nice to meet you."

It takes effort to peel my eyes from Clara in that dress and the thousands of dirty ideas it's inspiring. I turn to introduce myself. It's the polite thing to do. Another strange first: meeting the roommate. "Alexander. You must be Belle."

She hesitates, then finally nods. "Are you looking forward to this evening?"

"Yes," I lie. I can think of much better ways to spend the evening with Clara. All of them involve that dress coming off. Something that won't be possible at a sodding birthday party. "That is, I'm looking forward to the company."

Belle looks pleased by my answer. She inclines her head toward the hall. "Excuse me a moment."

At least, she knows when three is company. I step toward Clara, awkwardly presenting the flowers.

"I thought you didn't do romance." She sniffs them delicately, clearly surprised.

"Consider it a consolation prize," I say. "If you're going to put up with my family for the evening, you deserve a reward."

That's not why I brought them. Why the fuck can't I

just tell her she's lovely and take her hand and be normal? Why can't I bring her roses and sweep her off her feet?

Because as she said, I don't do romance. I've warned her, and yet, here I am doing exactly that and failing completely. Even worse, I realize that I've set her on edge. She's searching her cabinets for a vase with a barely suppressed frantic, wild-eyed panic. She's meeting my family—another first. I'd nearly forgotten, and so had she, apparently.

I can't watch her fret. Moving behind her, I grab her hips, willing her to be still for a moment. "Don't think about them."

"That's easier said than done," she whispers. "I barely know what's going on between us, and now I'm going to meet your family."

"It's not a big deal. Just remember that if they're jerks, it's because of me and not you." I try to sound casual, but my hands tighten on her. I'm leading her into the lion's den. I might as well display her on a silver platter. They'll be salivating to get a taste of her the moment we arrive. She'll be lucky to survive.

"That doesn't really make me feel better," she admits.

"Don't think about it." I draw her to me, feeling calmed by her body against mine. "Right now, I want you to think about what I'm going to do to you in that dress."

This earns me a smile. "I don't know how I'm supposed to concentrate with you looking like that."

"She does look fantastic, doesn't she?" Belle interrupts.

"Yes." I agree absently.

Belle finds the sought-after vase we've forgotten and brandishes it in triumph. "Here. Oh, wait!"

She whirls around and pulls something from a drawer.

"Sorry!" she says to me as she moves between us a moment later. When she steps away, a rose in full bloom is tucked into Clara's hair.

"Perfect." I can already imagine that being the only thing I allow Clara to keep on later.

"I need to go. Philip will be downstairs." Belle kisses her goodbye. "See you there!"

Clara looks relieved at the reminder that she won't be alone with me. I wonder what it's like to have friends at these things. Usually, I feel surrounded by snakes. It must be comforting.

"Shall we?" I offer her my arm. "If we don't get going, I'm going to spread you across the kitchen counter."

She bites her lip, but it doesn't hide the excitement glinting in her eyes. Is that because I'm taking her to a party or because she wants to be spread across the counter?

I shake away the temptation to find out. "Let's get to the car before we miss the party, Miss Bishop."

"Lead the way, X."

CHAPTER FOURTEEN

Norris proves himself once again by managing to keep our arrival and exit secret. It's no small feat. The press might as well have set up tents across from Clara's flat. She looks startled when I guide her away from the main entrance to her building to one tucked in the rear.

When we step outside, something primal awakens in me. I keep my hand on her back, watching the world around us as I help her into the limousine. My whole body is on edge, waiting for even the slightest threat. Relief washes over me when I shut the door behind her. Norris watches me from his place beside the driver's side door. He hadn't been keen on the idea of me picking her up and bringing her out alone.

"Are we good?" I ask.

He tips his head. "No trouble."

I allow my thoughts to return to Clara and her gown and all the wicked things I'm going to do to her.

"Do you know what I love about London this evening?" I ask, sliding beside her.

Her head tilts, and she casts curious eyes at me. Something else dances behind the curiosity, though.

"The traffic. I never appreciated it before tonight." I move closer, taking her face in the palm of my hand. Angling it for a kiss, I pause and marvel at her. Where did she come from? Why now? I shouldn't allow myself to want her like I do, but I'm finding that when it comes to Clara Bishop, I have little control over my feelings. Like how much I missed her when we were apart. Like how scared I am to lose her again. Like how desperately I need to kiss her. I give in to the emotion, crushing her mouth to mine. Clara reacts, clutching the hand I hold against her cheek. She presses it harder as if she craves the contact as much as I do. Her body melts against mine, inviting me to focus on the physical needs driving me instead of the questions my desire raises.

"Poppet," I say softly, "I've thought about you all week."

Her breath grows shallow as I move to show her exactly what I've been thinking about. Lifting her skirt, my hand slides up her soft thighs and urges her legs apart to discover nothing but bare flesh.

I groan, unable to contain my pleasure. "That's hardly playing fair."

"This dress doesn't work with panties." She speaks like it's an apology, but her coy smile says she knows exactly what she's doing.

"Personally, I'm of the opinion that no dress actually

works with panties." I decide to show her why, moving to my knees. Thank god, we took the stretch limo.

"No," she says. I do, but only out of respect.

"I don't like that word from you, poppet." I hate it, in fact. "I have a very hard time listening to it."

"No, I want you." Her tongue darts over her red lips like a teaser of what's to come. Namely me.

"And you can have me."

"No, I want to taste you."

I can't say no. Mostly, because I don't want to. Lounging back, I watch as she bunches her skirt to her thighs and kneels before me. She takes her time, and I say a prayer of thanks to whatever god is in charge of city traffic. A soft hand glides up my leg until it reaches the waistband of my trousers. She unfastens them and draws the zipper down, unleashing me into her hand. I moan in appreciation as her delicate fingers close over my cock. She strokes it, sending blood pounding to it until my every thought, my every sensation, is primitive. I barely control my need to pounce on her. I want to fuck her. I want to fill her. Before I lose control, her mouth closes over my balls, sating the need to have her. She's giving herself to me—giving me her luscious mouth. I spread my legs farther, allowing her better access—my gift to her.

The beast inside me takes over, grunting and groaning, as she continues her devotion up my shaft. I could come just watching her suck me off.

"You look so fucking hot with your red lips wrapped around my cock." I wrap a hand around her neck so I can feel each motion as she bobs slowly up and down until

I'm rock hard and ready to explode. "It makes me want to fuck you."

Before I can pin her down and do that, she sucks harder. Her cheeks hollow as her pace increases. I see it there. She wants me to come, and I want to fill her with me—in every way possible.

"Oh, Clara, you are so beautiful." I give in, falling against the seat as she drives me to my climax. "I'm going to come."

After the first jet of release, I manage to lift my gaze to her. She's not just swallowing. She's savoring. Each movement of her throat is greedy. She's hungry for me, and I need to give her more.

I lift her into my lap, kissing her like she's oxygen. I need to fuck her. Now. Flipping her onto the seat, I shove her skirt back up. I slide a finger along her seam, nudging it gently past the folds. "Sucking me off made you wet."

I love how she feels on my skin—velvet and wet and warm. I want to feel it surrounding my cock. I've never considered something so reckless before. But I trust Clara, and whatever we are, I know it's different for her, too.

"I need to be inside you. Nothing between us. Is that okay?"

"Yes, please," she moans. I don't need to hear anything else. I take my time, pushing inside her slowly. Every inch is a revelation. She's so fucking perfect. Tight and hot around my dick, but it's her face, glowing with bliss, that nearly undoes me.

"Not yet, poppet." It makes me want to do things to her—things I promised I didn't need. Lies I told, I realize now. I'll fight those urges to be with her. I'll take it slowly. I'll lead this lamb away from the safety of her world into the darkness of mine with deliberate care.

She whimpers as though she needs me to move faster.

I slip a hand between us and fondle her clit. "Think of a safe word, poppet. You don't need it now, but you might later, and when we're in that moment, you won't be able to think of it."

She shakes her head—beautiful, obstinate woman.

"I'm trying to control myself, poppet, but I want to make you feel safe. Choose a word that makes you feel safe," I explain.

"How about majesty?"

"Your safe word shouldn't be something that you might have to use for other reasons."

"Oh X, do you really think you're going to get me to call you Your Majesty?"

An involuntary smirk slashes my lips. "With what I'm planning to do to you, you might."

She looks torn between kissing me, hitting me, and ignoring me entirely. Finally, she whispers, "Brimstone."

It's an interesting choice.

"You could just say go to hell." I can't help myself.

"I thought you wanted me to pick a word that I would remember."

"Brimstone, though?"

"It was the last time I said no to you," she says softly.

Ahh. Now I understand. It makes me like it even less.

"You've said no to me since then."

"But I didn't really mean it those times," she says.

This changes things. I reward her honesty with a teasing twist of my thumb. "Whatever you wish, Clara."

"Then fuck me."

She doesn't have to ask twice. Instinct takes over. I drive into her. Over and over. Every part of me needs to fill her. I ache to see her eyes widen as I claim her. She's mine. I want to watch the moment she realizes it, too.

"Look at me," I command. "I want to see you as you come."

Her eyes flutter open, and I let go, releasing my last thread of control. My hips roll violently against her, and I empty inside her. She shutters and cries out, falling apart in my arms. When her body finally stills, her arms circle my neck as she sags against me in a boneless heap.

"I love knowing that you're full of me," I whisper into her hair. "All night I'm going to be thinking of being inside you, knowing that I've marked you. Knowing that you're mine."

She looks up, eyes sparkling, and kisses me. Something in them has changed.

Something in me has changed.

Will everyone see that tonight? Or will they simply focus on the stunning woman by my side?

"And I'll be thinking of your hot, naked cunt under this sexy dress. I want it to be ready for me if I need it."

"It will be."

I could linger here with her like this forever. She's so vulnerable and small in my arms. When she comes, she is a queen, and I'm her servant, driven to give her pleasure. Now? I've weakened her right before she'll need her strength the most. I help her adjust her dress grudgingly, stealing kisses as I do. It's a reminder that we're on our way to the ball. I won't be able to control what happens there. No one can control the press or my family.

"Stop, you fiend." She smacks me playfully, reminding me that right now, everything is perfect. Especially her.

"I can't help it. I can't keep my hands off you."

"I'm not wearing underwear," she reminds me. "You don't have to work so hard."

"We'll see about that." If she only knew. I sit back, brushing a loose strand of hair from her face. Her cheeks are flushed. She's so alive. She's nothing like them. She's nothing like me.

Clara checks her make-up. It's unnecessary. She's lit up from within. I did that.

What's going to undo it? Why did I bring her here? Why am I putting her through this? I take her hand, knitting her fingers through mine, and silently vow to keep her safe from the poisoned hearts waiting for us.

"Are you ready?" I ask. She stares at our hands before finally nodding.

When we arrive, I circle the back of the car slowly. Opening her door, I give her my hand again. I won't let her go until I have to. I do my best to shield her from the paparazzi. But it's no use. Cameras flash. The crowd shouts. Her eyes are wide and startled as she takes in the scene around us. I smile, hoping she finds it reassuring before I lead my lamb to the slaughter.

CHAPTER FIFTEEN

I slip into my shell as we make our way through the
lobby. There are friends and family and the bloody
paparazzi everywhere. Keeping Clara's hand tightly
clasped in mine, I weave through them. I don't bother
pausing for photo ops. No one wants those pictures of us.
They'll publish whatever they take that looks scandalous,
not some poised photograph of a happy couple.

Why the hell did I bring her here?

There's some relief when we reach the ballroom, but
it's short-lived. I survey the people gathered there. It's the
usual crowd—dignitaries and four-times removed cousins
and politicians and celebrities. All here to pretend my
father isn't a giant bastard for one night. I can't help
wondering who picked the safari theme or how much it
cost. Jungle ferns and birds flying overhead? It's beyond
ridiculous.

"Are you okay?" Clara murmurs in a low voice.

"I'm fine, Clara," I say, spotting Norris. "Excuse me

one moment."

My goal this evening is to keep Clara at a distance from my family. She'll have to meet them, of course. I can't get around that, and it was the point of bringing her here. I chose a public event on purpose—there's less chance of a scene.

"Alexander," Norris greets me coolly. He stands casually, but I have no doubt he's sweeping the room for security concerns. The man never rests.

"Keep an eye on my family, and I'll keep an eye on her," I say. "It's best we control all interactions."

"And do you know where she is?" he asks, each word as sharp as a knife's tip.

I turn to my side, my stomach flipping over when I realize she's not there. I turn and stare at the crowded room, searching for her. I left her. I remember now. What am I doing? How am I fucking this up already? I can't think clearly when she's near me—that point's been proven again and again—but this is a new low. "I told her I'd be right back," I say wildly.

"She's not a dog, Alexander. You can't expect her to stay put," he advises me quietly. His chin tilts to the corner. "She's with her friend."

I follow his gaze to find Clara laughing with Belle and another woman I don't recognize. Clara obviously knows her, though. The sickening pit in my stomach shrinks. I know it won't be gone entirely until I have her within reach again.

"I won't let her out of my sight again," I mutter.

"Is that wise? There are a few warnings you should

deliver yourself," Norris says. "You can't expect everyone here to behave without a little incentive."

"I shouldn't leave her alone."

"She's not alone, and she's perfectly safe here. No one will touch her inside." His certainty is reassuring.

Clara is safe—physically. But she's not in physical danger here. The wounds those closest to me will inflict are more of the mind-fuck variety. It's how my entire family communicates. Sticks and stones might break bones, but the old nursery rhyme fails to realize that words can be poison.

"I'm going to check on her first," I say. I owe her an apology at the very least.

I'm halfway to her when Pepper accosts me. Tonight, she's motherless and not playing the demure lady. She's on the prowl, and I've inadvertently stumbled into her trap.

"I've been looking for you." She makes a show of brushing some invisible speck of dust off my shoulder.

"I can't imagine why?" I bite out, still managing a smile. I brought Clara here to avoid a scene, but that means I must play by the same rules as well.

"Why are you acting this way?" She pauses and brings her gaze up to mine. "We're practically family. I was your sister's best friend."

"And you're fucking my father. Don't forget that," I say pleasantly, nodding to an old school acquaintance as he passes.

Her false smile shatters. "Don't be vulgar."

I know Pepper would like to remove the practically

from this sentiment—it's why she's shagging my father. What I can't figure out is where I play into it? Why bother with me when she's got his attention? I know she wants to secure a place in the royal family. I don't know why she thinks either of us is a viable option. I've made my feelings on marriage clear: I'm not about to continue this charade of a family any further, and I won't be adding to its number by marriage or otherwise.

"I'm sorry, I need to see to my date." I move away, but she follows at my heels.

"I want to be introduced," she says hastily.

"Why?" I stop in my tracks. No good can come of that.

"Alexander, no matter what you think, we are friends. We've been through so much together. We both lost Sarah." She blinks, and I swear she's near tears. "I don't want to lose you, too."

It's a ruse. It has to be. Pepper has two settings as far as I can tell: simpering sycophant and raging bitch. But they will eventually meet, and, at least, I can control the encounter here. Another time and place, I may not be so lucky.

"Behave," I order.

"I just want to meet the woman who finally captured your heart."

I cast a warning glare at her. "Don't try so hard to sell your act. It makes it easier to see through."

Clara's toasting with her black-haired friend—the one I don't know—as we approach. She hesitates, glass at her lips, body going still. Can she feel that too? The invisible thread linking us. She's tugging on her end now, calling me to her. I can't resist the pull—I don't want to.

"Clara," I say in a low voice as I step behind her. "I see you found a drink."

She spins around, startled, champagne spilling from her flute onto Pepper's dress. I fight the urge to laugh and win—but only barely.

"I'm so sorry!" She looks horrified, nearly dropping the glass as she tries to find a way to help Pepper mop it up.

Pepper shakes her head, plastering a smile on her face, but her eyes stay on the ruined fabric. "Don't worry about it."

Their eyes meet, and I wonder what they see. The two couldn't be more different. Pepper is tall and blonde and spends so much time at the gym it's practically her career. She wears her sexuality like a beacon. It's a siren song she howls at all times, and God help the poor bastards that fall victim to its lure. Clara, on the other hand, with her curvy body and dark hair, has no idea how sexy she is. She knows she's pretty. She's not exactly confident, though. She doesn't need every eye to turn when she walks into the room. I suspect she doesn't want that kind of attention. But any man who catches sight of her wants her. I know that. I've caught their stares this evening.

"Clara, may I introduce you to an old family friend, Pepper Lockwood?" I say stiffly, placing as much emphasis on friend as possible—and hoping they both get the message.

She smiles, obviously a little lost as to what to say, and before she can think of it, Pepper leans forward to kiss her cheek.

"It's nice to meet you, and I am so sorry." Clara is flustered, and I can't blame her. Surely, she senses the venom behind Pepper's greeting.

"It's just a dress," Pepper whispers like they're old friends. I don't catch what she says next.

Clara laughs, her body relaxing. Whatever Pepper said has lowered her guard. I shoot a pointed glare at my old friend.

This sham introduction is over, and she needs to move on. Pepper's eyes widen, but she collects herself quickly. "I should be going. I brought a date, and I've lost him."

Clara looks like she understands this a bit too well. She's in good hands, though, and no one will protect her as fiercely as her best friend.

This is good because it's time for Pepper and me to have a little chat. I brush a kiss over Clara's cheek and murmur a reassurance before steering Pepper away from her.

"I behaved myself," Pepper hisses when we're a safe distance from Clara and her friends.

"I wasn't going to stick around to see how long that would last," I say, dropping my hold on her elbow.

I start to turn, eager to be rid of her, when she blurts out, "So, how long have you known about Albert and me?"

"I'm not sure this is the place to discuss this," I say through clenched teeth.

"We could meet up. For coffee? Dinner?" she suggests.

"I'm fully booked," I say coldly. But there are things I want to say—need to say to her. Now is my best opportunity to do that without winding up with photos splashed all over the tabloids again. "And we both know that you're just hoping to make the front page again."

"We're news. I can't help that," she says, blinking as though she disdains the spotlight.

I'm news. I always have been. Looking back, I can't remember how Pepper became so close to my sister. Did she crave the attention even as a child? Was she groomed to seek famous friends? Knowing her mother, that seems a possibility. There's really not much I know about her at all. She's like a heat-seeking missile that's been tuned into my family's frequency. Or, at least, the frequency of money.

"Let's have a drink now," I say, nodding toward the bar.

Her chest puffs out, her chin tilts, nose sticking up in the air. She thinks she's won this round. Maybe she has, but losing one round might make all the difference in figuring out what she's really after.

"Two martinis," she says to the bartender.

I frown. "One martini—and a Scotch for me."

"I thought you liked martinis," she says, and I see her tuck away this encounter. For what? Further study?

"Not particularly." She's not getting more out of me than that. Our drinks arrive with the customary speed I expect. Being served first is one of the few perks of being born a sodding Royal.

"How did you find out about us?" Pepper asks quietly.

I'm almost surprised that she's been so discreet. An affair with the King? The scandal would be headline fodder for weeks. "You aren't as careful as you think you are. My father's weekend trips have doubled in the last few months."

"I don't see what that has to do with me."

"You've already confessed. There's no need to play innocent now," I advise her. Finding out was an accident, really. I'd sent Norris to dig up dirt on her, convinced she was the one who leaked the photo of me kissing Clara, and he'd stumbled on more. She doesn't need to know why or how I know—but that I know. That's what is important.

"No one can know," she says swiftly, dropping her hand on mine. "If Albert found out that you knew..."

"What?" I demand. "He'd call it off? Then I'm going to tell him because the thought of you two makes me want to vomit."

"You can't! You don't understand what's at stake," she pleads.

"Enlighten me." I frown. She's actually...scared.

Pepper pauses and draws a deep breath. For a moment, I think she's going to tell me what I want to know. But she's too calculating for that. She always has been. Whatever frightened her, she's got it under control now. "I know things, too. Let's not forget that. I'd hate to break sweet Clara's heart."

"She's smart. She doesn't get her news from tabloids." I abandon my drink and stand, disgust flooding through me. "You can't touch her."

"Would you care to wager on that?" A wicked smile carves over her red lips. "I like my odds."

"So do I." We glare at one another for a moment. It's a stalemate. We both have winning hands. We both know it. But who's cards are stronger? "I need to find Clara."

"That's a good idea." Pepper's eyes sparkle. There's not a single trace of panic in them now. "You wouldn't want her to fall into the wrong hands."

I don't bother responding. I simply make my way through the crowd. I need Clara in my sights. I need to touch her. Norris was wrong about her being safe here. I'd been foolish to think I could control this room—a symptom of how out of practice I am at being a royal. How many assassinations were carried out at court? I let my guard down.

My anxiety ratchets up another notch every minute that ticks by without spotting her. There are too many people in the crowd. I begin to look for Norris. Surely, he knows where she is. Then I see it: a flash of red tucked against her dark hair.

Clara scans the ballroom before continuing in the opposite direction. She's alone again. How could Belle let her wander off? Where is she going? I force my way towards her, ignoring the calls of friends, not caring that I'm practically shoving people out of my way.

I can see her. She's within reach, and nothing will stop me from getting to her.

CHAPTER SIXTEEN

S he pauses just out of reach and disappears behind a column. By the time I reach it and discover it leads to a darkened alcove, I'm sure I lost her again, but then I catch the curve of her hip peeking from the other side. Circling it, I reach around and grab her hand. I pull her towards the small privacy the alcove affords. I need my hands on her.

The weight on my chest lightens when I press myself against her. Clara fights it for a moment before melting against the alcove's marble arch. She needs this, too. She must after dealing with all the poisoned looks and self-serving introductions from strangers. My fingers sink into her, obstructed by the silk that keeps me from touching her bare flesh. Just the thought rockets blood straight to my groin, resulting in a painful reminder that there's too much clothing involved in this equation. But a kiss is all I can afford to risk. We've already suffered enough bad press. I won't allow a lack of control to result in more mud-slinging. I promised to protect her this evening—even if that means protecting her from myself.

It takes effort to pull away from her, but I do, brushing my palm over her bare upper arm. That's a mistake. Touching her again. I want to keep doing it. I step farther away and adjust my tie instead. "I needed that."

Clara stares at me, her perfect lips hanging open and giving me all sorts of bad ideas. We need to get away from this dark corner before I can commit another dark deed. I offer her my arm. She hesitates, dabbing at her lipstick, before taking it.

Does she know how careful she needs to be? A hair out of place? A smear of lipstick? It isn't something she can risk. Not with the attention of the room on her.

"You look beautiful." I hate that I need to reassure her. I want to kiss her senseless until her hair is wild and her cheeks glow, and then I want to lead her back into the crowd, looking like a woman claimed.

But tonight is a test. Of her. Of me. Of us.

And I'm determined to pass.

We're not two steps back into the ballroom when Stefan or Anton or whatever the fuck my father's latest simpering aide is named approaches us. He bows to me, which is completely unnecessary, but only nods to Clara.

I make a note to get him fired.

"Your Highness," he says. "Your father requests that you join the family for the toast."

"I showed up," I say through clenched teeth. "That should be enough."

"I'm afraid he's quite insistent," he says. "I suspect he'll just call you up in front of everyone if you don't—"

"Fine!" I toss my hands in the air, giving up and unintentionally losing Clara in the process. She's frozen next to me, still not speaking. What must she think of this? Of us?

"I'll see the young lady to a table," maybe Stefan says.

"She stays with me."

"But sir—"

"She stays with me," I say again. There's no way he'll dare question me twice. But in case he has a death wish, I grab Clara and drag her towards my family before I punch him. Maybe Stefan is only doing as he's told, I remind myself—it's something I should have sympathy for.

But I don't. All I can feel as I approach my father is dread.

CHAPTER SEVENTEEN

The entire family is here. Why do bastards always get so much attention? I'm not naive enough to believe the people gathered here came out of love. My father is a hard man to love and an impossible man to like. I suspect the only reason I tolerate him is our shared blood. Duty binds us together. If it wasn't for our birthrights, tragedy would have torn us apart a long time ago. He's not responsible for the loss of my mother or sister. I'm to blame for Sarah's death. But I'll never forgive him for how he treated me after. And while no one killed my mother, that's never stopped him from treating my brother like the unwanted third wheel.

We look nothing alike, except our eyes, I'm told. He's British in every sense of the word. His light hair, once sandy blond, is now fading to grey. Lines crease his face. He stands like he owns the place, a trait that came with his crown. Maybe that's why we've never gotten along. No one owns me. He knows it. That's a trait that came with my mother's Greek blood. It's why the man will probably outlive me out of sheer determination to keep the throne from falling into my hands.

He says I'm too volatile to be King. He's right.

Edward is dutiful by his side, and guilt washes over me. I can only imagine how many insults he already endured. I thought when I came back to England I might find their relationship had changed, but it's worse than ever. Edward might keep his romance a secret, but he can't hide anything from our father. No one can. It's a perk of having a secret service at your disposal. My brother raises an eyebrow, his face written with warning as though I'm not already expecting whatever hell is about to be unleashed. "Remember, this is about me, Clara," I whisper.

She nods, but she's too busy gawking at the others to mean it. I can't blame her, but I need to get through to her. This is going to be ugly, and most of the nastiness will be directed at her. It's my family's favorite strategy: bully the new blood until they break—or prove as indestructible as they are. I take her chin in the palm of my hand, turning her eyes toward mine. I've resolved that Clara is part of my life. Everyone else will have to fall in line with this reality—especially her.

Her eyes flutter wider, framed by dark lashes, and she stares through me like she can see everything I try to hide. I feel something inside me slam closed, unwilling to feel so vulnerable.

I can't. Not here. Not now.

Her gaze dances over me, momentarily puzzled,

before the slightest smile appears on her lips as if she'd seen that thought, too. It's as though she witnessed my defenses raising. Is the smile congratulatory? Is she pleased to have figured me out? No. It's something else. For a moment, I'm reminded of my mother, and that's when I understand what the smile means: she's reassuring me. One simple smile to let me know that she's here with me. For a second, I let myself believe it will be okay, and I can't help but lean to kiss her softly. She's everything I need without even trying. "Good girl."

"Alexander," my father calls, stealing the moment like he always does. "You've kept us waiting long enough."

"I'm sorry, father," I force the apology out. I'll play nice and keep my claws retracted until we're alone. Brushing a hand down Clara's arm, I try to give her an ounce of the reassurance she just gave me. "I lost track of my date."

"How careless." He beckons me away from the others. "May I speak with you?"

I shoot Edward a look, and he tips his head so slightly no one will notice. He's on Clara duty for the moment. I can trust him with her. The others? Not so much. They're already closing in from all over the room, drawn like sharks to blood in the water.

My father waits until we're out of earshot before he begins. "I don't remember telling you to bring a date."

"I don't remember caring," I say, adjusting a cufflink that loosened during the ride to the party. My mind flashes to Clara's bare skin, the feeling of her warm sex clamping over my cock. Suddenly, I'm looking for a fight.

It will be an excuse to leave—to take Clara back to her flat and fuck her until all memory of tonight is gone.

"You have a reputation to consider," he hisses, his eyes darting out over the pawns he's gathered for this sham of a celebration.

"Clara is an Oxford graduate whose family is worth several millions and who works in philanthropy. Might your standards be a tad high?" I ask.

"Don't pretend she's not a slut. I saw those texts. It doesn't matter what her file says. Any woman who allows that isn't suitable," he says, his voice rough with rage. "She's not the kind of woman you marry, Alexander."

"That would be a shame, wouldn't it? I wouldn't want to disappoint the family," I storm.

"Your proclivities are an embarrassment," he lowers his voice again. This is one subject he's desperate to keep quiet. It's why he sent me away. "If you need a woman to fulfill your perverse fantasies, so be it. Pay someone. Someone discreet so that I don't have to hear about it. But don't walk them through the front door."

"Is that how you keep Pepper quiet?" I've been saving this slight for the right moment—waiting to use it.

"I have no idea what you're on about." His eyes dart away, his body going rigid. I've cornered him.

"I'm talking about the fact that you're shagging your daughter's best friend." I won't allow him to feign ignorance. It's time for a reckoning.

"I have no idea where you heard this—"

"It's more about who confirmed it," I stop him. "I

think you might want to aim your discretion lecture toward your bitchy bedfellow."

"You think you're so clever with your poisonous barbs and little games, son, but you have no idea how unprepared you are for your role in this family," he warns me. "That girl will only be a distraction. It's time for you to get serious about your duty to your country."

"To this country or to you?" I spit back.

"I am the King. I am the country."

"You're a mascot for a dying breed. No one needs the monarchy." I mean it. Every word. He can't deny we're little more than ceremonial puppets who serve for photo ops and charity functions.

"You have no idea how wrong you are," he says, shaking his head. "No idea what this family is up against."

"Defunding?" I say coldly.

His fist tightens, and I wonder what will happen if I push him just an inch farther. Would he rescind invitations to future engagements? Or would there be a fistfight and another scandal for the wretched tabloids? "Find your pretty girl and dance with her," he advises me, shaking off the tense rage with a shrug of the shoulders. "Play with your toy. I don't have time for your childish behavior."

"Oh, but it's a party. Aren't we all supposed to cut loose?" I say, even as his words strike like a knife in the back. I know what he's doing. He's manipulating me—twisting me into the irresponsible prodigal son that feeds his ego. If I won't kiss his ass like everyone else, he's left with no other choice.

My grandmother steps between us, shielding her son as though she senses how close we are to coming to blows. "You disobedient little bastard."

"Grandmother," I say dryly. "Lovely to see you this evening."

"How could you bring that...that American here?" She makes the word sound like a slur. To her, it is.

"You're a terrible snob," I inform her. "She's half British."

"Half British! There's no such thing as half British," she says with a sniff, as though the very idea is an affront.

"As much as I enjoy a good flagellation"—I aim this barb at my father—"I should see to my date."

Grandmother mutters something about disgusting and attitude and my mother under her breath. I force myself to ignore it.

"Good night, Alexander." There's a finality as he dismisses me.

At least he won't care if I leave, now.

Turning, I spot Edward talking furiously with David. He glances up, our eyes lock, and he shakes his head helplessly. I cross to him in three strides.

"Where's Clara?" I demand, searching for a red rose in the crowd.

"She left. David saw her—"

I don't wait to hear the rest of his explanation. A few people try to stop me as I push through the crowd, but there's only one person I care about, and she's out in the night—alone and unprotected. I have no idea when she left, but when I slip out into the night, the steps are empty. There's no trace of her. There's only darkness, along with a few lingering paparazzi, who snap to attention and begin taking photos. Maybe she didn't come this way. Maybe she's still inside. But I can't sense her presence. It's as though she's fled the ball, rushing home to her safe, ordinary life without leaving so much as a glass slipper behind.

CHAPTER EIGHTEEN

This is why I don't do relationships. The first reason is my wretched family. The second is the goddamn paparazzi. The third is that, apparently, having a girlfriend also means having a nauseating pit in my stomach all the time. A photographer dares to get too close, and I snarl, snatching his camera and tossing it on the pavement. "Get a sodding life!"

"You owe me two thousand pounds." He shakes his fist at me as he stands up with the remains of his equipment. He takes one look at me and blanches white.

"You know where to send the bill," I spit back. I wonder how they'd feel to have every second of their life captured and dissected on a global scale.

The others back away, too shy to get close, but don't stop taking photos. Tomorrow there will be pictures in the tabloids—pictures of me without Clara. I can only imagine what fun they'll have with that after we arrived here together. The leeches probably saw her, but there's no way I'm going to ask them about it. The last thing I need is a story for them to sell along with their candid shots.

I yank down the cuff of my tuxedo, which scares the closest paparazzi back a few more steps. What little men with sad lives. I'm about to tell them this very thing when a firm hand closes over my shoulder.

"Your Highness," Norris says evenly. "I've been looking for you. I found what you're looking for."

Relief floods through me, but I'm not about to show weakness, not while I'm being photographed. I round, shrugging off his grip, and stalk back inside the lobby.

"Where is she?" I ask as soon as we're safely inside. I keep my voice low. Knowing my father has spies stationed everywhere, reporting my every move back to him.

"One of my men is following her," he says, tacking on "at a distance" when my eyes go wild.

"Following her where? Take me to her."

"She's on her way home."

"Home?" I repeat. "How? Why didn't you take her?"

"Miss Bishop left in a...hurry." Norris looks slightly embarrassed to reveal this fact. "Naturally, I had someone keeping an eye on her, so he followed and alerted me."

"How is she getting home then?" I don't understand how we can be here calmly discussing this while Clara is somewhere in the city. Perhaps in a nondescript taxi or, even worse, on the tube.

Norris draws a deep breath. "She's walking."

"Walking!" I explode. I'm halfway back at the door before he steps in front of me.

"Many Londoners walk home," he reminds me.

"Many Londoners aren't sleeping with the heir to the fucking throne." I'm getting tired of his zen routine.

"She's being protected, but it seems she needed some space."

"Take me to her," I order him.

"I'm not certain—"

"Now." I don't leave room for further discussion.

I spend the ride to Clara's flat fuming at my family for driving her away and at Clara for being so reckless. She needs to understand that her life isn't her own anymore.

Because of me.

I'm not sure that's something I can undo. I dragged her into the spotlight this evening. I'm the reason her face keeps showing up on trashy magazines. They're not going to leave her alone until I move on. The trouble is that the only thing I'm more certain I can't change than the media frenzy is my feelings about her.

Feelings. Fuck.

That wasn't part of the arrangement.

What will have to change is her lax attitude toward her own safety. Without warning, a vision of her naked from the waist down, bare ass in the air, bent over my knee, swims to the front of my mind. There are ways I could drive the point home. If she won't listen to reason...

But that's not part of the arrangement, either.

Honestly, what am I getting out of this, anyway?

I can't even entertain the thought. I know exactly what I'm getting out of it: her.

In the end, she's the one who deserves more—more than I can give her, more than I can ever be. I suspect that if I spend every day trying to achieve the bare minimum of what a woman like Clara should expect, I still will come up short.

But that doesn't mean I can't have my little fantasy. Imagine what it might be like to have her under my control completely. She told me she can never do that, so that's all this will remain—a sick dream from my bastard brain. It might only be in my head, but my cock isn't getting the memo. Visions of Clara bound and helpless draw my mind away from my seething anger, sending the blood boiling inside me straight to my cock.

By the time we reach her flat, I'm rock hard and overheated. I toss my tuxedo jacket in the seat. Norris opens the driver's door, but I wave him off.

He might not be responsible for what happened this evening—I believe the fault lies entirely with my family—but I might take it out on him all the same. I'd rather not.

"I'm going to stay the night," I inform him.

"Sir," he starts.

I hold up a hand. "Many Londoners stay the night at their girlfriends' flats."

Two could act casual.

He lifts a bushy eyebrow as his mouth flattens into a thin line. I can't decide if he's annoyed at the not-so-subtle dig or trying not to laugh.

"Let me do something normal," I say quietly.

"I'm not certain showing up to Miss Bishop's house in a limousine after a ball is terribly normal," he says. That settles it. He's trying not to laugh. "I'll leave you to it."

I have no doubt he'll be parked around the corner all night, watching. There's no sense in fighting him about it, though.

I take the stairs to Clara's flat two at a time. I don't know if I want to kiss her or shake her. I definitely need to fuck her.

The only trouble is: she's not there.

An hour passes—or maybe a few minutes. I can't tell. I've managed to convince Norris to go back and look for her, but he left reluctantly. He's going to need to get used to prioritizing her safety over mine because she's much more important, at least in my book. Every creak in the old building, every tenant moving about in their flat sets me on edge. When I finally hear soft footsteps on the stairs, my entire body goes rigid. It's her. I know it. I can feel it. Still, relief floods through me when her silhouette appears in the stairwell, her shoulders slumping downward, shoes in hand.

"Clara." Her name tastes wonderful on my lips. She's here. She's safe. She starts at the sound of my voice and drops her shoes. For a second, she stares at me with a strange expression.

It's just long enough for my relief to turn to anger.

What was she thinking? Walking through London alone? Leaving without a word?

She must sense my rage because she scampers toward the door, keeping her eyes turned from me.

"Where have you been?" I demand. She's not getting away from this that easily. I've got her back against the door before she can find her keys. She looks tired, not just from the hour, though. There's a sadness in her eyes that twists my insides. One night with my family. That's all it took to hurt her this badly.

"Walking," she says wearily.

It still doesn't excuse how stupid she's been. I rake a hand through my hair to keep myself from shaking her. Can't she see that things are different now? "You leave without a word, and then you walk home?"

"You pushed me away," she whispers, something dangerous sparking in her low voice. "I didn't run. I made the choice to leave."

And now she's challenging me. I can't blame her exactly. It's one of the things that draws me to her. She doesn't wait around to be kicked by anyone—not even the King and his courtiers. But I'm not them. Why can't she see that? "You came with me. I expected you to leave with me. I need to know where you are. That's not a request, Clara."

"I'm not a child. I can take care of myself," she snaps.

"That was before," I say. How do I ask her to change and stay the same? How do I help her see that choosing me was dangerous? That she has to think more than she did before? "You made a choice, Clara, and when you did that, I assumed the responsibility of taking care of you."

Her answering glare tells me that I'm not making my point terribly well. "I didn't ask you to do that!"

"No, you didn't. But you chose to come into my bed. You chose to stand by my side this evening." Can't she see what that means? Her life isn't hers anymore. She belongs to the paparazzi and the people and the world now—and they will all want a piece of her.

She recoils, shaking her head. "Yeah, but we're not married or anything—"

"What message do you think it sends for me to bring a date to my father's birthday?" I stop her.

Her words fall away, leaving her mouth hanging open as she processes this. I'm as surprised as she is by what I've said, but I do my best not to show it.

Is that where this is going? Is that what I want? One look at her, and I know I don't want it. Not because I don't want her. I suspect I'll always crave Clara Bishop. Because I don't want her to live this life.

"We barely know each other."

"That might be true," I admit, "but we've been linked publicly, and after those texts were published today, people are going to make assumptions."

She needs to know what she's getting into. I thought I'd made that clear before. Now, I'm no longer certain.

"What kind of assumptions?" she explodes. "I really don't give a fuck what people who read TMI think of me!"

I study her for a moment, wondering if I can tell her a

pretty lie instead of the ugly truth. I stand a better shot of keeping her if I do, but I can't. She needs to know, even if it means losing her. "It won't just be TMI's leak for long. There will be more legitimate news sources reporting on it. I live in the public eye, Clara."

"Why?" she asks bluntly. "Why did you bring me tonight? You knew that assumptions would be made. It's hardly the first time you've been caught with your pants down. Why give them more to gossip about?"

So much depends on my answer. This is my chance to lie. To tell her that I hadn't considered it and we needed to end things. Or to tell her that she's reading too much into this evening and let her believe that I'm an overprotective wanker.

Instead, the truth spills out."Because I want to protect you. I need to protect you. I can't explain it, because I don't understand it. Maybe it's a compulsion."

And it's not enough. I will never be enough to protect her from this life. I will never give her enough to make up for what they're going to take from her. There's not enough of me to be what she deserves, and I know it.

"Compulsions generally aren't healthy," she whispers, the challenge gone from her voice. I find comfort there now.

And even knowing all the ways I'll fail her, I know now that it's too late. She's mine to watch over. It doesn't matter if I do it with her in my arms or from a distance. I will always protect her. I brush a finger along her delicate cheek, marveling at the sheer wonder of everything she is to me. "This compulsion is. You can push me away, Clara, and I'll still devote myself to protecting you."

How can one person make you feel alive at the same time that they torment you? How can someone fill a void that never existed before you met them? How can she be the answer to every question I've never asked?

Clara stares into my eyes like she's trying to read my thoughts, and before I can wonder what she's thinking, my mouth finds hers. She collides into me with a force that leaves no room for more questions. I become something primal. I'm no longer a man frozen in contemplation. I am in motion. I want. I take. I lift her off her feet, and we slam against the wall. I need more of her, so I take it. Turning, I press her body against the brick and capture her tongue. I taste her, but it's not enough. Setting her on her feet, I kneel and shove her skirt to her hips.

This is where I belong: kneeling before her, giving her pleasure, earning her.

"Spread your legs, poppet." I kiss her soft thighs, already breathing in her scent. Holding her to the wall, I continue my devotions until her fingers grab hold of my hair.

"I'm going to fuck you with my mouth, and I want to hear you come. I want you to let go," I order. It's met with a pleading whimper. I love the little sounds she makes— the anticipation in each one. I love the ones she makes when she comes even more, though. I push her legs apart, wanting more and taking more with each stroke of my tongue. Her body stills, tightening, and I know she's at the edge. I close my mouth over her clit and suck it until it throbs.

She's speaking, but I can't hear her. There's only one thing that matters. I pin her against the wall harder and continue to pleasure her. Stroking. Sucking. Thrusting. I've found my calling—the reason that I exist—and it's here between her legs.

Her release is violent. It overpowers her. My hand anchors her. My tongue centers her. For one moment, I am her whole world, too.

As the tremors fade, I become aware of myself again— or, at least, the painful hardness of my cock. I need her naked. Now. Standing, I take her handbag and find the keys. Clara slumps against the wall while I unlock her flat. Kicking the door open, I lift her into my arms. We make it as far as the kitchen counter.

I lay her across it as I unbuckle my belt then my trousers. "You are so fucking beautiful."

"Wait."

I have her for the rest of the night, so I'm able to pause.

She scoots off the counter and reaches for her zipper. A moment later, her dress flutters to the ground and pools at her feet. Clara sinks her teeth into her lower lip as she stands before me naked, offering herself to me. I take her again, lifting her into my arms and carrying her to the wall. Her legs circle me as she bucks against my groin. She pushes down my pants, and I step carefully out of them, my cock already pushing against her soaked sex.

"Slowly," I remind her as I nudge her entrance. "Now, poppet."

She does as she's told, sinking onto my shaft with teasing slowness until she's skewered. As soon as she's taken all of me, she thrusts her hips like she's hitting a power button.

I force myself not to laugh at her impatience. "I don't want to hurt you."

She grabs hold of my hair and pulls. "I thought you liked that."

I stare at her, trying to be sure I'm hearing her right. I can't be. She's been clear on her boundaries. But it's there on her face: an invitation to cross them.

She has no idea what she's dangling in front of me or how dangerous her offer really is.

"Tread carefully, Clara." I can't take it. No matter how much I want to. Pressing my forehead against hers, I close my eyes to her momentary lapse in judgment.

I don't need the pain or the control—not if I can have her. I'll make it work. She deserves that much. I kiss her softly, not daring to open my eyes before I move inside her. "This is enough."

Finally, I chance a peek. Ecstasy soaks her features, and I smile. She's enough.

But worry clouds her eyes, and I know what she's doing. I know what she's wondering. I never should have asked her to submit to me. Will that request always linger between us?

"Clara," I saw in a low voice, "stop thinking."

"I—"

I kiss her before she can finish the thought. "Be with me. Feel me."

I shift against her, pushing deeper inside her body. It's an effective distraction for both of us. Clara's face goes blank, even as I feel her swell over my cock. A throaty cry escapes her lips and becomes my name. "Alexander!"

It pushes me over the edge, and I release into her, savoring each surge. I may never get enough of Clara Bishop, but that won't stop me from giving her everything I can.

CHAPTER NINETEEN

Clara sags against me, boneless and spent. I make no effort to break our bonded bodies. I'm still too anxious to release her in any way after her disappearance from the party—even physically. She's barely hanging on, so I turn to carry her to the bedroom. I step into the hall and realize I have no idea which room is hers. I've never been farther than her kitchen.

"Right," she says so softly I barely hear her.

Her bedroom is at the end of the hall. A window overlooks the street below, but at eye level, I can see only the outline of trees cast by street lamps. There's a bookshelf, half-filled with novels, and a few boxes shoved against the wall. In the morning, I'll investigate further, discover more about Clara's life. Tonight? I just want to hold her.

Her eyes open sleepily when I lay her across the bed. She watches me with drooping eyelids as I strip off my tuxedo shirt and crawl into bed next to her. It's smaller than the hotel bed we've shared, but there's enough room for me to wrap my body around hers. The only space I leave is enough room to stare into her beautiful face.

Now that she can't run, it's time to face what happened. "About the party—"

A hand slides free from my arms, and Clara holds up her palm to stop me. "Don't worry about it. We both knew they weren't going to like me."

"They shouldn't have been so rude." She shouldn't forgive them this easily. Dismissing their behavior won't earn her any points with my family. It will only prove to them that they can bully her into silence. And if they can do that, they can bully her into disappearing entirely.

She bites her lip as if searching for a way to refute this. Instead, she says, "Edward was nice."

If only that mattered. I love my brother. I wish I could tell her that he'll stand with us, but he's got his own reasons for not rocking the boat. She needs to understand that he's only an ally to a point. "Yeah. Edward understands what it's like to be an outsider..."

I stop myself before I can betray his trust. Edward might not be her knight in shining armor, but it's not my place to share his secrets. Although, I know Clara won't care that he's gay or share his secret. Her silence suggests she understands that. I want to tell her to be his friend. I want to hope for that. But I don't know what that means. For her. For us. For me.

There's only one truth I'm certain of, and it's somehow the most unexpected realization of all.

This is the only place I want to be: here, holding her, ignoring the outside world. In this moment, I would choose her above everyone else. I would give up every-thing I am to be the man that gets to go to bed with her at night.

But for how long can I pretend that's possible? How long before someone in my family finds the right button to push? The one that makes her see I'm not worth the trou-ble? How long before my father sends me away from London and her on the premise of fulfilling my duty? How long before she realizes that a prince doesn't actu-ally mean a happily-ever-after?

"I'm home safe, and you've damn near screwed me to sleep," she says after the silence extends to a breaking point. "You should go back to your father's party."

"I don't want to go back to the party." I don't want to go back to that life.

"X, it's your father's birthday."

I suppose it's normal to see a family event as an oblig-ation. Most people don't think of them as torture sessions. Of course, most people don't have national celebrations of their birth. "Exactly, and he has hundreds of people there to kiss his ass. He won't even miss me."

"I doubt that."

I shake my head. She's still thinking like a normal person. That's going to have to change. "You're right. He might miss me if he needs someone to yell at."

"I'm just going to go to bed." She stretches, her soft body lengthening in my arms and yawns.

Does she really want me to go? Is that why she's pushing me to go back to the party? I prop myself up and study her for a moment before kissing her shoulder.

Maybe she's saying what she thinks I need to hear. It's time I make it impossible for her to push me away. "I want to go to bed with you. Earlier wasn't enough for me. I have things to do to your body."

"This body" —she yawns again— "needs to rest. I have no idea how you've got that much stamina. It shouldn't be physically possible."

Or maybe, she's had a long, emotionally draining day, and I'm a wanker. What would a boyfriend do? I catch her trying to hide another yawn. "We can sleep."

"You want to sleep here?" The question lurches out of her like she doesn't know what she's asking.

Maybe that's not what a boyfriend would do. I might have to resort to asking for pointers on this relationship thing if I'm going to get everything wrong. "Is that not okay?"

"Sure. Of course, it's okay," she says a little too quickly, rolling over so I can't see her face. I gather her against me, breathing her in, and wonder if she means it.

She's definitely putting up with me. I'll take what I can get, but I'm going to have to ask someone how to handle moments like this. If only I knew a single person with a normal relationship.

"Alexander," she says, drawing my attention back to her. "Earlier when you said you didn't want to hurt me..."

Of all the topics I thought might come up, I didn't expect it to be this one, especially not twice in one night.

"I had my reasons for saying no before," she continues, "but—"

"There's nothing more to say, Clara. You don't owe me," I stop her. "I don't need that."

I can't ask it of her. I won't take the one thing she begged me to leave her. Not when being with me leaves her at risk of losing everything else.

"What do you need then?" There's frustration in her voice. Maybe I'm not the only one wondering how to make this work.

Somehow that thought gives me hope. I'd rather be muddling through this together than fucking it up all on my own.

"You," I tell her, meaning it. "Sleep, poppet. All I need is you."

CHAPTER TWENTY

Where am I?

It's the first thought that filters into my brain. The answer doesn't come. Only heat. The smell of gasoline.

Pain.

Unbelievable pain.

I look down to discover my shirt is torn, stained with blood, under it, something white poking out of my side.

My rib.

"Fuck! Alex!" Jonathan's voice cuts through the air. "Alex! Your sister! Fuck! Your sister!"

Sirens cut through the night air as a camera flash goes off. The light illuminates the scene, and I see Sarah, her hair plastered to her forehead, her legs bent at an unnatural angle to the side.

"Sarah!" Blood gurgles up my throat, and I choke on her name. I try to claw my way across the slick pavement, fumes making it difficult to breathe. No, it's something more than that. More pain—like my body is trying to collapse in on itself. I try to push past it. "Sarah!"

Another camera flash goes off. Another. The cameras are everywhere. I can't help feeling like we're driving into an Austen novel as we approach the antique, wrought-iron gates. One of the leeches with the camera bends to help me, camera still in hand, and I swing instinctively.

"Alexander, wake up!"

I want to. God, I fucking want to wake up, but this nightmare is real. This is happening. Sarah won't move. I can't tell if she's breathing.

Suddenly, I'm all alone with her in an empty street. There's no car. No paparazzi. Just me and my baby sister. I lift her head, wondering if I should do CPR. Something hot and sticky coats my hand. Blood.

This can't be happening. I close my eyes. Night becomes day.

When I open them, I'm staring at an unfamiliar ceiling. I breathe in shallow pants, waiting for the searing pain to catch up with my waking brain. It doesn't come. Glimpses of the night before flash through my mind. The party. Arguments. A red rose.

Her.

The bed is empty. I turn instinctively to find her. She's staring at me, arms clutching her stomach. "Clara?"

She makes no move toward me, and that's when I realize one palm is rubbing her stomach. Her eyes are wary, alert—too alert for someone who was asleep until moments ago.

"Oh god," I murmur. "What did I do?"

I can only think of reaching her. Swinging my legs out of bed, I'm out of it and on my way to her with the trained response years of military service drilled into me. But Clara backs away, still watching me with wide, doe eyes. I stop, finally understanding what's happened. "I hurt you."

She doesn't speak. She doesn't need to. I shift direction towards the clothes I'd left on her floor. I'd known this would happen. Years of restraint and one night upends it all. Why did I think it would be different? How many times had my buddy Brex woken me in the barracks in the middle of a nightmare? Every time he'd been ready, fists up, trained to expect my violent, subconscious reaction.

Clara didn't stand a chance. She still doesn't.

"I'm sorry," I say, buckling my pants. I tug on my shoes. "I warned you. I'm so, so sorry."

She still hasn't spoken by the time I reach the door.

"What were you dreaming about?" Her soft voice asks behind me.

No. I won't burden her with any more of my crosses. I spin to her, shaking my head. "I won't ask you to carry my demons, Clara."

She finally moves, but instead of backing away again, she walks toward me with gentle eyes. I see the forgiveness in them, and I hate the hope that springs in my chest.

"Maybe you could just let me hold them for a while," she says.

"It's too ugly for you. You're beautiful, pure—"

"I'm far from pure." She smiles a little as if testing the

mood, but it fades when the air between us remains heavy.

She needs to understand that this can't be laughed away. Clara needs to know that I'm not some broken animal that can be fixed. God knows I've tried to fix myself. She needs to see me for what I am: a lost cause.

I wrap my fingers around her throat. She needs to see that I'm dangerous. I see the lines and cross them anyway. I can't help it. Maybe it's because of the family I was born into. Maybe it's my nature. Either way, I'm not her hero.

I'm her monster.

"You are my beautiful Clara," I say, and I mean it. She's every good thing I ever wished for but would never deserve. "That's why I want to protect you from the world. That's why I want to protect you from me."

Tears well and fall like rain as she tries to blink them away.

Yes. She understands. I've shown her the truth, so we can stop with the lie. I will never be the man she needs. I can only cause her pain.

But when her mouth opens, her words are small yet powerful. "You told me once that you wanted to hear me beg."

I recoil, sucking in a breath. "No. Not like that."

I'm tainting her. My poison is infecting her. I need to leave before she becomes someone she hates as much as I hate myself.

"Please," she whispers. "Please, X."

What does she want? Why does she keep demanding more? Why can't I tell her no—tell her to fuck off like I would to anyone else? Why do I always hesitate when I know I should leave?

"Do you want me to tell you that I dream about screeching metal and fire? That I wake up holding a pillow because I'm dreaming that I'm cradling my sister's broken body?" I ask, hoping to scare her. "And that every time I wake up, I'm no closer to knowing what the hell happened that night? I can't tell you anything because I don't know anything!"

She stares like this is a surprise, and a familiar surge of shame consumes me.

"Have you spoken to anyone—" she begins.

"I'm not going to talk to a goddamned shrink. My sister would be alive if it weren't for me. Period. End of story." It's not the end of the story, though. If she knew the truth, I would lose her forever. So, why don't I tell her? It's what I want. I want to liberate Clara from this mysterious hold I have on her.

"This isn't your fault." She places herself between me and the door. "It was an accident. Everyone knows that."

She is strong. She is beautiful. She is so hopelessly naive.

"Everyone knows what they were told," I bite out. "Don't be stupid, Clara."

I see the barb strike, but if it stings, it doesn't wound. She crosses her arms in defiance. "You are not the first person to have been in a car accident."

"It was a little more than a car accident." A sliver of truth to assuage the guilt I feel over the lie—the one I will continue to tell her. The lie I will continue to tell everyone, even myself.

She pauses, wheels turning in her eyes. I've done it. I've scared her. Now I have to find the strength to let her go.

I don't expect what comes next.

Clara holds out her hand—extends a lifeline when she should cut me off. "Come back to bed."

I can't save her. I can only destroy her.

CHAPTER TWENTY-ONE

My bones ache to go with her, but I can't deny what we both know. "You're not safe around me."

Clara's eyes soften like an invitation. "I'm only safe around you."

How can she believe that? Have I warped her this much already? She thinks she can trust me, but there's so much she doesn't know about me. Every ounce of me wants to carry her to bed and claim her as my own. I would if I thought it would end there. But I can't deny that I'm craving more from her than just her body.

"My life is dangerous," I start, unsure how to proceed. I pace a few steps, trying to figure out how to tell her the truth without revealing my secrets—secrets that don't only protect me but also the most vulnerable members of my family. "I'm dangerous."

"And I'm not going to break." She moves toward me, defiance drawing her face taut and determined.

Yes, she will. She'll break. By me. By them. I draw her body to mine and wrap one hand around her lovely throat. I could break her so easily now. She needs to see that. "You are fragile, Clara. Delicate. If my life doesn't break you, the things I want to do to you might."

She refuses to look away. Only the slightest fear hides in her eyes. "I'm not scared of being with you, X. I'm only scared of being pushed away."

Words won't be enough. So it comes down to one thing: a test. I don't ask. I take.

I give way to my primitive need, crushing my mouth to hers, forcing her lips to part for my tongue. She meets me at every step, offering more of herself while demanding more from me.

She thinks she can handle more? Fine. We'll see.

I grip her wrists tightly, forcing them behind her back, and hold her body hostage. Her body molds to my desires. She doesn't fight me. She submits like a bud blossoming at sunrise.

How can she say she doesn't want this but give it so naturally every time?

Lifting her off her feet, I carry her to the bed, unbuckling my trousers to free my cock. Clara's heels shove them down as I kick off my shoes. I step out of them, spreading her legs with one hand. Dropping over her, I thrust without warning, splitting her open without hesitation. I don't stop even when her fingernails dig into my back. I just keep taking.

And she keeps giving.

Her breathy panting draws attention to her beautiful

lips, her slender neck. I brace myself on my elbow, so I can grip her neck again.

"You are mine, Clara," I growl, crushing her throat, so she's forced to look at me—to understand what I'm saying. "I claim you. Do you understand?"

She stares up at me, her blue eyes swirling with words she can't speak. But she nods with a slight smile, as much as my grip will allow, as a single tear falls down the side of her smooth cheek. It only makes me fuck her harder.

But I'm not an animal. I am a man—a man who will take until she says no.

"I'm hurting you now," I murmur, "like you wanted, Clara. Do you want me to stop?"

I want her to say yes. I want her to end this before I can taste her stolen pleasure. Because once I do, it will never be enough.

"No." It slips out like a surprise.

I don't pause to process this. I just ram into her as hard and forcefully as I can.

She doesn't mean it. She can't.

"You like it, but you think you don't," I grit out between thrusts. "I expect you to come, Clara."

"I can't," she moans, her body tight beneath me. She's holding on to it: the last vestiges of her control.

"Accept the pain," I order. "Let go." Or I'll make you.

I release her neck, move to her breast, and suck her nipple into my mouth. She loosens a little, aroused, so I nip the sensitive flesh. She yelps, but I don't relent. I continue to knead her breast, biting and sucking—

tormenting her until she's forced to release herself from the cage she clings to.

She arches into me, crying and shaking, her face drawn with rapt bliss. And she is mine completely. I fill her. I taste her. I claim her. Until I become her entire world.

She implodes, pleasure and pain mixing into a beautiful, strangled cry.

Then she collapses beneath me, her hands covering her face, overwhelmed. I recognize this feeling. I know it well.

Shame.

We're not taught to accept our demons. What happens when we stop fighting them? What happens when we welcome them?

Are we ever the same?

I slow, still buried inside her, and slide my arms under her to pull her close to me. I can't always give my darkness control. Not anymore. More than that: I don't want to. I roll to the side, cradling her against me, and rock in and out.

Gently, I brush her hands to the side and bring my mouth to hers. I kiss her softly. I call to her. It's hard to find the way out of the darkness at first. I know that. These shadows can consume you, make you feel lost. Since I've met her, she's been the light guiding me from that depth. I can be her way home now.

"Clara?"

She peeks at me from wet lashes, and when our eyes meet, the final tension melts from her. Her palms flatten on my chest, and I see her count her breaths, see her count mine, see her find peace again.

I roll into her, still hard, my own pleasure locked inside me.

"Your pleasure is mine," I say softly. "I will push your body until it nearly breaks, but I will never hurt you."

"And can I break you?" She reaches to brush a hand along my cheek, her touch asking another question entirely.

If only it were that simple. "I'm already broken."

"Then maybe I can fix you," she whispers.

Her hands slip down, finding the hem of my undershirt, and I force myself to let her. I look into her eyes and remind myself I trust her. Her hand moves to my abs, my cock pulses inside her, unaccustomed to the touch.

A cry breaks the silence, and I realize it's my own broken moan. She pauses her movement, pressing her hand completely flat against my stomach. After a second, she slowly begins to move it up.

"Don't," I say sharply.

Her eyes close, and she stops.

For a moment.

But when she opens them again, she says the words I never knew I needed to hear, "I claim this body. You are mine, Alexander. All of you."

And she does. Her hand strays to my scars—the mistakes marring my body, the proof of my selfishness. Her fingertips brush over them, not knowing how to decipher what she feels. Instead, she continues to press forward. Her hips circle, reminding me of all the ways we're connected.

I lower my face to her breast, allowing my body to trap her hand under my shirt. My hands move to clutch her ass, and she grinds into me, taking and claiming until I empty inside her. I let go, releasing the last parts of me I've held back, filling her with me and salting her breasts with tears.

CHAPTER TWENTY-TWO

I wake to find her gone. It takes a moment to process where I am, and then the events of last evening rush back to me. The disastrous party and my sodding father. Pepper fucking Lockwood getting her hooks in Clara. The blind panic when I realized Clara had left the party without a word. The memories after that are painted in vivid strokes of red and black. Clara against a brick wall, the taste of her on my tongue. My cock shoved inside her, showing her exactly where she belonged. Fire and screaming—and then her, drawing me back to the light. Her hands drifting over my scars. Lies and promises and boundaries crossed.

My hand skims across the thin fabric of my under-shirt, wondering what she thought when she discovered the monster I hide beneath these clothes. She glimpsed him last night. I can never show her all of him.

"What the fuck are you doing?" I mutter to myself, rolling to the side and catching a lingering hint of her perfume on the sheets. My heart thumps hard against my rib cage, and suddenly, I need to find her. Drag her back to bed. Possess her. Show her the part of me she can...love.

Bollocks. That part doesn't exist.

And even if it did, it's not enough to make up for my father and his rotten courtiers. She deserves more than this life—and far more than me.

I slide out of bed, searching the floor to find my trousers. I yank them on, not bothering with anything else, and go to find her.

As soon as I open her bedroom door, I hear voices.

"Should I make a plate for Alexander?"

The question is accompanied by the smell of eggs and bacon, producing a rumble of hunger from my stomach. Apparently, last night's caught up with me.

There's no response, but Belle must be speaking to Clara.

Flatware clanks against the counter, followed by a harsh, male baritone. "Alexander is here?"

What the fuck? I'm two steps down the hall, fists clenched when I remember that Belle is engaged. I search my memory, trying to recall to whom.

"Who on earth did you think was making that noise last night?" Belle asks.

A smirk dances over my lips. She knows exactly who it was.

"A neighbor," her fiancé grumbles, and I can't help feeling certain whoever he is, he's a little man. One likely not capable of producing the noise Belle spoke of.

"What does Alexander like?" Belle asks, and I know she must be talking to Clara.

Why doesn't she respond? Is she tired? Sad? Did I frighten her? Is she hoping I'll leave without staying for toast and a chat? I wouldn't blame her for that. But I'm hungry and determined to prove I can be a boyfriend, even if I keep cocking it up.

"Tea. No milk," I announce, coming into the small kitchen. Clara startles, her hand flying to tug together her cream-colored dressing gown. I want to remind her that she's got nothing I haven't seen, but I think she might spontaneously combust if I remind her, judging from her deep, ruddy blush. She looks like every dirty dream I've ever had, her hair tumbling around her shoulders in waves, her mascara smeared just enough to make her eyes look smoky and mysterious. I have to force my attention back to the topic of food. "As for breakfast, everything. I'm starving. I worked up an appetite last night."

My eyes meet Clara's, and I grin so she doesn't miss the double meaning. First, food. Then, sex. Things will be clearer after that. She flushes more deeply, dropping her eyes for a moment, but I saw her thoughts wandering to the same place.

She looks over at Belle, frowning to discover her friend staring absently at me.

"I'll get it," she says, grabbing a plate to fill it for me.

There's something deliciously domestic about seeing her there, barefoot in the kitchen, bringing me food. It stirs something primal in me that wants to lift her onto the counter and fill her with my seed. I turn away before I can let that idea take root and spot Belle's fiancé. Suddenly, I recall why I didn't remember who it was because Sir Philip Abernathy is about as memorable as a piece of toast. There's not a lot of options in the small flat for seating, so I take a barstool next to him.

He doesn't bother to acknowledge me. I don't bother to acknowledge him.

Clara places the plate before me, and I murmur my thanks before devouring it.

The women hang back, eying us, before Belle turns on Clara. "What do you want, Clara?"

"Oh, I'm fine." Clara waves off the offer, and I feel surprisingly wounded. She must be hungry after last night. If she's not, I might be forced to throw her over my shoulder and drag her back to bed until she is.

"Absolutely not," Belle says with a firmness that distracts me from doing so. "What do you want?"

"Some eggs and toast, I guess."

She guesses. I shovel my own food more quickly, determined to make her have an appetite. But there's something odd at play. I find myself stealing glances, catching them doing the same. There's a lot being left unsaid, it seems, and I'm the one on the outside.

What's new.

The two share a look, and Belle quickly makes small talk. "What are your plans today?"

"Not sure," Clara hedges.

Belle brightens. "Let's go shopping."

Clara looks to me like she's seeking permission. Am I that controlling of her already? God knows, she could use the time to breathe. I'm smothering her, and my family is judging her. She should go with her friend and get away from all of us. If she has any sense, she'll stay away. "I have a family thing, and I'm certain my father will require a few hours of explanation as to why I left last night."

She mouths an apology, but I shake my head. I really am a monster if she's apologizing to me for my family's behavior.

"Then let's go!" Belle claps her hands, looking giddy at the prospect of time together—and I feel a sting of jealousy. I wish anything in my life were that easy, particularly where Clara is concerned. "There's a new boutique in Notting Hill."

"Notting Hill on a Saturday will be a madhouse," Philip finally speaks up, and naturally, it's to sour their plans. He's really an incredible wanker.

"I need to shower, and then we can go," Clara says before turning to me. "Are you sure you don't want to come?"

"I would love to, but duty calls." It's an honest answer if a somber one. I'd much rather spend my day attempting to lure Clara into dark corners.

Philip snorts next to me.

My fingers close over my fork more tightly. "Is that funny?"

"I find the idea of you and duty rather amusing," he admits.

"Philip!" Belle bursts out.

"I served in Afghanistan and Iraq for seven years," I growl. The time for courtly pleasantries is over. Sir Philip needs to remember his rung on the ladder, both socially and as a man. "I know more about duty than the average Englishman can fathom."

"And what of honor?" he presses. "Did you manage to find some over there? Or is it too late for that?"

I won't lower myself to answer stupid questions from a fragile man. He doesn't know me. He's chosen to believe the gossip and rumors, and I fear a moment longer with him will result in me wringing the bloody life from his neck. He deserves worse. I march to the bedroom and throw on the rest of my clothes, sending a message to Norris to pick me up. What on earth is Belle doing with a man like that? I can't help wondering if my initial impressions of her are wrong. She doesn't seem like a social-climbing bitch. I'd found her rather kind, a poor match for him.

He doesn't know anything about duty—about watching good men go to fight and come home in boxes. Friends. He's never given up his life for the family's reputation or taken the fall for a terrible secret. I can only assume, giving his inexplicable self-confidence, that he also didn't grow up being measured and found wanting at every opportunity.

Clara catches me steps from the door. "You don't have to go."

"I have things to do," I don't break my stride. I'm nearly gone when I remember that none of this is her fault. She'll blame herself if I leave like this.

Twisting around, I hook an arm around her waist and yank her to me, covering her lips—claiming her so that there's no doubt that I'm a man who takes what he wants —and fuck anyone who takes issue with that. Her body softens into mine, stirring dangerous thoughts. I pull away and brush a finger over her swollen lower lip.

"Have fun today," I murmur. One of us should, and if I had to choose, I'd want it to be her.

She nods and forces a smile. "We will. Notting Hill is my favorite place in London."

I pause and tuck away that tidbit. I want to know all of Clara's favorites—places and people and dreams. Now's not the time for that, though. "See you soon, poppet."

A door opens as I descend the steps and an older woman with unkempt silver hair peeks out. She looks me up and down, bites back a smile, and retreats into her flat. It's not been nearly as messy as I feared: staying over. But I can't help wondering how long that will last. I bypass the front entrance and a herd of paparazzi waiting outside it and turn to exit out a secret entrance Norris discovered after looking at the building plans. There's enough speculation about Clara and me at the moment. She deserves some peace. Norris is waiting for me as I step out. A few meters away, there's a bomb shelter—a holdover from the Blitz undoubtedly and the reason there's the unused door in the first place.

"I need to tell Clara about this," I inform him as he opens my car door.

"Sir?"

I shoot him a warning look, and he sighs. "Alexander?"

"The door. She shouldn't have to deal with all those sodding reporters."

Norris doesn't speak as he closes the door and circles to the driver's side. When he shifts into drive, he finally glances over his shoulder at me.

"I don't think that's a good idea," he says.

"What? Why? I can't leave her to fend for herself."

"Perhaps, you should speak to your father about a security detail, then," he suggests, adding a thoughtful, "if you plan to continue your courtship."

"Courtship? For fuck's sake." I bite out a laugh. "We're well past courtship, and you know what my father will say. The Crown doesn't protect non-royalty."

"Perhaps..."

"Perhaps what?" I ask, although I suspect that I know what he's alluding to.

"The Crown only protects royalty, as you said."

"I think marriage is a bit premature," I snap. "Clara doesn't know me. She doesn't know my family. She has no idea what she'd be getting into."

Norris maneuvers through a tight alley, exiting a block from Clara's building. There are no reporters in sight. As we merge into London morning traffic, he watches me in the rearview mirror. "It's interesting that your first instinct is to apply royal resources to protect her, though, despite knowing they won't be made available."

"They should be. She's being dissected by every tabloid in the country." In the world, if I'm being honest.

"Yes, but that won't stop with a security detail. If you want them to leave her alone, there is a simple solution."

I lean forward, gripping the shoulders of the front seats. "Which is?"

"Break things off," he says coolly.

"They'll still follow her."

"See another woman. Someone suited to the spotlight. Miss Lockwood seems eager for the opportunity."

Now he's just baiting me, but to what end? "I'd rather stick my cock in a light socket," I say grimly, "but you know that."

"Well, then you're at an impasse."

I retrace the conversation's twists until I'm back at what started it. "Why shouldn't she use the door?"

"They're going to keep coming after her. The more she hides, the more aggressive they'll become. You can't lock her away in a tower and take her out to play with her." He sighs as though all of this should be obvious. "If you want her protected, you have to protect her."

"We'll never leave the bedroom if I'm her bodyguard," I say shortly. He's got a point, but not a solution.

"Not you, exactly. But you have to decide what you can do to help her and keep her safe," he advises.

I do have resources—money of my own, holdings, titles, bank accounts. I rarely bother with any of it. Everything at Buckingham is taken care of. There are secretaries to see to most other needs. "A security detail. I'll need your help...unless you want the job."

"I'm happy to step in as necessary, but someone has to keep you from your own worst enemy," he says.

"Who's that?"

"Yourself," he says as though this is patently obvious.

"I'll look into it, and once that's figured out, you need to prepare her."

Is all romance so complicated? I feel as though I'm coordinating a military attack. "Prepare her for what?"

"For the day, she is royalty," he says evenly.

I laugh, half-surprised, half-awed by his balls. "That sure of her, are you?"

Norris arches an eyebrow and asks the one question I refuse to ask myself. "Aren't you?"

CHAPTER TWENTY-THREE

Norris's words stick with me as I stalk into Buckingham. Am I that sure of Clara? I know what taking her to my father's party signaled. When I'd asked her, I'd been desperate to win her back. Now, I have to consider that I've sent a very clear message to her and my family.

A message I didn't intend to send.

"This is why you don't do relationships," I mutter to myself as I force a grim smile at a passing housekeeper.

"Nice of you to join us," Edward says dryly when I enter our shared quarters. We'd moved into the space when we came of age. At the time, our father had opposed the idea of us taking residences at Kensington or Clarence House. I suspect he wanted to keep an eye on us—or at least pretend to do so. In truth, he never bothers coming to our rooms. We don't bother going to his. Most of our interactions are conducted in his private offices. Our family is a business. We sell tradition and ceremony and hundreds of years of bullshit.

I scratch my head as he sips a cup of coffee from a wing-back in the sitting room. His gaze scans down me, taking in my wrinkled tuxedo, half-buttoned and untucked. Edward, on the other hand, is already dressed for the day in a pair of blue tweed trousers and a crisp Oxford rolled at the wrists. The Omega on his wrist informs me that it's past ten.

"You left suddenly," he says. It's a prompt—his way of asking if I want to talk about it.

"There was no reason to stay." Our father made his position clear. I made mine.

"It didn't have anything to do with your date running off before the stroke of midnight?" He's not going to let this go. For better or worse, my brother's taken it upon himself to serve as my conscience since I returned to London.

"I expect our father is preparing his lecture," I say harshly. "I don't need yours." I continue toward the hall to grab a shower and brace myself for whatever shit storm I've started this time.

"Not everyone is out to get you," Edward calls. "Sooner or later, you're going to have to let someone in."

That seems to be the theme of the day. First, Norris. Now my brother. Clara seems to be the only one not planning our wedding. Still, she'd gone too far last night. And I let her.

I slip off my coat and trousers and toss them onto the bed, my shirt and pants following before I head into my attached bath. I stop there, looking at the man reflected in the mirror.

Most of him is nothing to be ashamed of. Years in the military—living off what they deem food, running drills, and carrying heavy equipment—had shaped him into a powerful man. Biceps, abs, the hewn V of an Adonis belt narrowing to my cock, legs that could carry him miles through the desert. But as my body transformed into the man before me, the scars from my accident had gotten worse. The pink, ruined flesh had stretched to cover one side of my body, and the harsh, cutting lines of my muscles only highlighted them. If I'd earned them in battle, I might look on them with pride.

But they were a reminder of the worst thing I'd ever done and the lie I kept to protect my family's darkest secret. I'd lived with both so long that I barely thought of either. I hated when others saw my scars because they only dredged up their existence and all they represent.

And Clara had touched them last night. She claimed them. She claimed me.

It's not how it's supposed to work, but still, I couldn't deny her. And worse? I didn't want to. Perhaps, that's why I can't shake what Norris said, nor Edward's offhanded remark.

I turn the shower to its hottest setting, but even it can't scald away the memory of her touch on my skin. My cock gets hard as I recall her touch pushing me past my boundaries. I'd come inside her so long, I thought it might never stop. I lean into the scorching water, planting my hands on the wall, and wait for my erection to wane. But there are only flashes of her. Porcelain skin and freckles. The soft hair curling over her cunt. Her teeth biting into the flesh of her plump, lower lip. Reaching down with one hand, I grip my shaft and stroke roughly—hard enough that it hurts. Unforgiving. Punishing. The water burning the sensitive skin. But I don't stop. I can't. Not while she's in my head. I have to get her out. My mind replays fucking her on a loop as I work myself toward release. When I reach the moment where I asked if she wanted me to stop, when she told me no, her blue eyes are there, wide and afraid and certain—and full of love.

I come at the memory. It roars out of me, and I brace against the wall, pumping it from me as the shower washes away the truth.

I'll never get Clara out of my system.

She's inside of me. She's my blood. She's my bones. She's the rotten organ beating in my chest.

Clara is my curse and my salvation. I hate her. I love her. She can never know.

I finish washing up and grab a towel. Wrapping it around my waist, I go to find clothes. After that, I need to figure this out. Maybe I should talk to Edward. He understands the impossibility of our position better than most. But as soon as I set foot inside my bedroom, I stop.

"It's disgraceful," my father says, his eyes flickering away from me. He's in his usual Harris tweed weekend wear. It's as close as the bastard gets to casual.

I don't bother to ask him what he finds disgraceful now. My scars? My behavior? Listening to my jack off in the shower? It hardly matters. Where he's concerned, every breath I take is a disappointment.

I continue to the closet and grab the first clothes I find —a pair of old jeans and a t-shirt. After I'm clothed, I find him standing near the window in my room—the one that overlooks the back gardens.

"You left my party without saying goodnight," he says, as though I need a reminder of how the evening had gone.

"You had plenty of people there to worship you. You didn't need me." I sit on my bed and tug on a pair of black leather lace-ups.

"As though you would ever bow to me," he says with a laugh. "Nor should you."

I hesitate, surprised by his response.

"You're going to be king one day," he continues. "I won't live forever."

I suspect he might do just that purely out of spite. The last thing he wants is to pass me the crown.

"You need a suitable wife."

"This again?" I say wearily. "I hardly think bringing a date to one party is a proposal of marriage."

"You know it is," he snarls. "I don't care who you date or who you fuck if you do it with discretion. You do not bring girls home. You don't invite them to the family birthday party. Or Christmas. Or whatever stunt you're planning next."

I bypass the accusation and opt to point out his hypocrisy. "Inviting the woman you're fucking means wedding bells? Well, Pepper will be thrilled."

"Pepper is part of our inner circle," he interjects

distastefully, "and our relationship is none of your business."

My control slips, and I take one menacing step forward. One move. One swing. He'd crumble. I force my fist to stay by my side. "Neither is mine."

"I'm a widower. I'm King. No one expects me to marry." He tugs on his suit cuff, showing no sign that he's concerned. "The whole world is watching you. Consider that before you invite her in the future."

"I don't care what the world thinks," I tell him as he walks to my bedroom door.

He opens it before turning back just enough to give me an amused look. "That's your problem. It's how I know she can never be a queen. Well, one of the reasons. You're so concerned with proving something to me—to the world. You haven't even stopped to think of what you're doing to her. You'll ruin her. You'll hurt her. In the end, you'll lose her. If you care about her, you'll let her go."

He steps through the door, closing it behind him, leaving me alone to deal with my choices and demons.

"YOU'RE AVOIDING HER," Edward tells me the next morning when I go out to grab a mug of tea.

I stalk back to my room, adding him to the list of people I'm avoiding under my father. Clara is at the top of the list. But my brother isn't so easily dismissed. He follows behind me.

I give up and sink into a seat by my bedroom's hearth. He takes the one opposite.

"Go on," I encourage him. "Keep telling me all the ways I'm cocking this up."

"I think you already know," he says.

"Then why do I keep making the same fucking choices?" I ask him miserably. I'd known what I was getting Clara into, and I did it anyway. Edward's right. I am avoiding her—for her own sake.

"Because we don't know any better." He sighs, a half-smile on his face. "We hardly had a normal upbringing, and, as for relationships..."

He has no memories with our mother. She died when he was born. My own can't be trusted given how young I was when she was alive. I remember a caring, beautiful woman. I remember how my father looked at her.

I remember how sad she seemed.

Locked up in a palace and taken out for special occasions on the arm of the King. There are other memories, fleeting and conflicting ones I never mention to Edward or anyone else, but especially not to my father.

"You know we can't do this to them," I say distantly, thinking of a memory that sticks out like a page in a photo album.

She was crying in her room. Again. I climbed onto her lap, and she held me close. I patted her smooth cheek.

"I love you, my precious boy," she whispered into my hair. "Always remember that first."

"I love you, Mummy." My own small voice is

foreign and unfamiliar. How could I have ever been so little? So vulnerable?

"Someday, you will meet a girl," she says, "and you will love her. She will be your princess."

I looked at Sarah, playing on the floor with blocks, then gazed at my mother with a doubtful shake of the head. "I don't like girls."

"You will." This made her laugh. My heart swelled. I liked to hear her laugh. It felt like a reward, especially on the days she cried.

"What am I going to do?" she murmured, stroking a lock of hair that had fallen over my forehead. She wasn't really talking to me. She did that a lot. Ever since she told me she was having another baby.

"Will this baby be a boy?" I asked hopefully.

"I don't know." More tears then.

"I'm sorry!" I squeaked, wishing I hadn't asked the question. "I'll be nice to it, even if it's another girl!"

"I know you will," she said softly, hugging me closer. "You're the big brother. You have to protect them."

"I will." I peeked up at her, breathing in her scent, which reminded me of walks in the garden.

"And someday, when you meet that girl, protect her, too."

I nodded, laying my head on her shoulder. I would protect my sister and the baby, and when I was old enough, I would protect mummy, too.

I would take care of her so she didn't cry.

"Why are you sad?" I asked. I needed to know if I was going to help her.

"Sometimes, it's lonely here. All these people rushing about, but no time to live." She shook her head when I gave her a funny look. She wasn't making any sense. "Sometimes I wish I could sweep you away to a different life where you could just be Alexander."

"I am just Alexander," I said seriously, but now I knew what she wanted. Someday when I was old enough, I would take her somewhere she could be happy. I might even bring Sarah and the baby.

"Of course, you are, poppet." She kissed my forehead, and I scrambled off to do something that had faded with time.

The memory fades until all I'm left with is her words.

"I think David knows that," Edward said glumly. "He's not returning my calls. At least, you're in love with a woman."

"I don't think that means much to him," I mused, still thinking of my mother's words.

"I've asked David to the country along with the usual group," Edward told me. "He'll come, but not to be with me."

"You have to let him be with you," I say, finishing the last of my tea.

Edward arches a brow. "You should take your own advice. Maybe you should invite Clara to the country."

"Trial by fire? Lovely." I can not imagine putting her

through another moment with our father. "They'd make her miserable."

Edward stands. "Then be the one that makes her happy."

I mimic his expression. "You should take your own advice."

He holds up his hands in surrender. "We both know it's easier to give advice than take it."

"So what do we do?" I ask. We should walk away from them both. We should protect them. It's the only way.

"Actually take each other's advice," he suggests. "Call her. Go to see her. Something. Don't cut her out."

"Be with David," I say.

"Maybe you could give me something smaller to work with," he says dryly.

"Tell him. Talk to him. Or let him go."

It's the advice we should both take. We're both too selfish to take it.

Edward leaves, and I cross to my desk, drawing out a crimson-red envelope and scrawl a note to her. I might not know what to do about her yet, but she deserves more from me—I promised her that.

Poppet,
    Have a less dramatic week at work. I'm tied up
with family business, but I will see you soon.
    X

She had a full weekend planned with her friend.

She'll get this at work tomorrow, and it will...buy me time? I fold it and shove it in the envelope before melting a spot of wax and stamping it with my personal seal.

Then I lift it to my lips and kiss it, knowing soon it will be with her.

The only place I want to be.

The last place I should ever be.

CHAPTER TWENTY-FOUR

The next morning, I'm no closer to knowing what to do when I'm called to a meeting.

"Alexander." My father rises from his desk and gestures towards a man I don't recognize. "I'd like you to meet my...associate."

I stick a hand out, and he surveys me with shrewd, green eyes. The man is my age, maybe a little older. His hair is caught between dark blonde and red. The suit he wears is expensive, as is the Omega wristwatch on his arm. All these things tell me he's rich, but there's little else to discern from his appearance.

"Smith Price," he says, without giving any more away. The man is locked up like a safe, and he's not going to show anything unless he wants to.

"Mr. Price is here to discuss a mutual friend."

"My friend or yours?" I ask dryly. I can't imagine that we have any friends in common. The closest we get to sharing a relationship is where Pepper is concerned—and I'd hardly count her a confidant.

"Mine." My father's lips thin into a flat line.

"Actually, we have a mutual acquaintance." Price picks a thread from his sleeve, eyes it with annoyance, and flicks it to the ground.

I bite back a smile. I can only imagine the palpitations that move gave my father, but he doesn't speak. I can't help wondering who this Smith Price is that he puts up with it. "We do?"

"Georgia Kincaid," he says her name casually, but his eyes are trained on me, waiting to watch the bombshell explode.

"I haven't seen her in years," I say coolly. My father shows no signs that he remembers the name. If he did, I doubt I would still be part of this conversation. I also suspect Mr. Price would be on his way out the door.

It's a message meant for me.

"And your friend?" I ask my father, keeping my eyes on Price.

"You remember Hammond," he says, his face pinching.

I shouldn't be taken aback. My eyes sweep to my father, but he won't look at me. Years have passed since he found me—whip in hand, with her at my feet, bloodied and bruised and blissed out—and he hasn't forgiven me.

"I'm surprised you count him as a friend," I say simply.

"You know what they say about friends and enemies," my father says.

"What is this about? And what does it have to do with me?" I ask, growing tired of the charade. "I haven't spoken to Hammond in years, either. I don't fit into his scene."

A smirk flickers across Smith's lips as if he spots my lie but doesn't say anything. He lounges in his seat, his arm slung over its back, and answers. "You have a problem."

"I do?" I ask.

"Yes," he says, and all trace of arrogance is gone. "You're going to need help."

"From you?" I guess. I don't know how he's found his way here or how he managed to catch my father's attention. "I doubt it."

"I think you should listen to him," my father says coldly. "There are things you need to know about— dangers you can't possibly imagine. Not just to you, but—"

My phone rings, interrupting him. I'm reaching to silence it when I see it's from Norris. I look up to my father and Mr. Price. "I'm sorry. This is an emergency."

"It's her, isn't it?" my father demands. "You're family is more important than some tart you're shagging!"

I ignore him, tipping my head at Price. "Sorry to cut this short."

"I understand. I'll fill your father in." He rises with me, bringing us face to face. He passes me a business card. "When you need me, come and find me."

I resist the urge to laugh. I have no idea what's going on, nor do I care to hear anymore. My father suffers under the delusion that everything is life or death. It's the power

going to his head. I'm still shaking my head when I reach
the hall and return Norris's call.

"Sorry, I was in a meeting," I say, but he cuts me off
before I can fill him in on the bizarre circumstances. "Is
she okay?"

Norris delivered the note this morning. Since then,
he's been keeping an eye on her office. After making our
relationship public at my father's party, I'm well aware
she's likely to face some paparazzi this morning. I want to
know she's safe.

"There's another story in the tabloids—"

"What's new?" I ask irritably.

"I think you need to read it," he says quietly.

His words creep under my skin. I hang up and open
my browser. Search results start appearing before I've
finished typing her name, but this time the story isn't
about me. It's about her. I scan the headlines, a pit
opening inside me as I see what I've done. I didn't protect
her. I can't.

And now, it's beginning.

CHAPTER TWENTY-FIVE

Norris is not happy with me. I tug the ballcap down as I make my way off the Tube at Stepney Green. No one noticed me on the train, which is hardly surprising. No one is looking for me. I'm just some bloke with his hands shoved into his pockets on his way home from work.

I make my way toward Clara's flat. According to Norris, who's watching her at her work, she's still there. I could have waited to do this. Norris wanted to come with me, but I wasn't sure what would be worse: sitting in a car going crazy or sitting in her room going crazy. In the end, I thought she'd be safest with Norris keeping an eye on her, ready to keep the camped-out paparazzi at bay.

I spot a food cart selling kebabs, making my stomach rumble. The man behind it tilts his head curiously when I pause to consider getting one, but the last thing I need is to draw attention. The reporters will be following Norris and Clara home, but if he's smart—and he is—he'll lose a fair number of them on his way. Even the relative calm of the car ride will be a respite for her after being mobbed by the tabloid leeches.

When I reach her building, I press the buzzer and pray that Belle is home. She strikes me as the type who's too busy planning her wedding—to that obnoxious wanker, Philip—to have a job. She answers within thirty seconds with a bright, "Hello?"

Clearly, she hasn't seen the tabloids yet.

"Can I come in?" I ask.

She buzzes me in without asking why I'm here. I take the steps two at a time until I'm at the door to her flat. It's already open, and Belle and an older woman regard me with an almost aristocratic surprise. It's the kind of response that bred into titled people—people who might one day be called upon to entertain their king.

Belle shoots a glance at the older woman, and I see her legs cross.

"Don't," I say before she can curtsey. "I'm just your flatmate's boyfriend stopping by unannounced."

Her crimson lips twist into a bemused smile. "I suppose I'll stop looking for the glass slipper then."

She moves to the side, nodding her head that I should come in. I step through and look around. The older woman has the same regal cheekbones and bright eyes as Belle, but her platinum hair is silver from age, not dye, and she wears it in a short, artful mess. She holds out a hand, her wrist jangling with bangle bracelets.

"Jane Stuart," she introduces herself. "Your highness."

"Belle's aunt." I take her outstretched hand. "Alexander, please."

"Can I get you some tea?" Belle asks, looking around like she's trying to figure out how I fit into the day.

"Scotch?"

She tips her head, then shrugs. "That bad of a day?"

"I assume you haven't seen the news." There's no point avoiding it. If anything, Belle might have some insight into how to handle this bloody situation. I'm at a loss.

She plucks the lid off a decanter and pours me a glass, then two more. "What happened?"

I don't know Belle, but I need all the help I can get. "I think a simple google search will clear it up more quickly than I can."

I sip the Scotch while she types on her phone. There's a pause, and then her eyes widen, her mouth forming a quiet O of horror. Her aunt reaches for the mobile, looks at the screen, and proceeds to down her drink in one gulp.

"Something tells me this isn't news to you," I say dryly.

Belle heaves a sigh, looking back and forth between her aunt and me. "It's not really my place to tell you about this."

"I can respect that." I nod. I'd rather hear it from Clara. "But it's true? She has an eating disorder?"

"She did," Belle hedges.

"She does," Jane corrects her gently, "and it's under control at the moment."

I understand what's being left unspoken. Belle

doesn't want to scare me off. Jane is wise enough to know
that ignoring a problem doesn't make it go away. I don't
press either for particulars.

"Fuck," I mutter, finishing my own drink. I whip off
the cap I'm still wearing, toss it on the table, and comb my
fingers through my hair.

"Is that a problem?" Belle asks defiantly, misunderstanding my reaction. "Because if you're not man
enough—"

"I'm man enough," I cut her off. "I just wish I knew. It
didn't come up..." I trail off before I give myself away.

"In all the research you did on her?" Jane guesses, her
blue eyes studying me shrewdly. She goes to the kitchen
and returns with the decanter.

There's no point hiding it. I nod.

"It doesn't matter how much intelligence you have or
who follows her and reports back. You can't know a
person until they show you who they are." There's a
warning in her words and more than a hint of challenge.

"I want to know who she is." The confession slips
from me before I can take it back. Maybe it's the Scotch or
the surprise of today's news. Maybe where Clara Bishop
is concerned, I can't focus long enough to restrain myself.

Belle doesn't respond, but she bites her lip thoughtfully before checking her wristwatch. "I need to meet
Philip," she announces. "Will you be okay waiting for her
here?"

"Yes." Relief floods through me. I need to talk to
Clara...alone. The last thing I want is to share her with
her friends tonight. Belle must understand this.

"I'll wait in her room," I tell Belle, and she begins to gather her things, then I turn to Jane. "It was nice to meet you."

"Let her tell you," she advises me. "Be patient. It's not easy to split yourself open like that. It takes courage."

"I will," I promise.

I amble into Clara's room, and I'm immediately bombarded by her even though it's empty. Her scent lingers in the air. A pair of shoes waits for her. She's everywhere, and my body responds possessively, growing more anxious as each second ticks by and she doesn't appear.

Belle's blonde head peeks in through the door. "I'll be leaving now. There's not much in the fridge, but make yourself at home."

"Thanks," I grit out, dropping into a chair by the window where I can watch for her.

"She usually leaves the office around six," she tells me. "And Alexander?"

I swivel to look at her as she steps inside the door frame. "If you fuck with her, I don't care who you are, I will track you down, cut off your balls, and hang them from the Clock Tower's little hand.

My eyebrows lift in a combination of surprise and respect. "Noted."

Since I've never had any doubt I would hurt Clara, I might need to increase my security.

"She needs to feel safe," Belle adds softly. "Give her that."

I swallow. "I will."

Belle leaves me alone with my thoughts and the ghost of Clara's absence, and I turn to keep vigil at the window. I'll do more than make her feel safe. I'll keep her safe—at all costs.

I LOSE track of the hours I spend waiting for her to come home. Norris is near her, ready to see her safely to her flat. The last thing she needs is me showing up, not with the media circus it would cause. When a familiar Bentley drives past, relief floods through me. Soon. She'll be here soon. And then we can sort out this mess.

A door opens in the distance, but I don't move. Footsteps in the hall slowing slightly the closer they get to her room. Finally, she fills the doorframe, dressed in a simple blue dress that hugs her curves—curves that make me mental. I frown, wondering if she's self-conscious about them. If she is, I'm going to have to fix that. She stands for a moment, mute, her hair cascading around her shoulders before she moves to the bed. She still doesn't speak as she plops onto it. Instead, she grabs a pillow.

I wait for her to open up.

She doesn't.

Make her feel safe. That was Belle's advice.

I only know one way to do that, but first, I need to know if this is just another exaggeration of the so-called press. I won't make the mistake of believing whatever they print.

It takes effort to go to her and keep my hands to myself. She blinks up at me, the evidence of tears smudged under her lower lashes. I want to reach out and wipe it away—wipe all of this away. But first.

"Is it true?"

Fear flits over her face, and I tense. "Yes."

Hearing her say it breaks me. It's not enough that she's had to live with it. The goddamn press believes they can drag it up to sell fucking tabloids. I turn away, afraid she'll see my rage and feel anything but safe near me. But I can't contain my anger. It bursts out of me, sending my fist slamming into the plaster wall.

So much for keeping control of myself. I pull my hand out, watching the plaster crumbling. This sends Clara shooting to her feet.

"I'm sorry," she screams. "I'm not perfect. I'm sorry you didn't know. But you need to leave."

I whip around to find tears streaming down her cheeks and realize I've made another mistake. "You think I'm angry with you?"

"I have no idea how they found out about it," she continues like she didn't even hear me. Her hands twist together. "I was in therapy before university, and I saw a private counselor my first year of college. There was a relapse a year ago, but that was all confidential."

"You no longer have secrets, Clara." I took that from you when I took you.

"I realize that now. I realize I owe you an explanation, but—"

"You owe me nothing," I cut her off, doing my best to keep my voice soft. I want to soothe her, not add to her stress. I close the space between us and take her chin in my hands, directing her tear-filled eyes to mine. "Do you understand that? You owe me nothing."

Her head shakes, and I understand her a little more. I know what it's like to cling to whatever control life gives you. I want to carry her away, somewhere safe where no one will ever touch her. But the only way to truly protect her is to walk away, and looking at her now, seeing her rise as they try to tear her down, I realize that's impossible. I'll never give her up. I want her too much.

"I need you to understand," she murmurs, still caught in her own thoughts.

Do I tell her it's not important to me? That seems wrong. It's important to her. Do I tell her everything will be okay? That's a lie. We both know it. I can only tell her the truth I feel as certainly as the beating of my own heart. "If you need me to, I will listen. But you don't owe me an explanation. Nothing you say will change anything between us."

"Then go." She yanks free from me, turning her face so I can't see her pain.

"I don't want to go." I step closer. I want to take away the hurt she's feeling. I want to show her that she's the one I want—that her flaws only make her so much more beautiful to me. "What do you think I'm saying to you?"

"I understand." Her eyes stay cast to the floor. "You don't need more drama in your life. You don't need a girlfriend who has to actively construct positive thoughts about her body and set alarms to remind herself to eat. I don't blame you for that."

Fuck, is that what she thinks? That I want some

plastic doll hanging from my arm? I never wanted anyone by my side until she stumbled into my life. I tried like hell to stop myself from falling for her, but how could I not? Why can't she see herself like I do?

"I'm not leaving you," I tell her. "I never wanted perfection. I wanted you."

She sways, and I catch her. If only I could always be near enough to do that, maybe we could make this crazy situation work. I guide her to the bed, holding her close. Nothing will convince her that I want to stay—except staying.

"I still want you to understand." She turns into me, nuzzling closer, and for the first time all day, I relax.

I nod, determined to listen.

Clara begins her story slowly, her voice shaking slightly, and I tighten my arms around her.

"It started at school. My mother insisted that I attend an exclusive academy in California, and as usual, my father gave in. I didn't want to go. I was fourteen, and my friends were my life, but I had no say in the matter. I guess that made the transition worse, and I had a hard time meeting people." She takes a deep breath before plunging forward. "Finally, an older girl took me under her wing. She taught me about makeup and boys. For some reason, I thought she was really popular. Probably because she seemed happy. And then one day, she went into the bathroom and threw up after lunch."

I tense. I hadn't bothered to read the lies the tabloids printed, so hearing the truth from her now is jarring.

"She pushed me to try it, and when I wouldn't, she

started dropping little hints. There was a roll around my bra strap. She slapped my thigh in the locker room and laughed as it jiggled. So one night, I went with her after dinner and threw up. It was hard for me, and it took so long for me to do it while she stood there and teased me. When I finally did it, I decided I couldn't do it again. I hated it, but she was my only friend." She manages a sad smile. "After all these years, I still feel stupid when I tell this story."

I force her to look up at me. "You are not stupid."

She needs to hear it, even if she won't believe it. I know because there have been so many times I needed someone to tell me that my demons were real, but that they didn't define me.

"I wasn't smart, though. I believed her when she said my parents had sent me away because they were ashamed. I believed her when she said the thinner I got, the more popular I would become. By the time I went home for Spring Break, I weighed less than a hundred pounds. My mom—" she breaks for a moment, and I kiss her forehead, hoping it makes her feel safe enough to continue. "My mom started crying when she saw me. They pulled me out of school, and she drove me to therapy every single day because she wouldn't let them admit me. That summer we moved to England. Dad thought it would be a better environment for me. Maybe he was right."

"He was right." I want to send him a goddamn thank you card for removing the ocean that was once between us, for bringing her to London, for bringing her to me. "Because you're here with me now, poppet."

Her hand presses against my chest for just a moment like she's checking to see if I'm real. "I've done really well with therapy. I learned my eating disorder was a coping mechanism that I used when I was stressed or lonely. I stayed in therapy until my second year at university, and then I met Daniel."

"The one who tried to break you?" She'd mentioned him before. I had the sense he didn't want to run into me any time soon.

"I should have seen through him." Her voice is full of regret.

"Don't make excuses for him." I hated men that did that to women. Men who manipulated and twisted. Men who were so fragile they used others like human shields.

"It was fine for a while, but then things changed. He changed. One minute he made me feel like the most important person in his life, and the next, I was the reason he was miserable. He criticized how much I ate, pointed out how little I exercised. He competed with me for grades. When my parents gave me access to my trust fund, we came home after my birthday party, and I told him I was tired."

I brace myself, afraid I know what comes next. I let her go, putting enough distance between us that if my rage takes over, she won't be in its range.

"He didn't like that," she continues. "He accused me of being superior to him. He said I was being elitist and that I was too snobby to fuck him. Things escalated quickly, and he almost—"

I jump up from the bed, needing more distance, certain I might actually detonate. Pacing the length of her room, I motion for her to continue.

She does, but there's a nervous edge to her tone. "But he didn't. Belle came home. She saw what was going on and threatened to call the police. That night should have been enough for me to see what he was doing to me, but I still thought I was in love with him. I refused to go to therapy, even though Belle pushed. I was fine. Things were under control, and then I fainted during class. At the hospital, they asked me when my last period was, and I couldn't remember."

I stop dead in my tracks. It's bad enough that any other man has touched her. If he...

"I honestly thought I was pregnant, and the thought of having a baby with Daniel made me so scared that I got sick. They had to put me on oxygen and give me a feeding tube." She forces herself to continue as she cries, "I realized that I wasn't scared of having a baby, but I was terrified of being permanently bound to Daniel. When it occurred to me that my child would have him for a father, there was a sadness deeper than any I've ever known."

Clara Bishop isn't a mother. I'd have found that during my research. There's no indication that she ever had a child. That only leaves one possibility. "So you ended it?"

"I didn't have to," she says with a hollow laugh. "The results came back negative. I wasn't pregnant. I was malnourished. My liver was barely functioning. I was shutting down. I hadn't purposefully stopped eating. I hadn't even realized I was doing it. The doctors quizzed me and suggested I go back to therapy, especially a support group. It was there that I realized I'd been clinging to an idea of control that didn't exist. Not eating was something I chose. Maybe because of the awful things he said about my body. Maybe because subconsciously, I desperately needed to control something. My group helped me see that I'd given him control over me instead. So when I say he broke me—that's what I mean. I loved him, and he nearly killed me. At least, I thought I loved him."

"And now?" I don't know why it's important. I shouldn't want her to love me. I shouldn't want to know her heart has never belonged to anyone else. But God, I want her to say no.

Her answering look is hard. A decision is being made, and her next words are carefully chosen. "Now...Let's just say that distance has given me perspective. Although after today, I feel like I've been thrown back in time. I suppose no matter how far I've come, I can't change what happened, and that means sometimes I have to face it."

She can't change it. She can only control it. She needs to control her body, and I...

"That's why you ran when I brought up submission."

She nods reluctantly as though she'd hoped I wouldn't put these two things together.

"I can't believe I..." I've spent my life in a perpetual state of self-loathing. For the first time ever, though, I hate myself completely. I hate that I need what she can't give me. I hate that I'm weak. I'm no better than men like Daniel, demanding more than is my right, taking more than I give.

"No, X," she says swiftly. "It wasn't just that. It was the idea of any relationship."

"My predilections certainly won't help you." And now she's trying to soothe me when I'm supposed to be taking care of her.

She shakes her head. "I thought that at first, too. But you aren't him, and I'm stronger now."

"And your body?" Do the scars of what he said and did to her linger? "How do you feel about your body?"

She hesitates, which is an answer in and of itself. "Most days, I don't think about it. I eat. I get dressed. I walk or run. Other days, I catch myself wishing I had a body like Pepper's."

That's what she thinks? That I want someone like Pepper when I have her? I'm in motion before I even realize what I'm doing. Lifting her into my arms, I carry her to the loo. I need to show her what I see. I need her to see that she is breathtaking. I need her to understand she is everything any man could want—and everything I need.

CHAPTER TWENTY-SIX

Kicking open the door, I carry her to the mirror and lower her to her feet. She looks skeptically up at me, but she doesn't fight my sudden actions. I spin her to face her own reflection and lean to kiss her neck as I draw the zipper of her dress down her back, revealing her smooth shoulders. "I've been remiss in telling you how I feel about your body. Your gorgeous cunt gets so much of my attention, but when I said your whole body was made for fucking, I meant it."

I want to rip her clothes off. It takes restraint not to, but I'm not rushing this. I need her to understand me when I say she's perfection. My lips cruise across her shoulder to the curve of her neck. "This—" I kiss the spot "—was made to kiss—so smooth and soft. When I'm burying my cock in your perfect cunt, I can't help myself."

I've fucked plenty of women, but none have drawn me to them like she does. I can't stop myself from kissing her soft skin again, but I want more of her. I want to devour her. Before I realize it, my teeth nip the spot, and she moans. I smile as I realize she liked it. That bit of pain dashed into the pleasure.

This isn't about you, I remind myself, moving back to undressing her as slowly as possible. My hand slides one strap of her dress down slowly, and I follow its path with hungry kisses.

"Long and slender. These freckles drive me crazy." I prove it by pausing to kiss a few. "And the way they feel when they're wrapped around me, clinging to me as I ride you—perfection."

I clasp her hand, lifting our entwined hands to her shoulder so I can kiss each knuckle. "Such clever fingers. I hate when they aren't intertwined with mine, unless they're on my cock, of course."

She nods absently, her eyes meeting mine in the reflection. I wonder if she sees how beautiful she is yet, how much I want her, how desperate I am to keep her. But she's watching me, not the magnificent body I've put on display.

"Look at yourself, poppet."

"I want to look at you," she murmurs.

That's only natural. "I don't blame you, but right now, I need you to pay attention. Follow my lips with your eyes."

I move between her and the sink, kneeling so that I don't block her view of the mirror. Gripping her wrists, I force her arms behind her back until she arches close enough for me to catch her nipple in my mouth. I take my time, nibbling at it, sucking it. I want her to see what I do:

how her body responds to my touch, her breasts swelling with arousal, her cunt plumping until a single touch could push her over the edge. "It's almost cliché to tell you that your tits are perfect, but they are. Full and supple. I can never decide if I want to suck them or fuck them."

This earns me a whimper. Clara is full of surprises. She'd been so prim the day we met, so shocked when I kissed her. And then I'd taken her to bed and unleashed something that surprised both of us. Her little moan is giving me ideas. "Would you like that? Do you want me to shove my cock between your tits?"

How the fuck can I resist that? I have to remind myself that I can wait. This is about her body and showing her what it does to me, but I can't quite keep a vision of her breasts dripping with climax from springing to mind—my cock springing along with it.

"Later, poppet." I mean it. I want to do everything to her. I want to show her pleasure she never knew existed. I want to watch her come again and again. I kiss across the other breast, capture her nipple and continue my exploration. My hand strokes down her stomach, taunting her with what she really wants. I feel the tension building inside her, noting how her hips wiggle a little wider open in invitation. "Your body makes me so fucking hot, poppet. I think about it all the time, imagining how I'm going to fuck you. When we're apart, all I can think of is getting my hands on you."

I grab her roughly, already imagining how good it's going to feel when I bury myself inside her. "I can't take my eyes off you when you walk. Do you sway your hips like that on purpose, knowing that I'm watching?"

She shakes her head. Of course, she doesn't see it. She's been taught to see her flaws. I have to show her her strengths.

"All I can think about is grabbing these hips and putting you over my knee," I mutter, ignoring a pang in my balls at the thought, "or holding onto them as my cock pounds you. They curve so precisely into my hands. I swear your body is fucking proof of evolution."

Her eyes shudder closed. I know she's imagining all my suggestions. I want her to see me do all the things to her. I want her to watch me fuck her. I want her to see what she looks like moments before she comes undone.

"Open your eyes, Clara," I command her, spanking her lightly. Her eyes fly open, and I resist the urge to smack her ass harder. Would she cry out? Would she beg for more? "I'll have to spend a whole day worshipping your ass. It's a pity that you can't see me do it, but I'll be certain to describe every single thing I want to do to it. Everything I'm going to do to it."

I press her thighs farther apart and nuzzle my face against her sweet cunt. "I suppose it would be too much to ask to be buried here?"

She giggles, and I kiss her lacy panties, earning another laugh. "I'm serious, poppet. I want my lips down here, breathing you in. Your scent intoxicates me, you know. I want them clamping against my ears as I taste you. But I also need them spreading open for me, circling around me as I fuck you."

"Yes, please." It slips out of her again.

I resist the urge to stand up and fuck her over the sink on the spot. She wants it all so badly, but she won't let herself have it. I have to coax it out of her, give her permission, show her she should never feel shame in my arms.

"You know how I feel about this." I brush across her again. "Your cunt was made for me. It's so tight it just squeezes my cock when I'm inside of you, draining every drop from me. But you know that. You know you have a greedy cunt, don't you? I want you to see it. I'm going to fuck you with my tongue, so you can see how fucking beautiful you are when you come."

I run my tongue roughly over her lace thong, tasting how she's soaked through it. So wet. So ready. "Watch, poppet."

I want her to see me claim her with my mouth. Pushing her legs as wide open as possible, I hook her panties and yank them to the side. My tongue thrusts her open to find her clit. I'm not watching her anymore, so I hope she's behaving. A man can't be held accountable when his mouth is on a perfect cunt.

"I want to see your cock inside me." Her request is tentative. She wants me. She wants contact. She wants to give me what she imagines I need. But this isn't about me. I ignore her and continue on.

Gripping her hips, I urge her against me, stroking until her clit is so swollen, I can catch it between my teeth. Once I do, I savor it. Her body tightens, and then her climax floods my tongue.

"Had enough, poppet?"

She shakes her head, stumbling dizzily and catching herself on the vanity. My hands hover near her in case she loses her balance entirely. When she doesn't, I stand, unable to wait any longer. My dick is so hard that it's trying to escape my jeans.

In the mirror, I see her tongue swipe over her lower lip.

Fuck me. I fist my shaft. "Do you want this?"

She hesitates. Her answer is surprisingly shy. "No. I want your body."

I freeze, realizing what she's asking. She felt the scars. Now she wants to see them. How have I let this happen? Touching is one thing. Facing them is entirely different. "You don't want that, Clara."

"There's no part of my body you don't want, right?" She pauses, looking at me expectantly. I can't believe she's playing this card. "There's no part of your body that I don't want."

If she really knew. "Clara—"

"I felt the scars. I know," she says softly. "And I want you. All of you, X. Your body—all of it—makes me so fucking hot."

The little minx has me, and she knows it. How can I argue with my own words? If I want to prove that I want every bit of her, I can't keep my own body from her. Still, she doesn't have any idea what she's asking. I take off my trousers as she watches in the mirror. I hesitate when I reach for my black t-shirt, and Clara smiles. Slowly, I draw it over my head, revealing myself to her inch by inch. Her eyes go distant. She's guarding herself like a woman approaching a wild animal. She must have some clue that I have a reason to hide this.

"All of you, X," she urges.

I whip the shirt over my head, searching for any of the arrogance I usually feel in abundance and finding none. She scans over me, her face unreadable. The scars from my accident are brutal, refusing to fade with time. As I'd gotten older, they'd become worse as I filled out after years of military training and service.

Clara still says nothing, and I reach for her, grabbing her hips, needing some assurance that she can't turn and flee from me. But when her eyes lift from my scars to my eyes, she whispers, "Take me, and don't be gentle."

I move my cock to her entrance and slowly breach her. She wants it rough, but I don't trust myself. Not after she's opened the cage that restrains me. I keep it locked for a reason. I rock into her, urging myself deeper until I'm fully inside her. Leaning down, I catch the curve of her neck, intending to kiss it. Instead, my teeth bite into her, and she gasps. I'm losing control. I try to dial it back.

Clara isn't having it. She pulls free from my hands and folds over the sink, allowing my cock to slam deeper inside her. She moans, moving her hips to encourage me, her hands gripping the counter.

She's giving herself to me, showing me what she thinks I need to heal. But this isn't enough to tame me. It's dangerous for her to think so. I close my eyes, unwilling to pretend that I'm anything more than damaged and angry and dangerous.

"Open your eyes, X," she says firmly. "I want you to see what you do to me. I want you to see what I see."

I can't deny her, but I can't hide the truth. She can't heal me because some scars run deeper than the skin. She can see the ones on my flesh, but not the ones that twist my soul. I stare at her, wondering when she'll realize how fucked up I am. She pushes her hips back into me. She might as well wave a red flag. Doesn't she see how she's provoking me? She thinks she wants it rough, but she has no idea what she's asking of me—or herself. I have to show her before it's too late. I grab a handful of her hair and jerk her up, so she's forced to really look at me. She wants to see me. She needs to see the beast. She can't look away, and I reveal my true self, pounding into her so hard I know it hurts. She gasps and grunts, her face wrenching with the sudden violence of my cock. But instead of begging me to stop, she tightens around me.

"Don't stop," she urges, breathless. "All of you. Give me all of you."

I come with a violent surge that blasts from me so hard that she has to hold onto the counter.

She enjoyed it.

I have to make her see. I keep going, my cock remaining hard as it moves into her soaked cunt. I ignore how impossibly good it feels to fuck her when she's full of me.

"Alexander," she calls, discomfort running through her voice.

"Need...need..." But she needs to see—see the real me, the real danger of freeing me. She still has time to put me back in my cage because once I'm fully released, I'll take her captive and never let her go. I'll use her. I'll control her. I'll ruin her. Or my world will.

Clara manages to free herself and turns around, leaving my cock pulsing with unfinished business. As soon as she's gone, I realize my mistake. I can't punish her for my past. I have to protect her, and now I've pushed her too far. I need to show her that I can be gentle, that I can keep the dangerous part of me locked away.

"Brimstone," she whispers.

No. Not now. I need her too much. "I need to be inside you."

She shakes her head. Not like this. Not taking. Together.

I wrap my arms around her and lift her to the counter. The pause gives me time to gather myself. I find my control. I find her. My cock is still hard, still desperate to be inside her. I tenderly move it across her swollen sex and watch her, hoping she understands this is about something else. She stares for a moment before wiggling her hips to slide herself over my cock.

I let her take the lead. I can't help feeling like I'm coming home as I join with her. This isn't about fucking. This is connection. She clings to me, her eyes locked with mine, and I know neither of us can deny everything between us has changed again. There's no longer a path without her—there's no future that exists outside of her and me. I don't know how to do this. She has to show me how.

CHAPTER TWENTY-SEVEN

Things are very normal. It's the only word I can think of, even though I don't have much experience with it. After last night, I might have thought things would be tense between us. Instead, I'm watching her get ready in the mirror, wondering why she bothers with even a drop of bloody make-up. She doesn't need it. Her eyes flit to mine in the mirror and rake down my body. There's not an ounce of reservation or disgust as she takes in my scars. If anything, she looks like she's thinking about the same thing I am.

"If you keep looking at me like that, I'm going to have to take you back to bed," I warn her.

"Yes, please," she whispers before sighing. "Don't even think about it, X. I'm going to be late already."

As if she could say no to me. "I warned you that I'm a man who takes what he wants."

I prove my point by throwing her over my shoulder and carrying her to her bedroom.

"Put me down!" Her palm smacks me. "I'm late."

"Stop fighting me, or you won't make it in at all." I can think of much better ways for Clara to spend her day than sitting behind an office desk, and I can think of several inventive ways to ensure she doesn't have a choice.

Of course, I might be able to convince her. I let her fall to the bed before dropping over and crawling up her body, giving me the chance to catch her skirt with my teeth. When it's at her hips, my fingers dive past her lacy thong to her wet cunt. "See, poppet? You're still dressed."

She moans as my thumb finds her plump clit and strokes circles over it.

"Although this bra is vexing." I want more of her. All of her. I don't want her to leave—not for work. Not for any reason at all. "Your tits belong in my mouth. Don't they, Clara?"

Her hands grab the sheets as she arches, her body tensing. She's so close to release, but I'm not ready for her to come yet. I pause and wait. She needs to learn that patience is rewarded. Plus, she hasn't answered my question. I brush my cheek against hers, my scratchy stubble scraping gently over her soft skin. "Clara?"

"Yes!" she squeaks, and I reward her by plunging my fingers inside her, drawing her orgasm from her with precise strokes. Her hips thrust against me. I'm not the only one who wants more.

I brush a fallen strand from her face, so I can drink in the pink hue of her cheeks and watch her slowly return to me from wherever my machinations just took her. I will never tire of seeing her like this, glowing with the bliss of her climax.

I want her underneath me every hour of the day, coming again and again. We can pause to eat. I lean to kiss her, about to tell her just that—but someone knocks on the door.

Who the fuck got past Norris?

I kiss her more insistently, hoping she didn't hear. There's another, much louder knock that makes her go rigid. I give up. I'm not meant to be happy for hours on end, after all. I give her my hand, and she stands on shaky legs, adjusting her clothes and looking around for her blouse.

I wish I was dressed because she takes off for the door before I have my jeans on. We're going to have to talk about answering the door. It's not safe anymore. People will try to get to her now that she's been linked to me. I'm slipping my shirt over my head when the yelling begins. It's muffled, but I make out enough through the walls to know she's not in danger.

She is, however, having a rather heated argument.

No one needs to know I'm here. It will only complicate matters for her, but I can't stop myself from padding into the hall. I'm about to go out to her when I catch an older woman say, "That's what you said before. When did you start seeing Alexander again? Don't try to deny it! Your appearance with him at that ball has been all over the internet. We have people who can help you spin this."

"I don't think that's necessary, Mom."

Mom. Fuck, I really don't need to put Clara through this. I don't want to give her mother the wrong idea, and Clara's already had to deal with my father. I step backward so I won't be seen and debate returning to her room. But I can't decide which she'll dislike more: being left to deal with her mother alone while I lay low or being put on the spot for an introduction.

She decides for me. I hear her loudly instruct her mother. "All I really want is to finish getting dressed. I need to be at work in less than an hour."

Her mother just speaks more loudly, ignoring her. "I called Lola this morning, and she thought that we might try—"

"You called Lola?"

I scroll through my mental file on Clara Bishop but can't recall a Lola.

"She's going into PR, and she's very savvy about social media," her mother says.

"She's twenty-one, and she's had fifteen majors since she got to university!"

"Lola is set on public relations."

"You know what?" I hear Clara stomp across the flat. "I've got this. I don't need you or Lola or Dad helping me out."

There's a pause and then an unmistakable sob. I'm nearly out of the hall before I realize it's her mother crying.

"You're cutting me out of your life, Clara. You know how dangerous that is. Does he even know? Have you spoken with him since the story was leaked?" she sobs.

Her questions reverse my previous decision to stay out of it. I don't think. I just know that I won't let Clara apologize to her mother for what the media did to her yesterday.

"He knows," I answer her mother's question, leaving no room for her to misinterpret what I'm saying. Clara's gaze falls on me, her eyes shutting for just a moment, and I know she's bracing for impact. But I won't let her endure it alone. I'm surprisingly good with parents. "You must be Clara's mother. I'm pleased to meet you, Mrs. Bishop."

I extend a hand, but her mother doesn't move. She just stares at me, her mouth hanging open. She's a lovely woman if a bit overdone. It's obvious who Clara gets her looks from.

"Mom," Clara says softly. "This is Alexander."

She looks between us twice, shaking her head and turning on me. "Well, I'm glad she told you. Relationships must be built on honesty. Don't you agree, Alexander?"

"Of course." I force a smile for her sake.

"I think it would be best for all of us, particularly Clara, if we had someone attempting to contain this story. I'm sure you agree with that as well." She taps her fingers, waiting for me to agree with her. I suspect most people don't bother disagreeing with her often. I'm not most people.

"Unfortunately, I can tell you from personal experience that it's very difficult to control what they publish, whether it's true or not," I point out.

She shakes her head, dismissing me outright. I'm reminded of my father. "We have to do something."

"I can't promise anything, but I do have my best man looking into the circumstances behind the story," I say.

Clara's eyes widen with horror. "You shouldn't be dragged into this."

"This happened because of me. It's the least I can do." Why does she have to argue with me? I don't know what it will take to convince Clara that she's going to have to get used to things like this happening—as well as allowing me to deal with them.

I suddenly find myself hugging her mum, who clutches me like a life preserver. I'm not sure she's going to let me go.

"Thank you," she whispers as Clara shoots a sympathetic look at me. "It's so nice to see Clara has found someone." She finally lets me go, and her tears are miraculously dried when she hits me with, "We'd love to take you both to dinner. Do you have plans tomorrow?"

"Mom!" Clara looks like she's going to kick her out.

I suppose it's fair.

"I'd love to," I say before Clara gets too worked up.

"You'd what?" Clara asks, but Mrs. Bishop is already linking her arm with mine as she makes her way to the door.

"I'll arrange everything." She pats my arm reassuringly. "You don't have any food allergies? I'll call Clara with the details. Harold will be so excited."

I swear that she didn't even pause for a breath. Clara's already at the door, trying to shoo her out.

When she finally manages it, she slumps against the door, pressing a hand to her forehead. "I'm sorry about that."

"She seems to be a bit of a handful." At least, her intentions are blatantly transparent.

"I can get you out of this," Clara says quickly. "Don't worry about it."

I frown. "I don't mind going to dinner with your parents."

"Are...you...sure?" She gawks at me. I must really be shit at this boyfriend thing.

"Stop staring at me like I need a straight jacket. Unless you don't want me to go to dinner with your parents." Is that what this is about?

"No!" she shrieks, startling a bit. "Of course, I do, but I understand if you aren't comfortable."

"Isn't this what boyfriends are supposed to do?" I ask. "Meet the parents. Charm them. Earn the privilege to debauch their daughter."

Clara continues to stare.

"Is something wrong?" I ask, replaying the last few minutes and looking for clues. I'd been polite. I'd agreed to dinner. "Did I do something to upset you?"

She swallows, shaking her head. "Nope. I just don't deserve you, X."

"You don't." She's not wrong about that. "No one deserves to put up with me."

Her finger presses to my lips, her blue eyes growing sad. "Don't say that."

"Where did you come from?" I ask softly. "Who sent you to save me?"

Clara's eyes pierce through me, and then her mouth is on mine. I don't think. I react. I press against her, urging her leg up to coil around me. I can feel her damp heat against my groin, earning the attention of my cock. It takes more than a little effort to pull away and remind her that we have other places to be.

"You have to get to work," I whisper, unable to resist tempting her to change her mind. My own plans for today can wait. "Unless..."

Her tongue flicks over her lips. "Unless?"

"You want to call in sick and let me show you what a good boyfriend I can be."

She takes a deep breath. "Sorry, X. I can't play hooky on my third day of work."

I let her go slowly, knowing that she has a real-life to return to. I can't cage her like I've been caged no matter how much I may want to.

"Tonight," I tell her.

"Tonight," she repeats.

My mobile rings as soon as I step out the back entrance. Norris is there, waiting by the Bentley.

"Yes?" I answer.

"I assume you're with her," my father says distastefully.

"What do you need?" I bypass his slight. I don't need my good mood ruined by him.

"I assume you're coming to the country this weekend. I wanted to be certain you didn't try to back out of it."

"I'll be there," I confirm, sliding into the car.

"Good. You need to get out of the city," he says pointedly.

And away from her. I know what he's thinking. "Clara will be there, too."

"Alexander, I don't—"

I hang up on him and smile.

"Home?" Norris asks me.

"Where's that?" I murmur absently. My home isn't ahead of me. It's behind me with her.

"I'm sorry?" he prompts.

"Yes," I say so he can hear, staring out the window as we merge into the morning traffic. "Take me home. I have a note to write."

CHAPTER TWENTY-EIGHT

I wait for Clara near a Tube station, unhappy that she insisted on taking one from work. I wanted to send a car, but she reminded me that it would be easier for her to slip out if my private security wasn't standing by.

I had Norris send a man in plain clothes to follow her anyway, just like he's doing now. He managed a security sweep of the restaurant Clara picked for this afternoon. I couldn't talk him out of it. But I'd been firm on wanting to do this—meet her family—on my own.

So far, I've only spotted two undercover guards casually milling on the same block. At least, they aren't planning to sit next to me at dinner and poison test my soup.

Clara arrives in a flood of passengers, pushing her way through the crowd, handbag on her shoulder. Her eyes scan in front of her, teeth sinking into her lip. A few others glance curiously at her as though they recognize her, but no one stops her.

I wonder how much longer she'll enjoy this already-questionable normalcy. She stops and lets the other passengers continue in a surge toward their own lives, and I wait, keeping her in my sights until she's the only one left lingering in front of the station. She's still wearing the light blouse and tightly fitted skirt from this morning. My mind skips to the lacy thong I know she's wearing underneath, and my cock stiffens.

Forcing myself to ignore the growing ache in my balls, I prowl toward her. Clara turns her head as if sensing me and startles for a second. Her momentary panic quickly shifts, though, and she presses her lips into a tight line.

"I almost didn't recognize you," she admits.

I catch her in my arms, pleased when she wilts against me. She reaches up and tugs the bill of my baseball cap.

"The Yankees?" she says with a raised eyebrow.

"I have a thing for yankees," I say meaningfully, stealing a swift kiss. Even the momentary brush of my lips to hers is like an electric jolt. But it's not centered in my groin this time. It hits directly in the center of my chest like I'm being brought back to life.

"Oh really?" She pulls gently away, slipping her hand into mine.

I let her take the lead, completely willing to be at her mercy this evening. She'll be at mine later tonight. "I think they gave it to me on my last American tour."

Clara stops, blinks hard, and lets out a deep sigh.

"Is something wrong?" I ask, instantly concerned.

"It's going to take some time to get used to hearing about things like your American tours."

"I've only been on one," I tell her, starting forward to keep us moving. "I think I was twelve. It's a bit of a blur."

"It suits you," she says, an undeniable note of affection in her voice. "You look very American. No offense."

"You're American, so I'll consider it a compliment," I murmur. Jeans and trainers had felt like the easiest way to keep a low profile. I'd even go as far as to put sunglasses on under the cap. I start to apologize for my casual appearance when she tugs away and darts over to a shop stall.

Adrenaline rushes through my veins, pounding harder with each step it takes to close the new distance between us. The shopkeep says something to her, and I fight the urge to snap at him. Clara holds up a book and responds before putting it back on the table with a laugh.

As soon as I'm closer to her than he is, I relax a little. By the time she turns back to offer her hand again, I've rearranged my face into calm.

"I love Notting Hill, don't you?" She asks with a sigh. "I'm always finding little treasures."

I nod, gripping her hand more tightly so she won't be able to let go of me so easily. I have never been to Notting Hill. I don't admit this to Clara. I've driven through naturally. I'm aware of it, of course. There are plenty of places in London I've never actually visited. Given that I'm usually surrounded by a security team in public, I don't adventure out often. Tonight, though, I find myself in the bustling neighborhood. There is something wonderfully ordinary about its streets. People move about, going to and from their lives.

And by some miracle, I'm managing to blend in.

"It is a little warm." Clara presses a hand to her neck, and I see it's slightly dewy. She points to an antique shop. "I should go in there. I need a lamp."

"From the nineteenth-century?" I tease.

"I like old, beautiful things," she says, pretending to be offended. "Antiques have better stories, I guess."

"You're going to love my house," I mutter absently.

Clara blows a stream of air from her lips and pulls me toward another stall. I can't blame her for wanting to avoid my family after the disastrous party. That's not going to make what I'm planning to ask her later any easier.

We wander down the streets, slipping into an easy conversation. As twilight deepens, Clara begins to check her watch, then fidget. Finally, we find ourselves in front of a cozy bistro.

"You're quiet," I say, after a few minutes of silence stretch between us.

She looks at me, a flame burning in her eyes. She blinks, and it extinguishes, but the ember remains. "Actually, I'm tired."

That's my fault.

"I feel like I should apologize for keeping you up half the night," I say, pulling her to me and kissing the top of her head, "but I'm not sorry."

She smiles at my blatant cockiness. "And I won't be getting any sleep tonight either."

"Hot date?" I ask.

"The hottest."

"Anyone I know?" My palm skims from the small of her back to her hips.

"I would say you're on intimate terms." She blows me a kiss that's more provocation than affection.

"You need to rest." I resist the siren call of that innocent gesture. "I'm sending you home alone tonight."

Her throat slides. "But I owe you sexual favors."

"And what did I do to deserve that, poppet?" What did I do to deserve her? "Tell me so I can do it again."

"You might not be saying that after dinner." There's resignation in her voice as she reaches for the restaurant door. I grab her hand and pull her back to me.

I trace a line down her profile, over her lips, and pause there. "Have a little faith. I can be quite charming when the situation requires it. I am a prince, after all."

"Prince Charming, huh? I don't remember him having a dirty mouth and an insatiable sex drive."

"He kissed the wrong girl," I whisper, angling my face for one last kiss before we face her family. "Or maybe 'happily ever after' is only code for multiple orgasms."

"The Brothers Grimm have nothing on you." Her tone is playful, but there's something thick hiding behind her words.

I feel it, too. That's why I play along and wink at her. "Wait until I tell you my theories about riding off into the sunset."

"Behave." She smacks my shoulder lightly.

"I love it when you get riled up. It makes me think of spanking your pretty, little ass." It's out of my mouth before I can stop it. I'd told her I wouldn't—that I didn't need to possess her like that. Before I can gauge her response, an amused voice interrupts us.

"Well, well, well. Can I get in before he mounts you on the spot?"

Clara looks over my shoulder, going slightly rigid in my arms. She pulls free as a woman with dark hair strides over and sticks out her hand.

I look from her to Clara, unable to miss the obvious resemblance.

"Alexander, this is my sister, Lola." Clara forces a smile. "Lola, allow me to introduce—"

"Oh, I don't think that's necessary." Lola doesn't shake my hand. She holds it for a moment as if taking a measure of me. "It's lovely to meet you. Clara has told me absolutely nothing about you."

I resist the urge to tell her Clara hasn't spoken of her either. I know she has a sister. That's come up in my research. Charlotte Bishop. Lola, it seems. But despite their similar features, there's something feline about Clara's sister. She looks not only prepared to pounce, but I suspect she might have claws.

Before she can show them, I step toward the door. "Ladies first."

"Ohh. A gentleman." Lola steps through first without hesitation. Her eyes skate over me, assessing. There's something abrasively American about her, despite having been here from an earlier age than Clara.

"She seems like a...handful," I mutter as I take Clara's hand.

"Mmhmm." Her hand tightens over mine, and I

realize I'm not the only one with family drama. Glancing down at Clara, I realize with surprise that she's not nervous.

She's protective.

I start to tell her that I'm not worried about facing the Bishops when a seating host beckons us to follow her to our table. Why tell her? I'll show her. I fall into step behind her, one hand on the small of her back.

BY FIVE TILL EIGHT, we're on the second round of cocktails and no food. I know the time because the entire bloody restaurant is decorated with hundreds of clocks, all of which are slightly slower or faster than the others. The result is a constant ticking that scratches at my nerves. I calm myself by stroking a hand down Clara's thigh. I resist the urge to order Clara something to eat. I don't want to overstep, but I'll be forced to once the hour strikes.

"I don't know what could be keeping him," Madeline Bishop looks at her silent phone, which has neither rang nor lit up with a text since we arrived.

I might be forced to intervene, but I could be polite about it. "I'm in no hurry."

"We should order," Clara declares when the clocks strike eight.

"Let's give him a few more minutes," her sister says, sipping her drink. "Tell us how you two met."

Clara shoots her a scathing look. "Pick up the Daily Star."

"I want to hear it from the source." Lola won't be put off so easily.

I can't risk Clara stabbing her with the fork she's clutching, so I jump in. "I was stuck at another boring party, trying to hide out, and then this beautiful girl showed up and started telling me off."

I lift her hand to my lips, my eyes meeting hers. I don't miss the amusement dancing there from my interpretation of events.

"Clara!" Madeline sounds absolutely horrified, but I only chuckle.

"No, I deserved it."

"So why did you kiss her?" Lola asks.

"Now that is a long story," I say, my grin widening as I recalled that day, "and seeing as it didn't make the papers, I'm going to keep it to myself. But I will tell you that I spent the rest of the day trying to find out who your sister was. She kept a low profile at Oxford."

Her mother sighs as though she disapproves of this fact. "She's not very social. I did my best, but sometimes nature has other plans."

"I find her company intoxicating." I'm speaking directly to Clara now. I want to shield her from the tiny slings and arrows being hurled by her mother and sister. I need her to know that she is perfect just as she is. "I want her all to myself anyway."

"Aren't you coy?" Lola says, still nursing her drink.

I shrug, not bothering to give her any more fuel to burn. Instead, I catch the waiter peeking in and wave him over.

"Are you ready?" he asks, looking at everyone but me. I'd abandoned my disguise in the private dining room. My hat was hooked on the back of my chair, and my sunglasses were shoved in Clara's bag.

"Can you bring us this evening's appetizers?" I ask. "We have another guest coming, but I can't allow these ladies to wait any longer."

Gratitude shines in Clara's eyes, and I wish I'd done it sooner. It had been polite to wait for a few minutes, but I wouldn't allow her to wait longer. Now I realize she hadn't wanted to defy her mother.

But her mother would never argue with me.

I can't help kissing Clara, hoping she'll remember that I'm doing my best to protect her. Her mother clears her throat in irritation, and I straighten, picking up my bourbon.

"I read up a little on your company, Mrs. Bishop," I say.

"Former company," she says. "Let's not talk business."

"She gets enough of that from Dad," Clara adds.

"That's true." Her tight smile calls out the lie before she does. "At least, it used to be."

Lola, who's cheeks are now slightly flush from alcohol and no food, leans forward. "Tell us about growing up in a palace!"

"Don't they have books devoted to that?" I ask.

"They do," she admits, "but I hear that the reality is quite different. Although I am a sucker for happily-ever-afters."

She looks from me to Clara. The sisters share some unspoken communication before Clara giggles.

"It's not as exciting as it sounds." I continue, wondering what's funny.

"Bollocks!" she cries, sounding more British now that she's drunk. "I bet you've been all over the world and that you grew up riding horses and hunting foxes."

I grin at the shift in her polished exterior. "I suppose I did. It's rather boring, really. Dinners with foreign dignitaries. Riding lessons. Although I've never enjoyed hunting."

"I'm a member of PETA," she says. "I don't approve of hunting."

Clara's lips turn down.

"Unfortunately, it's a tradition in our family. I'm not particularly interested in it either." That wouldn't get me out of it this weekend. Nothing would. I'd learned that lesson the hard way. "Actually, when I was eight, my father told me I was going on the hunt for the first time. I was incredibly excited. I'd had riding lessons before then, but I'd never been allowed to go with the men."

"I couldn't sleep the night before," I continue, glad to have found something that they all seem interested in, "so I crept to the stables to brush my Arabian in preparation. Anyway, I'm in there with my horse, and I see this red fox locked in a cage. I couldn't believe it. The second I saw him, I remembered all the hunts I'd watched begin at my family estates, and I realized we were going to hunt him."

"So I did what any eight-year-old kid would do. I hid him."

"Oh my god!" Lola giggles. "Where did you put him?"

"I didn't really think it through," I admit, still feeling a little stupid after all these years, "so I took him to my bedroom."

"I bet your parents loved that," Madeline says dryly.

Her interjection knocks me off course for a minute. Of course, I can't expect her to remember my mother had already died. "My mother would have, I think, but my father did not. In fairness, though, I did make one tiny mistake when I brought him inside."

"Which was?" Lola asks.

"My sister let him out of the cage." I still remember how brilliant Sarah thought that move was. "It took the staff two days to trap him, but the hunt was canceled!"

"So you were the hero," Clara says.

"That's one way of looking at it." I sink back against my chair, glad that my youthful idiocy amused them. "I doubt the staff thought so."

I couldn't help joining their laughter. Turning, I caught Clara staring at me, her eyes full of an emotion that I hadn't seen reflected toward me since long before I saved that fox.

"I apologize," a voice breaks in. "Last minute call and Tube delays."

I rise to meet Harold Bishop. We shake hands, his grip as firm as mine. Remarkably, he seems nonplussed by me. Perhaps, he lets his wife worry about matters like his daughter's love life.

"Again, I am sorry," he says, sitting next to Madeline.

"Have you been waiting for me? You should have ordered!"

"I called you," she says coldly.

"I got caught up at the office," he repeats. "We get such terrible mobile service there, but I should have found a phone and called you."

I don't have to look at Clara for confirmation of what I'm seeing. I do anyway, and it's there, written all over her face:

Her father is lying.

But why?

CLARA's quiet when we leave dinner. I wonder if her mind is on her parents and the tension that lingered between them throughout the meal. It seems I'm not the only one with family issues to deal with. I slide a hand between her legs, squeezing her thigh to draw her attention to me. "Clara?"

"Sorry, X." She shakes her head as if clearing it and climbs into my lap.

"Something's on your mind." I have no idea if she wants to talk about it. Lately, every moment we spend together seems heavy, reality weighing down our stolen moments. Part of me misses how this started when I could push aside my life and focus on burying myself deep inside her. But I can't look back. The strangest part is that I don't want to.

She sighs. "I was thinking about my parents. They barely spoke to one another."

"And that's not usually the case?" I wonder if I'm prying.

"My mom tends to be a little high maintenance. She was definitely giving my dad the cold shoulder."

She shrugs, something shifting in her face as she turns to wrap her arms around my neck. Her face angles to mine, sending a clear message that she's done talking. She wants to be distracted, and I'm more than willing to oblige. I trail a finger over the rounded line of her cleavage. It's far from innocent, but I'm surprised by her reaction. Clara rocks into me, and I hook a hand around her neck, pulling her mouth to mine hungrily. I'd behaved myself during dinner. Now I'm ready to appreciate dessert.

"I owe you sexual favors," she murmurs, her hand reaching to my belt buckle.

I can already imagine her soft hands on my cock, but I can't put off talking to her about my plans any longer. I cup her face with my hands, hoping that I can seduce her into agreeing to deal with my family again. "Come to the country with me this weekend."

Her eyebrows ratchet up, but she gives me a pleased smile. "Do you even have to ask?"

"I'm not asking," I tell her, knowing she won't be as thrilled when she hears the rest. "I already told them you would be there."

She stills, zeroing in on the most loaded word. "Them?"

"My family." There's no way around it.

"You want me to spend a weekend in the country with your family?"

"There will be some friends there as well. Edward has invited a group." I think she likes my brother—or she will when she gets to know him. I know he'll be kind to her. With his help, the weekend might not turn into a disaster.

"X—" she starts

"You said anything," I remind her. "I said that I wasn't asking. I expect you to be there with me."

"Don't you want to spend some private time with them?" Her voice is impossibly small because she knows how ridiculous the question is.

There's a reason I'm taking her because if not, I might murder half of them in their beds after the first evening. But also because they need to understand that Clara is part of my life now. "The only person I want private time with is you. Three days apart is too long. I need to know you're being taken care of."

"I can take care of myself." She swallows, and I regret saying it. I don't want her to think I see her as fragile, but I can't imagine not worrying about her being stuck in London to deal with paparazzi—or her mother, for that matter.

"You can get dressed." I realize I'm going to have to play dirty. "You can eat and drink and sleep, but you won't have everything you need."

I press my erection against her ass to tempt her.

"You raise a good point," she says breathlessly.

"Do I?" I have her. I know it. But it won't hurt to give her a preview of why she'll be glad she came.

"Mmhmm." She circles against my cock. "You owe me."

"I thought you owed me sexual favors." I smirk.

"I promised that before I found out I'd be dealing with your family for a whole weekend. Let's call it a draw, X, or you'll end up repaying me for a long time."

"Oh, poppet." My hand creeps under her skirt as I kissed her neck, her collarbone, reminding her that I would make it worth it. "I am more than happy to be in your debt."

It's a debt I'd start repaying now. My fingers find the thin elastic of her thong, and I rip it off her. I toss its remains on the seat, Clara looking like she might come if the wind changes.

"You know there are finite resources in the world. You might spare a few pairs of panties," she says in a saucy voice that has me dreaming of putting her over my knee.

Later. Right now, I need to sink inside her and remind us both that no matter what's coming, there's one thing that always makes sense. I have her on her back in a second, her thighs opening like a flower bud. "I'd love to hear more about your panties. Later."

"But—" she starts to object, but I cut her off with a kiss and a quick thrust of my hips.

Clara gasps against my mouth, her body clenching around my cock as she shatters. Her head lolls back as her fingers clutch my shoulder blades, holding onto me as she unravels. As much as I love watching her come, I'm not satisfied.

Still, I can't deny that I enjoy the tight heat clamping

my shaft. I piston inside her, rolling my hips to put as much pressure on her tender clit as I can.

"Oh fuck," she moans, panting. "I can't—"

"Yes, you can, poppet," I coax, continuing to work her towards her next orgasm. "For me. Consider that a command."

There's a warm gush of arousal around my cock. She loves being dominated, told what to do, freed to give in to her every desire. Someday she'll see that. Someday she'll trust me enough to hand me total control—after I earn that trust. Not before. For now, I'm more than happy to relish the subtle gifts her body gives me. I hammer into her, taking another moment of rapture from her, this one claiming me with it.

"You win," she says between pants as I gather her into my arms. "I'll go to the country."

I tip her chin up with my index finger and kiss the tip of her nose. "Of course, you will."

She never had a choice.

CHAPTER TWENTY-NINE

I've lost my bloody mind.

The thought occupies me so completely that I barely speak to Clara on the drive to Norfolk. There's no way to prepare her because I hadn't bothered to look at the guest list my office sent me. It's not hard to guess who will be there. The usual sycophants always turn up for the hunt. There's nothing more appealing to the aristocracy than chasing down a helpless animal and murdering it.

I just have to make sure they stay focused on the fox and not the woman at my side.

I'm out of the car as soon as we pull into the front-drive, making my way to Clara's side of the car to help her out. I need to keep her with me as much as possible. It's the best thing for her. A few valets are already bringing our bags inside. She pauses, looking around like she's not sure if she should offer help or not.

"They'll take it to your room," I tell her.

"My room?" she repeats. "I thought I was here with you."

I lift her knuckles to my lips, kissing her hand. "First rule of country weekends. Propriety must be observed."

"So we sleep in separate rooms? Will they be sending a chaperone with us?" she asks dryly.

"You'll find my family is all about appearances, poppet. Separate bedrooms are one thing, but that just leaves people to find new, exciting places to fuck," I tell her in a lowered voice as we climb the stairs.

"Is that so?"

"I'll prove it to you," I say, allowing my wicked thoughts to edge into my voice. Finding dark corners to drag her into is about the only aspect of this weekend I'm looking forward to.

Manfred, Norfolk's head butler, greets us at the door. "Everyone is in the parlor, Your Highness. Your bags are being taken to your rooms. Perhaps, you would like to freshen up before joining the guests?"

"Please," I say.

"I will have Charles show Miss Bishop to her room," he says.

"Is that necessary?"

"Your father asked for her to be placed in the southern wing," he tells me stiffly.

And my room is in the north. "Naturally." I force myself to stay calm. It's not as though it matters where they put her. No one bothers to worry about the bed-hopping that goes on after dark, but I dislike sending her off.

"It's fine," she says, squeezing my hand before letting it go. "I'll find you back here?"

I nod as a young valet appears to show her away.

"Will you require any more assistance? I can send a valet up?" Manfred asks as they disappear from sight.

"I haven't needed anyone to help dress me in years." I stride off in the direction of the family quarters as Edward appears in the hall.

"I thought you might have changed your mind." He swirls a glass of Scotch.

"I should have," I admit to him, looking around to be sure we're alone. "They put her in the fucking south wing."

Edward snorts. "Geography never stopped you. I still remember you trying to explain it when father caught you sneaking across the grounds at dawn when you were eighteen. I believe you said you'd been out for a run."

"I had been exercising." I smirked, trying to remember whose bed I'd been visiting that night. In truth, those times all blurred together. It had probably been one of my sister's friends. "Sarah's friends were always good for a little overnight aerobic activity. This is different, though."

Edward fell into step beside me. "You didn't really expect them to make you two a bed? Why have thirty guest rooms if you don't use them?"

"She's not a guest," I bite out. "She's my girlfriend."

"I'm aware," he says dryly. "Honestly, I'm shocked

you got her here at all. Father's been on a rampage all day."

"I didn't give him a choice." I cast a meaningful look at my brother. "Sometimes, you have to take what you want and say sod the consequences."

"Let me know how that goes for you." he says with a bemused smile, taking a sip. "Speaking of what I want, I better go back. I left poor David with them."

At least, everyone plays along with Edward, pretending not to know about his secret romance. That means that while he and David are miserable at these things, they aren't targeted. I have no idea how my father will punish Clara for being here, but I expect the others will be just as bad.

"Edward," I call before he gets too far. "Help me keep an eye on her?"

"She's really important to you, isn't she?" he asks.

I hesitate, uncertain how to answer that. If anyone might understand loving someone you can never have, it's him. I settle for nodding.

"Will do. I haven't been asked to join the hunt, so I will shield her as much as possible."

"Thank you." I stalk toward my room, finding it exactly as it's always been. Apart from the lack of dust, there's no sign that anyone's stepped foot in here. No waiting bags. They've been unpacked already, I assume. Crossing to the wardrobe, I find a suitable change of clothes and begin to undress.

I have a part to play this weekend, my suit is the costume, and everyone around me is an ally or antagonist.

It's tradition to take a weekend in the country each summer, everyone ready to flee the heat of the city. But I know better than to think this will be an escape. I've walked Clara into hell itself. Who knows how badly we'll get burned?

CHAPTER THIRTY

I lounge in the hall, hoping to catch Clara before anyone else does. When she finally emerges, she steals my breath from me. There is something effortless about her. She's not trying to impress anyone. She is simply beautiful. Her navy gown skims along her curves, pulling my thoughts in indecent directions and bringing out her blue eyes. It reminds me a little of the dress she wore that first time—in the lift. Thankfully, it's not that exact same dress, or I'd already have her against the wall. "Poppet?"

She sighs as I find my way to her side. I hate that I'm not the one making her make those sounds. "Save those for me."

"I'm not allowed to sigh?" she asks sharply.

"Oh, I insist that you sigh." I lower my lips to her jaw and whisper the words across her skin. "And whimper and moan when I'm fucking you. I demand it. I'm a selfish man, and those noises belong to me."

"I'd be happy to comply." She grabs my suit jacket, and I'm struck by how forward she's becoming, channeling the possessiveness I display toward her back at me. I rather like it.

I have to pull away to keep myself from carrying her off to a room, locking the door, and not leaving the bed the entire weekend. It's what I want. I don't want to waste time on the simpering idiots that finagle invitations to the country every year, but I also need to prove a point. My father needs to see that Clara will be at my side whether he wants it or not. "Don't tempt me, or we'll never make it to our scheduled appearance."

"So I'm not the only one with a printed itinerary?"

"Unfortunately not." I offer her my arm. At least, hers doesn't include a bloody fox hunt. "To the Billiard Room?"

"Yes. I was lost."

"I would have found you." I would always find her. In a crowd of people, she will always be the first one I see. It's as though there's a thread attaching her to me, always tugging me in her direction. I can't explain it.

I sure as hell can't ignore it.

The usual wankers are present in the Billiard Room. The only friendly faces are Edward and David, who are making a good show of being there alone. Although as we enter, I catch Edward's eyes sweep toward David as though he's checking on him. I want to wish he'd come out and say what everyone suspects, but I know all too well the position that will put David in. It's why I edge slightly closer to Clara now as though I can protect her from the vipers circling around us.

I lead her into the room, dropping my voice to a whisper. "An hour. Do you want a drink?"

I'm not sure if that's good self-preservation instincts or not. I'm about to tell her just that when a valet enters the room, glancing around until his eyes fall on me. I'd expected my father to raise a bigger fuss about Clara's presence. The valet comes to me and whispers, "Your father would like to speak with you, your highness."

Of course, he would. I grab Clara's arm as he adds, "Alone."

Naturally. "I need to attend to something. Edward will look after you."

I motion for Edward, who strides toward her. I'm already thankful I spoke with him earlier. I don't have to explain in front of her where I'm going or worry that she'll be left to deal with the rest of these snakes.

It's not just my father waiting. His mother is there as well. My grandmother Mary looks like what happens if you leave a princess out in the sun too long. The skin around her lips is pinched from age into a permanent scowl of disapproval. Her once blonde hair is now silver, carefully styled into a helmet of curls. She sits across the desk from him.

"Grandmum." I move to her, kissing her cheek before taking the other vacant seat. "You look well."

"You brought that girl," she responds disdainfully.

I force a tight smile.

"I told father I invited Clara. We all have friends

here." I don't look at him as I say it, but I saw Pepper in the Billiard Room. It's no surprise that she's here, but it's hardly his place to lecture me on bringing a woman for the weekend.

"She's just a friend then," Grandmum says carefully.

"A girlfriend," I admit.

She gasps as though I struck her, and my father grunts something under his breath.

"Would you rather I call her a friend and take her to bed in secret?" I ask him pointedly. Our eyes meet, the one trait we share, and he knows I'm calling him out. I have no idea if his mother knows that he's screwing Pepper, but I doubt he wants me to bring it up.

"You have responsibilities," he says, his face returning to a more neutral passivity. "Clara is very pretty, but you can't make life decisions based on what your dick wants."

I cross my arms to keep myself from lunging across the desk to strangle him. "This is the twenty-first century. Clara is well-bred—"

"She's American," my grandmother says like I've invited a mutt into the house.

I turn my glare on her, challenging her to continue explaining what she means by that statement. The Royal family are the original snobs, but nothing gets under their thin-skin more than Americans. The country didn't have the decency to close their eyes and think of England.

"You need to be prepared to assume my role—" my father continues.

"Are you planning to retire?" I half expect him to live

forever to prevent me from ascending the throne. I want him to, actually. I have no desire to be king.

"I do not approve of your flippancy," Grandmum lectures.

But my father looks as though he's got a headache. It's how he's looked most of my life. I recognize the temple-rubbing frustration from every conversation we've ever had. "There are situations that you need to be briefed on, and yet you're busy screwing that—"

This finally sends me to my feet. "Choose your words very carefully. She is precious to me."

There are lines that, once crossed, will force decisions neither of us wants to make. I know my father well enough to guess the lengths he'd go to in an effort to separate us. He once sent me to face death itself to avoid bad press. What will he do to avoid an unwanted addition to his precious bloodline?

Before he can speak, Clara steps into the room. Her eyes are hollow, worn down, and empty. Edward is nowhere in sight. How long has she been standing there? How much has she heard? "I'm going to bed."

It's nothing more than a declaration of intention, but it's a loaded statement. She's drawn a line in the sand. Them. Her. What team will I choose?

"I'm coming with you." I cross to her, taking her hand but carefully angling my body so that I can step in front of her like a shield if necessary.

"We are not finished speaking," he says, his jaw tightening as I choose her over them.

"This conversation is over." I dismiss his objection.

I'm through with pandering to their snobbery and power games. "I'm not debating this with you any longer. I've made my decision."

He pauses, his eyes scanning the woman next to me—assessing and dissecting. This isn't over. Finally, he simply says, "Good night."

When we reach the door to her room, we pause. Clara sinks against it, her hands wrapped behind her back.

"This is me," she says. "Where are you?"

"The North Wing," I tell her. "My old room, full of precious memories." I don't bother to hide the bitterness from my voice. Coming here is torture. It's being forced to swallow poison one toxic drop at a time. Why did I bring her here?

"I suppose I'll see you in the morning."

I nod, steeling my resolve to walk away. She said she was tired, and after what she overheard, I can't blame her for sending me away. "Clara, I..."

She waits for me to finish that statement, but I started it without knowing the words on the other end. Instead, I settle for a kiss. My lips linger on hers, wishing I could wipe away what she heard, how they make her feel, everything.

But my kiss isn't what wakes her from this nightmare. It's what started it for her.

Her hand fumbles for the knob as we break apart.

"Good night," she says as she steps inside.

The door closes, shutting her away from me. I turn and begin making my way across the house. Why had I brought her here knowing what she would be subjected to? Because I hadn't wanted to come alone. Because I couldn't stand the thought of a weekend with these people.

No.

I couldn't stand being without her.

The corridor is dark. My footsteps echo on the marble floors as the shadows close in around me. I'd left the only light in this fucking place behind me. I don't want this world or its secrets or its shame. I want her.

My body realizes before my brain does, carrying me back to her door. By the time I raise my fist to knock, it swings open to reveal Clara, a look of stony determination on her face.

"I don't want you to go to the North Wing," she blurts out when she sees me.

My hands grip her face, crushing her mouth to mine as I back her into the room and kick the door closed. Clara's hands slip under the lapels of my suit jacket and shuck it off my shoulders. I release her face and step back, unbuttoning my vest. Clara watches, firelight catching her eyes from the hearth before she reaches behind her and slowly slides down her zipper. I shrug off my vest and begin on my cufflinks. Clara watches as though she's in a trance. Then I start on the buttons of my shirt. The movement jars her back to life. Her gaze skips down as if surprised to find me undoing my shirt. Somewhere, in the back of my mind, I realize I've never done this before: causally undress in front of her. Without thought. Without hesitation.

When I reach the last button, I let it fall open before I strip it off.

There's nothing left standing between us. We've stripped it all away.

Clara's hands slip up to her shoulders, and she pushes her dresses to the floor. White lace cages her breasts, her nipples poking against the sheer fabric. It's the only stitch of clothing left on her body.

We collide, unable to stand another moment of separation. I lift her into my arms, her legs circling me possessively as I carry her to the bed. Our tongues tangle, seeking the answers we can only find in each other. Laying her across the bed, I straighten and unbuckle my belt.

"Tell me you're mine," I command as I slide it free and push my trousers to the floor.

"Always," she promises as I step between her legs and take what's mine.

CHAPTER THIRTY-ONE

Clara Bishop is going to be the death of me, I decide as I pause to take in the poor excuse for a skirt she's wearing. It hits mid-thigh, but the wind from an open window catches it, lifting just enough for me to catch a glimpse of her ass before her hand flattens it down. I'm going to buy her one in every color. She turns and catches me drinking her in.

She's frowning.

"Have you decided to run?"

She'd asked me to leave last night after a few hours in bed. Part of me wanted to, but more than ever, I know that we need to stick this out. The only way we make it through this is together. She seems to consider my question longer than I'd like before shaking her head.

I cross to her, pleased, and trail a finger down her skirt. "This needs to come off later."

"Cancel the hunt, and you can take it off now," she tempts me.

"I'll only be gone for two or three hours." I force myself to stay cool. I don't want to leave her here with them any more than I want to go with the others.

"That's long enough for them to eat me alive." She pulls at her too-short skirt.

"I'm told they're serving sandwiches." The joke falls flat. "But I'll remind them that they have to answer to me if anyone upsets you."

She considers, her head tilting and sending her thick brown hair curls swirling over her shoulders.

"You've got that wicked gleam in your eyes, Clara. What are you thinking?"

"Nothing." She brushes a hand across my chest, but the glint remains.

"Something tells me that you're going to be fine." Maybe Clara isn't the one to be worried about. My grandmother has a heart condition. "Try not to be charged with treason."

A hand clamps on my shoulder, and I find Jonathan standing next to me. "You're going to let that fox get away, Alexander. Although it doesn't look like you're hurting for tail."

Clara smiles tightly, but we both manage to bite our tongue. When it comes to a man like Jonathan, it's best not to engage.

"Don't be vulgar," I tell him.

"It's all in good fun. I'm sure Clara doesn't mind." He laughs off my concern and continues out the door toward the stables.

I turn, expecting to find that Clara very much minds,

but her attention is pinned on the latest arrival to the dining room. I don't bother sparing Pepper more than a passing glance.

Rather, I hook my arm around Clara's waist and lean to kiss the delicate spot behind her ear. "I will see you soon, poppet."

I leave before the urge to throw her over my shoulder and carry her back to bed can take hold.

Edward catches me at the door. "David's going with you. Try to keep him from getting shot."

"Clara's staying here," I mutter. "Keep the vultures at bay."

We clap hands on each other's shoulders in silent promise before I continue outside. It makes me feel better to know he's there with her, even if she slipped through his fingers the last time I left her in his care.

"I thought you were going to make us wait," my father greets me with an icy glare. "I sent Manfred to wake you this morning, but he said you were already gone. I had no idea the walk from the North Wing took that long."

I hook my foot in a stirrup and swing my leg over. Once seated, I urge the Arabian into a steady trot before answering him. "I didn't sleep in the North Wing."

"For fuck's sake," he growled in a low voice, leading his horse into step beside me, "there are expectations—"

"Fuck your expectations," I shot back, pressing my heel slightly into the stallion's side to increase my speed.

My father matches me. "Do you have any idea what you're doing? You're going to destroy that girl like you destroyed—"

But I'm already leaning forward, guiding my horse into a full gallop, and leaving him behind. I need to put some distance between my father and me, especially with a hunting rifle at my side.

BY THE TIME the hunt winds down, I'm sore and impatient. I guide my horse to a trot alongside Norris, who I suspect came along simply to ensure I didn't shoot my father.

"Ride ahead and tell her to meet me outside? I'm going to take her out to show her the grounds." It's half question, half command. I've used up too much of my patience to offer more.

He responds with a bemused smile. "I'll tell her to change."

I think of her filmy skirt and shake my head. "Don't."

He cocks an eyebrow but keeps his opinions to himself. Pressing his own horse forward, he shoots ahead of us. Unfortunately, his absence leaves space for Jonathan to ride up beside me.

"So, tell me, man to man," he begins.

I refrain from commenting on his use of the term man to man. It's not that I hate Jonathan. I nothing him, which makes it impossible to take him seriously—especially when he says shit like that.

"An American?"

"She's half British," I say in a clipped tone. Jonathan doesn't know what dangerous ground he's treading. I consider warning him.

Before I can, he continues, "I mean, I don't blame you. She's hot, and I bet knowing your father hates it makes it hotter."

"My father has no influence over my feelings." I grip my unused riding crop in my hand, wishing it were his neck.

"Feelings?" he repeats. "You're not actually serious about this girl?"

"Of course, he isn't," my father's icy voice interrupts.

"Let me know when I might have an opinion on my own life." My blood heats inside me as I feel a familiar rage take hold.

"When you accept who you are," he says.

Or rather who he wants me to be—who they all want me to be.

"Excuse me, I have a date." I press my horse into a faster canter before either can respond then to a full gallop. I need to see Clara and remind myself they're wrong about her and me. But no matter how fast I ride, I can't seem to outrun the truth behind their words.

I said it myself when Norris implied things were serious between us. I'm not sure why everyone thinks they are—half of bloody Britain is planning our wedding already. Clara and I have an arrangement. Yes, some of the terms have changed. Yes, we're no longer fucking but dating. Yes, I met her parents and brought her to the country.

But that's not a ring on her finger.

I won't do that to her because a ring like that isn't a

promise. It's a shackle. I will not clip her wings. I will not tether her in a cage.

As the house comes into view, I spot her moving across the veranda. It's as though an invisible rope tugs me toward her.

I might not bind her to this life, but, my God, I am bound to her. I slow as I approach, giving time for some of the others to catch up with me while I wrestle with this realization.

Clara continues down to the lawn as I approach. I smile to see she's still wearing the light blouse and short skirt but that she's tugged on a pair of riding boots. Pushing away all the serious concerns, I concentrate on the shapely lines of her legs.

She raises an eyebrow as I approach, and I realize she's looking at the riding crop still clutched in my hand.

"Father insisted. Of course, if you know what you're doing, you don't need one." I shrug.

"I could have used one this morning," she says dryly, and I nearly grin.

I guess brunch went well.

"I suppose it would have its uses." She might be on to something. Maybe I should bring it to dinner. I keep this thought to myself and extend a hand. "Come."

A knowing expression—half relief, half desire—takes hold of her face, but she gestures to her ensemble. "I'm wearing a skirt."

The wind catches it, lifting it high enough to show more of her bare thighs and a slight glimpse of the apex between them before she shoves it down.

"Believe me, I noticed." I dismount, ready to throw her over the saddle if necessary—no matter how barbaric the gesture. Pulling on my helmet, I toss it to a waiting servant. "I need to get you away from these bloody people. I want you all to myself."

"Where are you taking me?" She takes my hand, and I know I have her. Blessed relief washes over me.

But we're still on display. I need to get her away from the prying eyes all around us. They were all asking that question, too. "You're asking the wrong question."

"I am?" She bats her lashes at me, and the innocent gesture fans the primal instinct I'm trying to keep under control.

At least until I have her alone. "You should be asking what I'm going to do to you."

That gets her full attention. Her mouth drops open, giving me even more wicked ideas.

"Ever heard of the term saddle sore?" I continue. "If I don't ride off with you right now in front of all these people, tonight they're going to wonder why you're walking so strangely."

She blinks as if she's processing what I mean. I watch as it becomes clear. "So the ride is an alibi?"

"It's all part of what I plan to do to you." I yank her to me before she can concoct another question and silence any further objections with a kiss. There's no further resistance when I lift her onto the saddle. She carefully arranges herself, pushing her skirt under her sumptuous ass—as if that will do her a bit of good. The truth is that I want her to be sore and raw. I want to see her delicate skin red and tender because then I can make her feel things she never imagined, even in her wildest fantasies. A gamekeeper appears to collect my gear. I think better of giving him the riding crop. I'm not certain how Clara might respond, but today, after everything, I can't help considering its use. My balls ache as I consider what it feels like to take it to her. I pass the rifle to the waiting gamekeeper before mounting the horse behind her. Wrapping one hand over the reins, I coil my other arm around her waist. She settles against me, and it's as though a missing piece locks into place.

"Alexander!" My father's sharp voice slices through the moment. "We have guests."

"Clara is my guest," I say, uninterested in pursuing another fight with him. "I'm taking her to see the grounds. We'll be back for dinner."

He scans her with disapproval. "I expect you to be properly dressed at the table."

"C'mon," I say gruffly, hating him more for making her feel inferior. He'd done the same to me my whole life, but it's different somehow when he does it to Clara. I needed to get her away from him, from all of it. I press the horse faster until it's behind us: the house, the expectations, the family. I don't slow until we reach a valley that dips low, obscuring the estate. It was June, but the country air held the remnants of spring this afternoon. The skies overhead were grey, even though there was no other sign of an impending rain shower. Then again, out here, a storm could strike at any moment with even less warning.

"Beautiful," Clara whispers, and I wish I could see the world through her eyes.

I can see her, however. In my arms, she's all I see, and I have to agree. "Yes."

"You have me all alone," she says, settling into my embrace. "What are you going to do to me?"

I allow a breathy laugh as I move to kiss the freckles on her neck. "Not yet, poppet."

Instead of relaxing, though, she goes rigid. I tighten my hold on her, assessing where things have gone wrong. I've been so wrapped up in my own thoughts, I nearly forgot that she spent the morning in a den of vipers.

"You're unhappy," I finally realize.

There's a pause before she nods. "I don't belong here."

"Oh poppet." It's a feeling I know all too well. "Neither do I."

There's no escaping it for me, though. If I can stop being so selfish, she might still escape. Except I am selfish, and no part of me wants her to break free. "But you are wrong about one thing. You do belong here with me."

Clara spins in the saddle, twisting her body so she can claim my lips. Does she sense that I belong to her as much as she belongs to me? Judging from the reckless hunger in her kiss, she must.

"So are you going to take me for a roll in the hay?" she asks when we break apart.

"I'm planning much more depraved things. And I'll start by..." I slide my hands from her waist under her skirt, stopping on the elastic lace of her knickers. "You are such a tease in this little skirt. I've had blue balls all morning thinking about your barely covered thighs. Do you know what it's like to spend the whole day hiding an erection from half the monarchy?"

"I can't say that I do," she says breathlessly.

"Exactly." I rip them off her, sliding the ruins lace roughly from her and shoving it in my pocket. It feels like a trophy, but she's the true prize. I lift the back of her skirt and examine my reward appreciatively. "This gives a whole new meaning to bareback."

Her body softens in submission, waiting for me to take her. But I'm not ready for this to end. I want to tease her. I want to torture her. I want to make every nerve in her body sing with hopeful arousal.

Pressing my heel into the horse's side, I urge us forward slowly. Her bare skin slaps against the leather. There's a slightly wet smack with each beat of the hooves beneath us. I resist the urge to stop and bury myself inside her slick heat. It's harder to resist the temptation when she starts to squirm. Her hips trying to signal that she wants my hand to move from its place on her belly to the want between her legs.

I grind my cock into her backside instead, knowing this will both drive her wilder but also let her know she's not alone in her desperation.

After a while, her head lolls back, and she gazes up at me with pleading eyes. I slow to a trot and lift my hand to brush her cheek. "Yes, poppet?"

I want to hear her say it.

"Please."

"Please what?" I could come just listening to her beg.

"Please, stop. I...need...you." She struggles to ask. After meeting her parents, I can see why. She's been taught to take her place and take what's given. I want her to learn to ask for what she wants. I want her to ask for every filthy pleasure she's ever denied herself.

And then I want to give them all to her.

"Say it, Clara," I coax.

"I want you to fuck me," she whispers, the words sounding hesitant on her lips, even though truth coats them.

I wait for a moment. "Want or need?"

Her throat slides, and something changes in her face. She gives in.

She submits—not to me but to herself.

"I need your cock. I need you to fuck me until I can't take any more. Please."

I can't give her all of me. I won't burden her with that curse, but I can give her this—and I will.

CHAPTER THIRTY-TWO

Dismounting the horse, I turn to find her swinging her leg over to follow. I catch her, stopping her from sliding from the saddle. Clara doesn't protest as I guide her legs open and slide my palms along her bare thighs. Her cunt is a dark, rosy pink, aggravated and aroused by our ride. It's nearly as beautiful as she is.

I want all of her. I need all of her. I help her to her feet but only so I can lay claim to her. Clara seems to have the same idea as she rips at my clothing. She manages to get my jacket off before I grab her arm. Pinning her wrists together with one hand, I lift them. She's an innocent caught in my snare. I lash out, forcing off her skirt before tearing off her blouse. Buttons scatter around us, but Clara only relaxes more with each predatory move. I slide my fingers into her bra, popping her breasts free from its constraints but leaving the lingerie to lift her nipples.

I take one and suck it like I could swallow her whole.

Then the other. I continue until her breath comes in shallow pants, and she sways on buckling knees. I catch her before she crumbles—and more importantly before she comes. "Not yet, poppet."

She moans but doesn't fight me, so I push it farther. Dropping her arms, I order her. "Take off your bra."

Clara obeys, her eyes locked with mine as she shrugs out of her ruined shirt. Her bra follows. Then she waits as though she understands the game we're playing. I run my eyes along her bare skin as she stands before me in nothing but a pair of leather riding boots.

A thousand ideas war in my head for attention. "I have half a mind to set you back on that horse and watch your tits and ass bounce across the countryside."

"I have something else I'd rather ride," she says with well-deserved annoyance.

I try and fail to keep a smirk off my face. I love when she submits, but I don't mind a little sass mixed in.

"You get off on this, don't you?" she asks when she sees my grin. "Nearly driving me half-crazy until you fuck me?"

I've never pushed her this far before giving her what she wants, and part of me longs to savor her desperation longer. "I do, poppet, which is why I should take you over my knee and smack that sass right out of you."

A tremble of pleasure races through her, so intense that she shivers. She wants it, too. But she won't ask for that.

But I think she might give it.

"In fact..." My eyes skirt to the saddle where the riding crop's been abandoned. I brace myself for a crush of disappointment as I lift her hand to kiss it. "I need to know that you trust me."

"I thought I had proven that already. I've never been with anyone like I've been with you."

"I assumed that much." I try to sound casual. If she knows how strong my urge to dominate her is, I fear she'll give in just to please me. I want her to want the domination. I want her to crave it. It's the only way I can be truly satisfied. "That doesn't mean you trust me."

"Do you trust me?" she hits back, to my surprise.

For a second, I wonder how she can even ask that. How can't she see the truth? "I think you're the only person I've ever trusted."

"Yes," she whispers, as though she finally understands why we're here. "I trust you."

It's the last part of her I'd left unclaimed. At least, I couldn't be certain until now it was mine. She's given me her body over and over again. This is something more, something deeper than I've asked or she's offered.

I will not take the gift lightly. "Do you remember your safe word?"

She nods and murmurs it once as proof, "Brimstone."

Hearing her say it unlocks the final shackle caging the man within. I allow him out with hesitation. A weight lifts from me even as I remind myself to take this slowly.

"Turn around and face the tree," I order in a strained voice.

Clara does it, and I step toward her. Guiding her arms over her head, I help her brace against its trunk, pleased the bark is not terribly rough. I allow my hands to explore her: the flat, soft plane of her abdomen, the plump fullness of her hips, the rounded curve of her ass. Every delicious inch of her belongs to me.

"Close your eyes," I say in a low voice.

She waits, not daring to move, as I retrieve the riding crop. I drink in the sight of her, her creamy skin smooth and elegant, contrasted with the dark trunk of the tree. Overhead the cloudy sky casts filtered light on her figure, posed and waiting for me to deliver whatever dark pleasures I wish.

"Spread your legs," I demand as I move closer. "That is a fucking beautiful sight."

I want her to know how perfect she is. I wish I could show her how I see her—how much I want her. I press my body to hers so she can feel the proof of it in her soft backside and smother her sex with my palm.

Fuck. "Your cunt is so wet for me. Feel how wet you are."

She lowers one arm from her braced position, and I guide it to her swollen sex. There's a breathy groan of satisfaction as she feels her own arousal. But then she slips a searching finger between her folds. I push it away. "None of that."

She whimpers, and I wonder how much longer she can last. I wonder if I can make her come without my hands or fingers or mouth. I step back and test the theory, hesitating for just a moment before handing control to my other-self. I loose a single well-aimed lash. It bites against her clit, and she cries out in surprise. I slide the leather bit along her singing flesh, waiting for an objection. None comes. I pull back, pause, and then spank her ass with it. An angry red line appears on her pale skin. I close my eyes, memorizing the sight, as I reach out and rub away any lingering effect. Two lashes. I want it to be enough.

It's not, but I wait for her response.

An eternity passes before she moans, "More."

My eyes close in silent relief, and I move closer, planting a kiss on her neck to show she's safe. I step back, take a deep breath, and let the crop fly—harder and faster this time.

Her knees buckle as it cracks against her skin. I might be concerned save for her pleasure-drenched cry of "Alexander!"

"Wider, poppet," I grunt. I want to make her come. I want to deliver her to a place she doesn't know exists—yet.

She spreads her legs more for me, and I push the crop between them, rubbing its tip over the swollen bundle of nerves there before I smack it hard. Tensions coils in her limbs. Another lash, and she sobs, "I need you." Her cry stops my hand before it can fly a third time. "I need you inside me. I need you to fill me."

"Are you sure, poppet?" It's not what I want exactly, but I can't deny the ache in her voice. I feel it not just in my painfully stiff cock but echoing through my own chest. I unzip my pants before she responds, already knowing her answer.

I slide one finger barely inside her to check that she's ready. "You bloom for me like a flower."

Her body, still rigid with undissipated tension, relaxes just enough to let me know that she's ready. I position my cock against her heat and warn her, "I need to fuck you, Clara. I don't know if I can be gentle."

Her answer is unrestrained. "Don't be."

I grab her, groaning at her words, as I shove inside her. Once I'm buried inside her, I linger for a moment to appreciate the sensation. I brush her hair over her shoulder so that I can bring my body in closer contact with hers, hunching over her to capture as much of her as I can. And then I let go. I slam into her. I yank her hair, jerking her head back to claim her mouth with my own. I take and take and take. I move deeper and harder. Not caring if I wreck her. Not caring if I hurt her.

I break the kiss to savor the grunts of pain and pleasure spilling from her as though neither her mind nor body can quite process what I'm doing. I release her hair, and she clutches at the tree, allowing me to drive inside her even more violently. She tightens around me on the verge of climax, and I give my final order. "Come for me."

Her pleasure is a strangled cry. It wracks her body, overtakes her limbs, strips away every ounce of self-control she clings to until she is a mewling mass of orgasm centered on my cock. I enjoy every depraved second as I watch from the brink of my own release. As her trembles fade a little, I let myself fall. I plummet into the depths of my own darkness, unleashing the monster within me as I flood inside her—tainting her innocence with my perversion. "Clara. My Clara."

Her name on my lips brings one thought: now she's mine.

I revel in it until the last drop fills her, and the leash clamps around me once more.

What have I done?

CHAPTER THIRTY-THREE

I gather her in my arms, her body too spent to hold her up. Then I help her to the grass, glad the day is warm and balmy. Overhead the grey afternoon gives way to the sun, but my mood remains dark. I spread my jacket across the field and help her lie down. She smiles dreamily at me, her eyes blinking slowly as she lifts one arm against the daylight.

I stalk to the horse and check the saddle. I'd crossed a line. Clara doesn't seem to mind—yet.

There's that word again. It seems rules don't matter. I'll break them. I told her I didn't need her submission. But I've been pushing her toward it slowly and surely, letting the dominance inside me out to play for stolen moments while I look the other way. But that? I just gave him the keys to the cage, and I'm not certain he'll let me lock him up again.

I turn to find Clara watching me with hooded eyes,

her arm shading them from the sun. She hooks her index finger and beckons me over.

I prowl toward her, looking for an apology that might fit the situation on the way. Given that she doesn't seem to mind the brutality of the encounter, it's a tall order. I sigh as I move over and realize I don't know how to apologize to someone that doesn't know they've been wronged. Clara's gaze is adoring. Undeserved. I force a smirk. "You were giving me a come-hither look."

She arches against me, her teeth sinking into her lower lip, and I feel the shameful surge of blood pooling in my cock.

"That's a shame. I meant to give you a come-fuck-me look," she simpers, bucking her sex up to the bulge in my pants.

"Now I see the difference." I give in as she reaches to free my cock. She takes it out, her hands warm and soft before she releases my balls and shows them some rare attention. It's a welcome distraction from the thoughts crowding my head. "Christ, I love it when you play with my balls."

I need to make her feel good. I need to remind her that I can give her pleasure without such a dark price. I capture her breast in my mouth and begin to suck. She melts into it before she moans, "I want to suck you off."

The sky darkens overhead again, beginning its slow descent into rest and taking my resolve with it. I push against her, unable to resist the appeal of seeing her pretty mouth wrapped around my cock. I'll make it worth her while, though. "If you do that, I'll only be able to fuck you longer."

"How long do we have?" she murmurs.

Not long now, a shadowed voice says in the back of my mind. I push it away. "Not nearly long enough to satisfy me. I want to fuck you in the twilight and under the stars and as the sun rises."

"Yes, please." She licks her lips, doubling down on her mouth's promise of distraction.

"You're so fucking hot for me, poppet. Do you know what that does to me?" I push onto my knees, sitting back on my heels, and grab my cock. "You've got such a greedy cunt. All I want to do is fuck it. Fuck it hard. Fuck it slow. I want the absence of my cock in your pretty little cunt to feel abnormal. It belongs to me, and I'm going to take care of it as often as I can."

Clara's eyes narrow as she crawls toward me. Then I feel the hot lash of her tongue glide up the length of my dick. I clutch her hair and lift her into a kneeling position before standing myself. I keep my grip on her as she starts to suck me off. She isn't giving me a blow job. She's devouring me. My eyes close as her mouth closes over my balls until I can't wait any longer. I pull away to warn her. "I'm going to fuck your mouth now."

Before I can, she leans forward and swallows my length, taking me so deep I groan. The message is clear. This is about her, not me. She's claiming me. Through the heady satisfaction each stroke of her tongue brings, confusion sets in. She had been clear about her boundaries, but instead of guarding them, she opens the door each time I push against one.

She fucks me with her hands and mouth until I can't hold back any longer. But there's no hesitation when the first spurt of my climax hits her throat. She's greedy with it, and when I finally look at her, the wantonness written across her face keeps my erection from diminishing in the slightest.

I need her in my fucking mouth now. "My turn."

I drop to her, lowering her onto her back. She parts for my hips, but I can't think of anything else but tasting her. I trail kisses down her stomach, stopping on her soft inner thigh. "Do you know why I use the wax seal on the notes I send you?"

She nods down at me. "So they remain private."

"That's the practical reason." I stop and trace her seam with the tip of my tongue. "The crest is an old family one."

"I had no idea they were so official," she whispers, so breathily it's hard to make it out.

"Traditionally, red was used in correspondence to the church," I explain, my fingers spreading her open like a present. I don't know how else to tell her what she means to me. I don't know the words or the actions. I lift my eyes to hers so there can be no mistaking what I'm trying to say. "You are my religion, Clara Bishop. Sacred. Lovely. I want to worship you."

She gasps when I drop my mouth and begin to do just that. I take my time even as the sun fades and reality beckons. I want to linger in this perfect moment forever. She comes too soon. I love how she clenches against my finger, but I'm not ready for this afternoon to end.

"You taste so fucking good," I murmur, stealing one last lick. Her thighs clamp against the intrusion, putting my head in a vice grip. I push away, fist my shaft, and stare down at her.

She lays spread before in welcome, legs fanned open, hair haloing her head. Is this the last time I'll have her? I shut away the unwanted thought. Maybe it doesn't have to end. Maybe she's changed. Maybe I have. Maybe I'm too weak to give her up.

There's only one way to silence my mind. I nudge inside her, and Clara's head lolls back and forth. "I can't."

She trembles beneath me, her body still raw from the last orgasm. I don't care. I can't.

"I say you can," I bite out. Her body agrees with me, relaxing open. I reward her by circling the pad of my thumb over her clit. "Put your legs over my shoulders."

I help her hook them over my shoulders. The position allows me to thrust deeper. Her eyes roll back, teeth sinking into her lower lip, hands searching the grass for something to cling to as I drive into her.

"Wait," I instruct as I feel the first telltale squeeze around my shaft. "I say when you come this time."

I pull out, and she cries out, arching her back like I've taken her heart along with me. I brush the tip of my cock down her sex. "I love watching your eager, little cunt opening for me."

This earns me a whimper, but I want more. "Tell me what you need, Clara."

Her eyes flicker to mine. Her answer is simple. "You."

"You have me."

I think maybe she'll have me forever even when I let her go. Is that how this ends?

"I want your cock," she says desperately, calling me back to her and away from my thoughts.

"I had to make sure you were ready," I say with a lying smile. "I needed you relaxed and wet, so I can fuck you hard." At least, that part is true.

"Please," she whispers. It's the please that does it—the please that undoes me.

I don't know if I'm giving her more or taking more of her as I plunge back inside her body and lay siege. Our bodies crash and collide until she swells around me, and I empty into her. We collapse onto the ground, still wrapped together.

This is all I want: stolen moments with her in the quiet. "I could do that for the rest of the night."

"Let's," she murmurs.

It takes effort to peel myself away. "I love that your body is so needy. It's quite the challenge to keep your beautiful cunt satisfied."

"It's only needy for you." Her breath catches when I dip a finger inside her where the proof of our union is still hot and sticky.

"Yes, that's right, poppet. Only I can give you pleasure." Because I'm selfish. Because I won't give her up. Because I can't. "And I will give you more tonight after dinner."

Her eyes close, and she says, "Promise?"

Pleasure is all I can give her. The rest will cost her too much. "Everything I say to you is a promise. When I say I'm going to fuck you, that's a promise. When I say I'm going to make you beg, that's a promise. And when I say this beautiful cunt is mine, that's a promise."

And then, because I'm selfish and cruel, I kiss her, moving between her legs to prove it one more time.

WE'RE quiet as we ride back to the estate. I don't press Clara to share what she's thinking. She doesn't ask me. I only want to linger in this private moment where she is in my arms, safe and removed from my world. By the time we reach the stables, shame has a hold on me entirely. My jacket is tucked around her, but it does little to hide the obvious state I've left her in.

At least, I'd been gentle with the crop. Otherwise, it might not only be her clothes showing signs of my filthy deeds. I keep a hand on her back as a bumbling stable-hand helps us. He averts his eyes, but he saw enough to know what I did to her.

She clutches my jacket like a life preserver as we walk, hand in hand, toward the house. When we reach it, I stop her and peek inside. The last thing I need is a confrontation with my father. The corridor is empty, and I gesture that it's safe. She takes one step inside, and panic seizes me. It's as though I hear the clock being wound. I'm not ready for it to begin its countdown. My lips find hers and the answers I want to believe. I'm lost to her until her fingertips graze down my shirt and linger on my scar. I grab her wrist, yanking away like I've caught a snake.

"No, Clara," I snap.

Tears well instantly in her eyes, but she plasters a smile on and tugs against my hold on her. "I'll see you at dinner."

"Clara—don't." I tighten my grip. "Not here. Not in this place. I can't explain it to you."

"Try," she says, losing patience. Until now, I'd been concerned she came with an unlimited supply of it.

"I can't." I'll never be able to. I won't ask her to carry my burdens or bear out my vices. "It's not you, Clara."

She sighs. "It never is. I thought after this afternoon—"

"You need to change for dinner, poppet," I interrupt, some sense of self-preservation kicking in. There's an itch in my brain. If I admit it—if I let her talk about us—it will cost her everything.

"Maybe I should just go home," she says.

I think it's a bluff, so I answer. "No."

Her eyebrow quirks up, and I know I've responded incorrectly.

Can't she see how precious our time is now? Can't she feel the sands slipping away, each already spent? "I want you to stay, but I'll understand if you go. I'd leave if I could."

"Then leave with me." Her voice is coated with fear. She does feel it, but she doesn't understand it.

"It's not that simple, Clara." This has to play out. If she leaves now—before our time is up, before my father's threats can be carried out, before I can ruin everything between us—I won't be able to let her go. I need more time. "I can't run from this. Not anymore. But there's something you should know."

She stares at me, waiting for what I have to say. I'm not even certain what to expect until it slips out of my mouth. "If you run, Clara. I will follow you."

ONLY MY FAMILY is staying in the North Wing, which is why I'm momentarily surprised to see David quietly slip out of a room—until I realize it's Edward's. He turns, startling to find me standing there. He takes a deep breath and relaxes.

David shoves his hands in his linen trousers, his toe tracing a line on the tile. This must be his innocent act. "I needed to borrow—"

I wave off whatever concocted excuse he plans to give me. "I know, remember?"

"Actually, I'm leaving. I came by to say goodbye, but he's not here."

"Do you want me to pass a message?" I ask.

"What's the point?" David shrugged. "If he cared—"

"He does," I cut him off. "It's complicated, though."

"Yeah, I know." His jaw twitches, and I realize he's wary of another lecture. I wonder how often he gets them from Edward. "It's always complicated."

"Always?"

"No," he admits. "Not when we're alone—away from all of this." He gestures to the walls, and I look at it through his eyes. Priceless paintings owned by my family for generations. Antiques so polished they look as though they were acquired new yesterday. And outside, acres of carefully kept land. All given to us because we won some fucking lottery by being born.

"Is it?" I ask, genuinely curious.

"Yeah." David nods. "You're lucky. You can be here with her, out in the open."

"With a target on our backs," I add ruefully. We both understand we're being hunted. David might resent keeping to the shadows, but it made him less obvious prey.

"Royals have always been targets," he reminds me. "I think that's why he keeps me secret."

This time, I'm the one who nods. "He loves you, you know."

David laughs. The sound is hollow like the echo of a dry well. "So, he says."

He turns and makes his way down the hall. I watch him leave, knowing the weekend in the country has claimed its first victim. Edward was daft to bring him here. I shouldn't have brought Clara. We both know it.

Maybe self-sabotage runs in the family.

CHAPTER THIRTY-FOUR

After our ride this afternoon—and my father's none-too-subtle threat during the hunt—I'm feeling possessive of Clara. I'm not sure if she had to sew her outfit tonight or what's taking her so long because dinner's started before she appears in the hall, Edward at her side. A strange sensation grips my heart seeing them together, arm in arm and heads bowed in whispered conversation. I want them to be friends, but I'd rather not share her. Not today. Not knowing how far my father is willing to go to keep us apart. Not knowing that I need to let her go.

As they get closer, I grow more impatient. "You're late."

"Alexander." Edward shoots Clara a look and drops her hand as though he senses he's on my territory. "I was just escorting your lovely girlfriend to dinner."

Clara's eyes dart to the floor, her embarrassment a strange contrast to the scrap of clothing she's wearing. I give Edward a meaningful stare that says, are you responsible for this? He shrugs, a bemused smile playing on his lips.

"I can handle that." I offer Clara my arm but find myself wondering if she'd prefer to be escorted by my brother. The two seem to be getting along, and she needs all the friends she can get. Clara must sense my hesitance because she rolls her eyes. Edward continues on, leaving me for a moment to address her appearance. I run my eyes down her, appreciating how the fabric under the black lace of her dress nearly matches her own skin. She might be completely covered, but she's giving me ideas. "In this light, you look naked."

Her giggle suggests she knows how provocative the dress is, but does she know how hard it's going to be to sit at the table with her while sporting a rock-hard erection?

"We're late for dinner, X," she simpers.

I open the door just enough to let light into the dark corridor and get a better look at her. It's worse in the light. It's also better.

"What are you wearing?"

Her hand grabs my chin, and I realize her shoes have brought her to nearly my height. I glance down and see how long her legs look streaming from a pair of heels that basically beg me to turn her around and fuck her on the spot.

We're never going to make it to dinner.

"I wore something sexy for you."

For them or for me? There's something different about Clara tonight, and I can't quite put a finger on it. She's acting boldly, and I worry any brash confidence she exhibits will only draw more bullying her way. She doesn't need to try so hard to impress anyone, least of all me. "You always look sexy to me."

She responds by kissing me so deeply that I forget my worries for a moment. I slide a hand down her hip and around to cup her ass. There's no resistance from her clothing. It's practically hanging out, ready to be spanked. "Christ, this is short. Suddenly, I'm not hungry."

But it's clear she's got other plans. "I'm ravenous."

Despite her proclamation, she totters as she pulls away, and I catch her. I can't help pressing closer to her, so she can feel my cock straining against my trousers. Maybe I can convince her to skip dinner if she knows what's on the table.

"Oh X," she murmurs, "Don't you know that good things come to those who wait?"

"Screw waiting." Before I can just lift the skimpy excuse for a skirt up and pin her against the wall, she frees herself from my embrace and moves quickly to the dining-room door.

"Delayed gratification, X."

"Clara," I call after her. I'm going to need a moment to adjust myself before I dare head inside, and she shouldn't enter alone. But she ignores me, continuing on, her ass swinging dangerously as she makes her way to her seat at the table.

I can see everything through the crack in the door that she's left ajar. Dinner's already begun, and everyone stops to stare at her as she passes. She might be a guest. She might be an American. She might be the ruin of this family if my father is asked, but at this moment, she's a queen.

It's so obvious that she rises above all of them.

A server moves toward her, and instinct takes over. No man, no matter how innocent his intentions, is getting near her when she's dressed like that. I burst through the doors, tossing a nod at my father, and make my way to her. Clara's own instincts must also be kicking in because she doesn't move. She doesn't take her seat. She watches me—only me—as I find my way back to her. I dismiss the server curtly and step behind her chair. "Clara."

She sits, and I take the seat next to hers, trying to decide if I'm angry or turned on. What on earth has made her think a power play is a good idea? The weekend is already going badly enough. Her hand strays under the table to squeeze my knee, but I push it away. I don't think my cock can take even the barest touch from her anywhere on my body.

"Nice of you to join us, Alexander," my father says disdainfully.

I watch Clara as I speak. "I had no idea I was a necessary aspect of your meal. You certainly didn't need to wait for me. I'm not a fork."

I wish she wasn't here like this, showing herself off. I wish he couldn't see her.

"If you're finished with this display of machismo, I'd like to eat dinner."

"So would I," I say, speaking to him but looking at Clara, my eyes saying something entirely different. I have somewhere to be—namely, balls deep inside you.

"Doesn't Clara look fabulous, Alexander?" Edward asks, forcing me to address the scandal in the room.

"She's a bit overdressed for dinner, don't you think?" Pepper says, sniffing a bit but earning eager laughs from her harem of vipers. "Or under-dressed, depending on how you look at it."

"Jealousy doesn't suit you." Edward doesn't bother looking at her. He just picks up his butter knife and smirks. "It makes your complexion look all green. Clashes with your dress."

"We all know you're an expert on the subject," Pepper says, turning to Clara. "I saw that dress at Tamara's. I had no idea you had even heard of her. I thought she was a bit more exclusive."

But Clara doesn't miss a beat. "She can't be terribly exclusive if you know who she is."

What is going on?

"I'll have to speak to her," Pepper says.

"When you do, give her my love." Clara dismisses her cattiness with a casual disinterest that only makes her place as the center of attention more clear.

"I will." But Pepper won't back down. She's never known when she was in over her head. That's probably how she wound up shagging my father. It's clear she'd meant to get her claws in me and settle down.

Clara turns her attention to her soup, and I do my best to focus on the first course. But the only thing I'm hungry for is her. It takes dedicated focus to lift my spoon to my mouth and eat.

When Clara places her napkin on the table, she whispers, "I'm sorry."

"For what?"

"You seem upset."

I can't stop myself from smirking, meeting her eyes to assure her that I'm not. "We still have a lot to learn about one another, Clara. I wasn't upset. I was turned on. I didn't think I could stop myself from throwing you across the table and ripping off those shameless excuses for knickers you're wearing if you touched me again."

She blinks, her eyes widening just a little, and there is my Clara. Not the Queen of the castle, but the pure soul that I've fallen for. She's so unlike the rest of them.

It's almost dangerous.

"Maybe you should," she murmurs.

"Don't tempt me, Clara. A man only has so much restraint." I grin again, wondering if she'd even stop me if I spread her across the table and had her for dinner. It would certainly put a stop to all the ridiculous gossip going on around us. Clara's hips wriggle in her chair, and I know I've made her wet. I know she's picturing the same thing. "Soon, poppet."

I watch her eat a few bites of her salad, her mood increasingly restless. Why are we here wasting time with all these snobs when we could be alone? David was right. Maybe there is a future for us away from all of this. I should have kept her home this weekend in London. Bringing her here, while a statement, can only make matters worse. Everything would be better if we were cozied up at her flat. Instead, I've lit a fuse on a bomb I don't know how to diffuse.

As a server places my plate in front of me, I don't bother looking to see what we're eating. Instead, I decide to goad her a little and enjoy watching her squirm. "Eat up, Clara. You'll need your strength tonight."

Her eyes shutter, lost to some waking dream of what I mean by that, when Pepper's caustic voice interrupts, "I do hope you aren't having an episode."

I'm about to intervene when Clara takes a bite, chewing it slowly and glaring so hard at Pepper, I think she might set her on fire with her thoughts.

This does nothing to distract her, though.

"I was so surprised when I found out about your little problem," Pepper says. "Usually women with eating disorders are thinner."

I'm vaguely aware of laughter followed by silence.

"Pepper, be careful," Edward finally warns her. "Your bitch is showing."

"Edward," our father cuts in.

"Oh, you aren't deaf," Edward turns on him. "You're just pretending to be oblivious to what's right in front of your face."

"Something you count on," Pepper mutters, batting her eyes meaningfully.

I don't dare speak to defend either of them because when I do, lines will be crossed. It's what Pepper and my father want: for me to take them on. If I do, there will be no turning back, and I'm fairly certain that if I don't get control of myself, I'll wind up throwing one of them through a window. I grip my silverware like it's an anchor while also reminding myself that it's not a weapon.

Pepper turns to me. "You should probably get your girlfriend some help before her eating disorder gets her on more tabloid covers."

It's the last mistake she'll make in my presence, but before I can deliver that news, Clara responds serenely, "Pepper, I can't help noticing you haven't touched your plate or your salad or your soup. The only thing you've had your mouth on is that rocks glass. I'm happy to lend you my doctor's name after I finish eating."

"Enough of—" my father starts.

"You don't get to say enough, not if you sit and watch as she's slandered," I say in a voice low enough that everyone stills to hear me.

"Don't be melodramatic," Pepper says, as though it's all innocent teasing. The telling slide of her throat undermines her arrogance. She knows she's made a mistake.

"You're here as a guest of this family," I tell her, "because of Sarah. I'm now rescinding that invitation. I'd like you to leave."

Pepper gawks at me, her mouth falling open. Around her, everyone starts talking at once.

"This is my house," my father booms, knocking his fist against the table.

"And surely you stand by your son's request to have a fair-weather friend removed from our table," I say, my own voice rising to match his. "Unless Pepper is here at your invitation."

Checkmate. He knows I have him. Unless he wants

his dirty secret unveiled to the entire dinner party—many of whom will eagerly sell the information to the press—he has to play along with my edict. He nods in agreement to my wish before leaving the room without another word.

I have no doubt I'll pay for getting his little toy sent home early. He'll have more time to fuck with my relationship now, but I couldn't allow Pepper's behavior to continue.

"Pris?" Pepper looks at her friend, but Pris isn't going to leave with her. Pepper might enjoy attention from her little crowd, but none of them are loyal enough to abandon their own standings with the family.

Next to me, Clara has stopped eating. I want to take her away, but not until I'm sure she's been fed.

"Finish your dinner," I urge her.

She stares at her plate as the rest of the dinner party fumbles to continue the evening.

"Now," I growl under my breath.

She does as I command. One bite after another until her plate is empty. Then she stands and looks at the rest of us. "The meal was delicious and enlightening. Please excuse me."

Before I can stop her, she runs from the room.

CHAPTER THIRTY-FIVE

I finally find her standing on the back veranda, staring out at the sweeping lawns. Opening the door, I cross to her and pull her into my arms.

"Alexander—"

I press a finger to her lips before she wastes effort sharing her thoughts. "I won't apologize for her, Clara. I won't waste any words on her."

"I have a few that wouldn't be wasted on her." Her voice shakes, some of her confidence eroded.

Pepper stole that from her. My father enabled it. That's what she's going to face again and again if I persist in this affair.

"Poppet." I take her face in my hand and kiss her, wiping away the evening from her mind. I have the power to do that. She submits to me, going limp against my body as my tongue plunges hungrily in her mouth. I want her. I don't know how to deny myself her. I can't. I push her hand against my erection to prove how powerless I am in her presence. "This is what you do to me."

She reaches for my belt buckle, but I won't let her. Not tonight. I need to push her. After what my father said today, after tonight's dinner party, I know what I have to do. If she runs, it's for the best. I'll go away, ask for a new assignment in the middle east or go off on tour. I'll find a way to keep myself from her.

It's for the best.

I simply have to show her just how out of her depths she is.

"No, Clara. When I say," I demand. She's let me be dominant before, but not like this. "Right now, I want you to turn around."

I'll use her. Possess her. Humiliate her. I'll do everything she's asked me not to do, and then she'll see what I really am.

Then she won't love me.

Leading her to a stone railing, I push her over the edge and lift her skirt. She's staring at the house in front of us, at its open windows, at the occasional passing movement as someone walks down a hall. Anyone could look out and see us. That's the point.

"When I saw you before dinner," I say, leaning down to whisper, "I wondered where you'd left your skirt."

She laughs, but there's a nervous edge to this. I'm taking her outside her comfort zone. "I like this dress."

"Oh, I like it, too," I tell her. "I like that I can do this."

I slide a hand under her skirt, giving in to every

fantasy that I've had about claiming her like this before the world.

"I must admit I didn't like sitting next to you, so close to this—" I press my palm to the heat between her legs "—so close to what is mine, knowing I had to wait for it."

"Antici...pa...tion," she teases.

"That's exactly what I had in mind, poppet." My fingers move under her thong, gliding between her swollen, wet seam. "Do you want to step out of these for me?"

She sighs as I stroke her softly. "You're giving me a choice?"

"It's come to my attention that we have finite resources on Earth," I remind her, "and that I should spare a few pairs of panties."

"How forward-thinking of you," She reaches to her hips and wiggles the panties free.

"I think you'll approve of my planned call to action." I bend and pick up the lacy undergarment. Then I shove it against her face. "We're so very close to the kitchens, and I want to keep all those sexy little noises and cries of yours to myself."

I expect her to cringe as I push them into her mouth, but she whimpers instead. Fuck, that's not how this is supposed to happen.

"I'm actually jealous, poppet," I say, stroking my free hand down her neck. "I'll bet you can taste that sweet, little cunt of yours on those panties, something I've been dying to do all night. I suppose I need to do something about that."

I push her high enough on the railing that her feet come off the ground, her ass rising in the air. She's completely on display, and I force her legs farther apart, leaving her exposed to the world around us. She continues to moan, and I realize that she's enjoying this. I'd expected her to be shyer this close to a house full of people. But she's always had a way of surprising me. How much farther can I push her? I lightly clutch her neck, moving my other hand up higher to spread her cheeks open, revealing the pink pucker of her ass. I push my thumb against it slightly.

"Relax," I command her. "You belong to me, Clara, and I want you. All of you."

Her body tightens, tensing despite my order. I push my thumb inside her anyway, plunging in and out while she squirms.

"I'd like to take your ass, Clara," I muse. I would have eventually. "Remember it is mine, and I will claim it when I choose to."

Her moans grow louder, muffled by the panties gagging her, but it's clear that she's enjoying this. So much for pushing her too far.

"Not tonight." I need to try a different tactic. "You aren't ready, poppet. But you can't deny me my desire to play with you after you teased me all night in this poor excuse for a dress. They're scared of you, you know. So different, so confident. You've unraveled them just as you've done to me."

I begin fucking her ass with my finger before slipping

two more fingers inside her cunt. I don't hold back as I roughly claim her pleasure. She's practically crying as her body moves closer and closer to the edge.

"I love that little cry of yours. It sounds so helpless as if you're begging me to rescue you. Do you want to come?" I ask, already knowing the answer.

She nods, and I curl my finger, hitting the spot inside her that sends her orgasm exploding from her. She drenches my hand as she comes on it.

I wanted more. Withdrawing, I bend and suck her clit into my mouth as her thighs protest from the additional stimulus. Before she can squirm free, I push my thumb inside her ass again, and she comes even more powerfully a second time.

I can't stop, even as her legs clamp against me. Even as she pleads for me to. How can I ever give her up? "I need to be inside you." I rise and yank the panties from her mouth. Bringing her to her feet. "Ask for it."

She shakes her head, wobbling on her feet. "I...I can't."

"Wrong answer," I say and unzip my pants.

"Too much," she moans.

"Poppet." I know she'll take it. I know that she'll take anything I give her. I'll never convince her to run, which means that I'm going to have to force her to, and nothing I can to her body will be enough to push her away. I'm going to have to break her heart.

But first, I need her one more time. Maybe if I know this is it, it will somehow be enough. I stroke my cock along her swollen cunt. Her legs try to shift, but she keeps them closed. She's battling herself—and losing.

I kiss her shoulder. I won't force it. Not anymore. Not if it's going to be the last time.

"I need to feel you, X," she finally says, something foreign in her voice. "Your skin on mine."

I understood what she meant. Not my cock or my mouth. She wanted me—all of me. The parts of me I'd only given to her. It's the least I can do. But as I unbutton my shirt, I know selfishness drives my actions. I want this, too. I want to be with her, completely bared to one another, nothing between us.

Except for the whole world.

I draw her body up against me, pressing my skin to hers, giving her the parts of me that only she will ever claim.

"I want your cock. I want you to fill me," she cries, and I groan, thrusting inside her, meeting no resistance in her slippery heat.

My hands slide across her, wanting to feel her. I grab her breast. I hold her to me. For this one moment, she's mine, and I'm hers, and nothing can change that.

"I'm going to come inside your beautiful cunt." I couldn't hold out much longer. I needed to empty inside her, feel what it's like to mark her one more time. "Christ, you're milking me. You want me inside you, don't you? You want me to pour inside your cunt, because you know it's mine."

"Only you," she promises.

"Only you." It will only ever be her. I know that, and

the revelation sends my climax rocketing to my cock. I release inside her as she falls along with me.

When she crumbles forward, I catch her. Lifting her into my arms, I carry her towards the house, away from what might have been to what has to happen.

I carry her inside to break her heart.

CHAPTER THIRTY-SIX

I watch Clara wander around my bedroom. She pauses to survey a photo of me with my mother and Sarah. I can't even recall where it was taken or when. Most of the memories waiting for me in this room feel as though they belong to a different man living a different life.

"She was beautiful." Clara picks up a photo of Sarah on one of her horses. The photo was taken on the grounds. She must have been fifteen years old. Was that the last time she was here?

"She loved to ride horses," I share, trying to remember the last time I saw her ride.

"What happened?" she asks softly.

I've been waiting for Clara to ask me about the accident since the morning after we slept together the first time. I know all too well how many women will get in bed with a prince to get a peek at the family secrets. But Clara never presses. She waits. She offers. She means it when she says she wants all of me, and she's willing to wait for me to give myself to her.

I wish I could.

"Clara, I honestly wish I knew." I hesitate. Why tell her this so near the end? It's not how I want her to think of me. But part of me feels she has to know this, as though it might help her see why she doesn't belong in this world. She's too precious to risk to the reporters and the courtiers and my own flesh and blood. "I remember flashes. That's why I continued to invite Pepper to events."

She smiles, not a radiant, bright smile but a small, understanding one. She's listening.

"I was drinking, and my sister showed up. She was underage, and I yelled at her for being at a bar." I shake my head. The night is so blurry, even after all these years. I've replayed it over and over in my head. Her palm moves to my shoulder. "For some reason, we left. I don't remember much after that. And what I do remember, I can't burden you with."

"Nothing between us, X," she murmurs. "No secrets."

No secrets. Sarah is proof there will always be secrets. My family clings to them, especially the ones we keep from ourselves. If we never admit we know the truth, it's not a lie. It's how we protect ourselves. It's how we continue to do our duties.

For some reason, I can't stop talking about that night, though. I thought it might serve as a warning for her, but now something else is driving my confession—something I don't understand. "I remember how slippery her blood was on my fingers. She sagged like a rag doll. I remember the heat of the fire as it blazed across my skin, but I couldn't leave her there, even though I couldn't carry her. I was so scared that I didn't even feel the frame of the door in my side. I'd been impaled, but I wouldn't leave her, so we burned together."

Clara claps a hand over her mouth, but I hear her sob of horror. "And Pepper?"

"She'd been flung from the car. Broken bones," I say. "If she remembers more than me, she's never admitted it."

"X, what happened was horrible." She brushes the hair from my forehead, trying to get me to look into her eyes, but I won't. "But it wasn't your fault."

"Why don't you see the monster when you look at me?" I ask. "Everyone else does."

"They don't see you like I do." She takes a deep breath before plunging forward. "They don't love you like I—"

"I'm sorry," I cut her off. "I just need a minute." I move to the loo, locking the door behind me, and sag against the wall. She'd almost said it. I'm not sure I could let her go if she did. I haven't heard those words since they died. Not from someone close to me. Someone who knows me. Girls shout it at me on the streets, but behind closed doors, no one loves me, and I love no one. Sarah rarely said it and usually only out of formality. I haven't truly heard those words from anyone since I was a child.

Clara is wrong. I'm the reason Sarah was there that night. She'd followed me. She had a crush on Jonathan. I should have let her stay. Dance. Have fun. But I demanded we leave, knowing what the papers would say the next morning. I was already fighting with my father about university. I didn't need any more attention paid to me. Instead, the morning's papers told a different story—one that changed my life forever.

One that sent me into hell looking for redemption. One that showed me how little anything mattered in the larger scheme of the world. And one that ultimately put me on a collision course with her.

No good came from that night. Its poison taints my family's blood. Leading me to her was only its finally temptation. Would I damn her soul along with mine?

I can't.

I will never hold Clara on blood-soaked pavement. I will never dictate her every waking hour to duty and ceremony and all the other bullshit a royal has to deal with. I will never take her freedom to steal joy from this half-life I've been born to.

I will let her go.

A low voice floats muffled through the door. My father's arrived, come to seek me out for another round. I resist the urge to open the door and save her. I can't do that anymore. Letting him threaten her is the first step in my plan. The only way to save Clara is to break her heart.

I wait for a minute or an hour. It hardly matters. I open the door to hear my father say, "You're his toy, and when he tires of you, he'll get a new one. There's nothing you can do to secure your place in this family."

"Has it ever occurred to you that I am not looking for marriage?" she asks, her voice pitching up a bit. "Or a place in this family?"

He laughs at her, and my blood runs cold. "All women are looking for marriage, whether they know it or not."

Clara turns, spotting me in the door. She starts toward me, but I narrow my eyes, lifting the veil to the rage that always simmers just below its surface.

"I see that since you couldn't sway me with your threats, you switched tactics," I speak to him, ignoring Clara as much as possible.

"We both know how this ends." He meets my glare with one of his own. "The tart's quite pretty, but you aren't serious about her. Why do more damage to her reputation?"

I force myself not to look at her. I tell myself I can't show her I care about his cruel barbs. It will undermine everything.

"You know the expectations," he says. "I've given you far too much latitude since you returned, but it's time to accept your role in this family."

And then I play my final move—I let him win at last. "I know."

I can't bring myself to look at her as I sacrifice the match to save the queen.

"I should leave you two," he says, his eyes ticking back and forth between us. "Good evening."

He closes the door, and a second later, a book flies across the room. I still don't look at her. I keep my eyes on the door.

Walk through it.

Walk away.

Escape.

When I finally turn a cold gaze on her, she collapses to the ground. I do nothing. I command my limbs to stay locked in place—to ignore my heart crumpled on the ground. She blinks up at me, waiting, the last gasp of hope on her face.

My eyes flicker away.

There's movement, and when I look back, she's standing. Her eyes pierce through me, and I know she sees me for what I really am: cruel and controlling and irredeemable.

She steps in front of me, effectively forcing me to look at her.

She doesn't touch me, and her voice trembles when she finally speaks, "I love you, Alexander."

I close my eyes as the words hit me. Had I thought I could stop her from saying them? Had I even tried? My heart closes around them, tucks them away, and locks them in the darkest, deepest space inside it. It will be enough to know they're there. I can't let this change anything. It's proof that I'm doing the right thing. She deserves a life I can never give her at my side—a life I can only give her by letting her go. I summon all the hatred I feel towards this place, towards the past, towards my birthright, and let it overtake me before I open my eyes. "That wasn't part of our arrangement."

I don't stop her when she turns to run. I don't go after her, even as I hear her wrenching sobs. This is always how it had to end. I'd known that from the beginning, and I'd been too selfish. Now she had to pay the price. I wouldn't take any more from her.

After a few moments, I leave the room and walk across the hall, knocking softly on the door.

Edward opens it a crack, and I spot a note on the bed.

"Alex, I found a note from David. I think I really coc..." he trails away, tilting his head to study me. "What happened?"

"I broke her." I won't lie to him. He needs to know. He needs to see. There are no happily-ever-afters for men like us. That's the stuff of fairytales. "Find her. Get her home?"

"Are you okay?" he asks in a low voice.

For some reason, I laugh. "It doesn't matter. It's done."

I turn away and walk into the darkened corridor, disappearing into the shadows. I watch as Edward leaves to go after her. When he's out of sight, I follow, sticking close to the many corners and nooks in Norfolk to hide me. Coming around one, I stop and move back into the shadows as Edward leans over her and whispers something.

From the darkness, I see her lift her head. "I fell in love with him."

She doesn't have to say more. Edward picks her up and carries her off—away from me and this world. I continue to follow behind them, watching as he helps her throw clothing into her bag. I lurk as he hugs her and places her in a car bound for London. When it's driven far enough from the estate to be nothing but a speck in the summer twilight, I finally step from the shadows and move towards his side.

"Why?" he asks, not looking at me.

"You know why," I say gruffly, not trusting myself to talk this through.

"You can still go after her," he says, sensing my thoughts.

"Why prolong it?" I turn from him back to the house where my future waits—my duty and my punishment.

Edward calls out before I take another step, "Do you love her?"

I pause. I hear what he's saying. This isn't only about her and me. This is about this world. "Does it matter?"

I leave him there and return to my prison, ignoring the hollow space in my chest as my heart races back to London.

It's for the best.

CHAPTER THIRTY-SEVEN

"So we're back to this?" There's no hint of disgust in Edward's voice. Instead, he joins me, dropping into a chair across from me and grabbing the bottle of Scotch. I hadn't bothered with a glass. He doesn't either. After a long swig, he stretches it out to me.

I accept and take another drink.

"David still not talking to you?" I ask. I'm not entirely certain where the saying 'misery loves company' comes from, but it's only half wrong. Misery doesn't mind company, mostly because misery doesn't give a fuck. That's the point.

"He'll come around." I envy his certainty. Edward looks better than I do. He's dressed in real clothes, or at least, fresh ones. His hair is combed, and his face clean-shaven. He pushes his horn-rimmed glasses higher as if he's performing a similar inspection of me.

I know what he sees. My shirt and trousers weren't wrinkled when I put them on yesterday. I'd been determined then. Right until the moment, I found a stack of newspapers next to my breakfast, each one containing speculation on the abrupt departure of Clara from the country this weekend.

"Do you know who sold the story?" Edward asks, guessing why I'm upset.

"Does it matter? All my friends are silver-tongued serpents. I have no one."

Edward pauses a beat and reaches for the Scotch. He takes a steadying drink. "You have me, Alex."

I blink, realizing he thinks I've lumped him in with Pepper and Jonathan and the rest of the troop of sycophants. "I know."

"Do you?" he presses.

I swallow and force myself to confront the truth. During my days on the front, I had friends, close friends. They were scattered to the four winds now, vanishing to different lives. I knew better than to think a man like me would ever have a family like that again, makeshift and ragtag as it was. But I never really considered how alone my brother must have felt all these years. He'd been a kid when I left. Part of me had persisted in seeing him that way. But he's not. He's my brother. A friend. A place to start building a new family of my choosing. "I do."

"So we're friends?"

"Yeah," I say slowly.

"Good." He settled into the chair, dark eyes narrowing like a hawk. "So, how are you going to win her back?"

"I'm not." My jaw clenches, and I wonder if all of this

is some manipulation. But for what end? Clara will never want to see me again. She offered her heart, and I ripped it to shreds. I hadn't even had the decency to see her safely home.

"Why?" The question is pointedly simple.

"Because I'm no good for her," I growl.

"You are not your title," he says in a soft voice.

"You sound like mum," I say wearily and wish I could swallow it back. "Edward, I'm—"

"It's okay. I suspect that's a compliment." He'd never met our mother. She'd died giving birth to him. No one had expected her death, especially our father.

"It is," I say carefully, "but that doesn't mean I'm wrong about being no good for her." Edward didn't know about the darkness that consumed me. He didn't understand my affection came tainted with a brutal, consuming need to possess.

If I expect sympathy, my brother delivers the opposite. He shoots to his feet, his voice shaking, "What is your fucking excuse, Alex?"

"What's wrong with you?" I look up, surprised by the volatile outburst. It's not like him to take such a strong turn toward anger.

"I live every day in secret. I keep my boyfriend hidden. We sneak around. We endure snide comments. Because we aren't an approved set. And you sit there: a man and a woman."

"Thanks for the anatomy lesson." He ignores my snide interjection.

"I live in two worlds. But you"—he points a trembling

finger at me—"you can walk down the street with her, dance with her, kiss her, marry her."

"I don't want to marry her," I bite out.

He barks a laugh. "You do, and you know it. She's the one, and you aren't too stupid to see it."

"I'm not?" Fury seethes from me, and I put down the bottle before I throw it at him.

"You see it. You feel it. It's there every time you look at her. It's why our father has been acting like a toddler for weeks. It's why every tabloid is hanging on your every move. You're not stupid or blind—you're punishing yourself." He pauses, his chest heaving from his tirade. "Still. Stop punishing yourself. You can be happy. Be happy."

"That's a ringing endorsement," I say dryly. Straightening up, I shrug my shoulders. "Why would I punish myself?"

He only hesitates for a second, but the pause gives him time to soften. "I know everything...about Sarah, and after..."

"Everything?" I lift a brow. "I doubt that."

"You don't deserve pain," he says in a quiet voice.

"I don't deserve happiness." It slips out before I can stop it.

Edward throws his hands in the air as if giving up. He stalks toward the corridor that leads to his apartment. "Take it anyway. One of us should."

I want to yell after him, demand he takes the advice he so easily throws at me. Instead, his words stir inside me, mixing to form an idea. I never wanted this world. It's poison. Even now, with my brother, my friend, it sullies everything. It taints me. It cages me. I told myself I'd never let it do the same to Clara.

But I've never stopped to consider there might be another way. I don't want this world. I never have, but I've never had a reason to make my own world.

I do now.

CHAPTER THIRTY-EIGHT

I t's the longest night of my life, waiting for dawn. I should have put a time on the note I sent, but somehow I'd known the more I demanded, the less she might come. I wait for her until dawn cracks along the horizon and seeps through the windows of the house.

Our house.

If she'll have me. I push against the thought and the swell of hope it sends ballooning in my chest. If she comes, that means I have a second chance. This time I'll get it right. I'll demand less. I'll protect her more. I'll separate her from my world, so we can build our own. I just need her to show up.

Instead of lingering on the clock, I get up, toss on jeans and pull a shirt over my shoulders, not bothering to button it. I should shave, but tea seems necessary given how little sleep I'd managed. I place the kettle on the hob and glance out the window. A splash of crimson catches my eye, and without thinking, I find a knife in the drawer and head outside.

The house in Notting Hill is lovelier than the pictures. I hadn't stepped foot inside until the papers had been signed, and Norris had arranged a private security team—all necessary measures to keep the matter as anonymous as possible. It's meant as a gift—or, rather, an olive branch. It will be our private sanctuary, tucked in a discreet corner of her favorite neighborhood.

I can't help marveling as I pad down the steps and into the garden at the sheer freedom. The stone path is warm underfoot, not yet heated by the summer sun, but the flowers are opening, spreading in welcome toward the daylight. A warm morning breeze carries their perfume as if to say hello. I find the rose that caught my eye from the kitchen window and clip it. Spotting it felt like an omen, and I know what I need to do. Taking the flower with me, I pause and tuck it into the door handle. It's a message and a warning.

Clara must know I sent the key. I'd used my seal even if I hadn't signed my name. But if somehow she didn't, the rose will confirm it for her. One final choice. One final crossroads.

I return to the hob to find the water boiling in the kettle. I turn off the flame as a car door shuts on the quiet street.

My heart stops—knowing before I do. I dare to look out the window again, and it restarts. She's standing at the gate. She looks at the key. She looks at the house. I step back enough that she won't see me gawking at her from the window and feel like a coward. The sound of the gate creaking open inflates me with hope again. I make it to the door, my hand on the knob before I remember the choice I've left her.

A heartbeat passes. Another. Time slows, then stops altogether. I feel her on the other side of that red door. It takes all the restraint I can muster to wait, but as the seconds tick by in agony, I give in, unsure if I'll find her there or already gone.

It's harder to open the door than it should be, as though part of me doesn't want to do so. But she's on the other side, bathed in sunshine, the rose in hand. Her head whips up, cornflower-blue eyes meeting mine and instantly welling with tears. I drink in the sight of her. Her luscious curves are sharper than the last time I saw her, and there are bluish smudges under her eyes. And she is the most beautiful creature I've ever seen.

I continue to study every inch of her: the rose flush of her cheeks, the freckles dusting her bare shoulders, the white shirt and the nipples peaking through its threadbare fabric. My gaze lands on a single drop of blood welling on her fingertip. She pricked herself on the rose. I reach for her hand, lift the wound to my lips, and swipe it away with my tongue. A copper tang floods through my mouth, and I feel my knees buckle slightly. I kiss the spot before hooking an arm to pull her to me.

I slant my head over hers and take her mouth before the heat burning in my eyes falls freely. The tears escape on contact, a strange mixture of relief and anxiety and hope and longing. She pulls away, blinking, and before she can process any of it, I'm on my knees. I draw her to me, rest my head against her belly, pleased to find some lingering softness there. But it's too easy to circle my arms around her waist.

"You're thinner." It slips out. It's my fault. I'd thrown her to the wolves. I'd failed to protect her. And she'd born the cost of those choices.

But she's here now, and that has to mean something.

"I'm okay," she murmurs. "I haven't had much of an appetite, but I am eating."

And now she's reassuring me as though she needs to defend herself against the pain I've caused her.

"You can't..." I say in a strangled voice. "Not because of me. Promise me, Clara."

There's a beat of silence before she does as I ask. "I promise."

I linger there, holding her, afraid that if I move, she'll slip away once more. Finally, she breaks the silence, "Where are we?"

I take it as an invitation. Standing, I weave my fingers through hers and lead her into the house, not yet trusting myself to speak. Part of me wants her inside as if a stupid door is obstacle enough to keep her here. I watch as she takes in the living area. It had come mostly furnished, but I'd managed to trick Edward into helping me choose the rest of the decor on the pretext of giving a shit about my own apartment at Buckingham. I suspect he realized the truth, but he didn't press for answers. My brother is good like that. Her eyes skip over the deep sofa, upholstered in cream linen to the marble hearth to the paintings on the wall. She doesn't say anything, so I find myself answering the question she asked on our doorstep. "You're asking the wrong questions."

I can almost swear I smell her dampen with arousal, but maybe it's wishful thinking.

"Twenty questions again, X?" she asks, sounding tired. Too tired. Maybe she didn't sleep last night either.

I shake my head and dart a nervous tongue over my lips. "No games, poppet."

"Why are we here?" she asks a new question.

Maybe she wants to play after all. I take a step toward her, drinking in her scent: rosewater and vanilla, and under it a soft, heady musk that beckons me to the apex of her thighs. I resist the urge to follow it. "You're getting warmer."

"Whose house is this?" She practically mouths the final question.

I lean in to whisper, "Ours."

Clara shoves against my chest, glaring at me. "I don't understand."

"This is our normal," I say with a note of careful surrender. "This is our sanctuary."

"How?"

"The house is in Norris's name," I explain as she begins to pace the living area. "I pay for it, of course, but this way, we maintain our privacy."

I'd considered all the angles after my talk with Edward. We needed a space of our own. We needed normalcy. We needed things my world could never give, but my power could easily take.

But Clara sounds rattled. "You mean to maintain secrecy."

"Privacy. Secrecy," I say with a shrug. Of course, I want to keep this from the tabloids and my father and the whole rotten lot. Doesn't she? "Here we can be Alexander and Clara. Nothing between us."

"Except the secrets."

How can I make her see? I cross to her, take her in my arms, certain she'll find the answer she truly needs there. "Not between us. Nothing between us."

"Oh, X." My pet name is heavy on her lips. "Everything is between us. Can't you feel it?"

"I don't want it to be." With time, it won't be. I just need a chance to show her.

"Your father expects you to get married. He has it all planned," she speaks in a measured, neutral tone, but there's a rumble of thunder under her words.

"I can't control what he plans, but that doesn't mean he can force me to do anything."

"Did you know about his plans?" she asks.

I can lie and shrug off her concern, but then I'll be putting another obstacle between us. But not an invisible one: a glass wall that she'll see through but have no hope of shattering. Or I can tell the truth and hope she recognizes that I'm trying to give her all I have to give. "Yes."

Is what I have to give enough?

She jerks away from me like I've hit her. "I've spent the last two weeks trying to figure out what I'd done wrong. Because I don't believe loving you is wrong."

I hate that word on her lips. I hate how much I want

to hear it. I hate the way it cracks open my chest and reminds me there's nothing inside the hollow space. "Perhaps not for you. I stayed away because I felt it was unfair. I felt like I was leading you on."

Loving me can only hurt her, destroy her, steal all the light inside her.

"And this isn't doing just that? Why are we even here?"

Suddenly, I realize she's right. And wrong.

I'm not leading her on, but that doesn't mean I can give her more than this. I'll never ask her to carry the burden of my life. She thinks I'm keeping myself from her, but I'm protecting her. Why can't she see that? Why can't she give us whatever scrap of happiness we can salvage? "Because I need you."

It's harsher than I mean it to be because I'm angry. Not at her but at myself.

"But you don't love me," she murmurs.

Lie. I try to say I don't. The words won't come. I can't tell her I love her. I can't tell her I don't. I shove a hand through my hair, frustration taking hold of me. I'd expected a fight but not this much resistance. "I told you I don't do romance. I don't do long-term."

"What mixed signals you give me, Your Majesty." There's venom in her voice, the result of weeks of stewing in her own anger and pain. "That's a dangerous thing to do with a girl like me. What is this? A place to fuck me in? A little hideout your father doesn't know about so you can keep your tart a secret because you can't have me showing up in the press?"

That's what she thinks? "That's not what this is!"

"Then tell me what it is," she says, shifting into a wide-eyed offering before me, "because I'm trying to understand. I really am."

I look away. I can't stand the need I find there because I know I will never, ever be enough to fill it. And that even if I try...

I've told Clara about my past—some of it. She knows about my mother. My sister. If she knew the truth...I set my jaw, determined not to make my ghosts her own. When I turn on her, she takes a step back as I find the only words I can to explain, "Every woman who has ever loved me is dead."

"I'm sorry, X," she says softly, and my rib cage cracks open a little wider revealing more of the emptiness inside until she continues, "but I'm not dead. I'm right here— and you can't make me stop loving you."

For how long? I lock the question away. I have to make her see. I have to make her understand. I take her in my arms, lifting her chin, so her eyes meet mine. "I won't destroy you."

"You already have," she whispers.

Instinct sends my arms falling to my sides. "I never meant for this to happen."

I didn't. Clara was just a pretty girl at a party, and then one kiss changed everything.

"I know, but I'm a big girl, X," she says. "You can't control me. You can't control who I love."

"Stop." It's an order—a stupid one that she's no more capable of following than I am.

"That's why I can't stay. I can't pretend that everything's okay. I can't pretend not to love you. I think that would hurt worse than leaving you. I'm sorry, X. I can't be your secret."

She's slipping away like stars fade into the sun, just as impossible to catch. I try to hold on to her anyway.

"One night," I blurt out. "Stay with me one night, and if you can walk away in the morning, I'll let you go."

It's the last play in my hand. I've shown her all my cards, but she can't resist. I know it. The desire hums between us, filling the air with a crackling tension. But this isn't about fucking.

I finally realize the truth. I can't say it. "Let me show you."

She studies me for a moment, and I resist the urge to reach out and take her. She'd let me. Her body is as much mine as hers now. But that's not the way to show her that I...

I can't even think it.

Finally, she answers but not with words. She pulls her shirt over her head, discarding it to the floor, followed by jeans and a bra. She strips away all the tangible barriers between us and stands before me, exposed and vulnerable. "One night."

I only need one.

I claim her. Carry her to bed, devouring every inch of her neck and throat. Trailing greedy kisses along her jaw. Her palms are hot on my chest, sliding over my scars like she can heal them—heal me.

God, I want her to. I want to be the man she needs.

I will be that man.

Placing Clara on the bed, I steal over her, tasting her as I move between her legs. But I don't wait. There's only one way to show her she belongs to me. I kiss her breast gently and plunge inside her. She arches at the sudden fullness. I swallow the sound of pleasure she makes, more precious than my own. That's when I realize my mistake.

Clara Bishop doesn't belong to me.

I belong to her.

I've taken from her. I've taken so much. I need to give her what she really needs. I have to find a way. I sit back, and her eyes flash, a frustrated cry escaping her at being abandoned.

It takes effort to bite back a grin. I love to drive her crazy, but that's not what this is about. If I only have today and tonight, I will give her everything I am. I will fill her with me. I will give her pleasure, but I'll give her every bit of myself I can.

Scooping her up, I gather her into my arms. She understands, aiming carefully as she sinks into my lap. Her eyes meet mine. Neither of us can look away. I don't think we would if we could.

A tentative finger finds my face. She traces its lines and curves, runs it over my lips. She asks questions with each touch. I lift my mask and let her see all the things I hide—all the things I can't say. Her hips circle furiously, her breath growing shallow and desperate. I see that thing I dread shining in her eyes. I see the thing I crave.

I see what we can't escape because I want it too much to let it go.

I swallow against a dry throat, "Say it, Clara."

"Alexander," she murmurs my name like an incantation and then casts her lovely spell, "I love you."

I break at her words, erupting into her as she shatters on my cock.

"I love you." Another surge.

"I love you." Another.

"I love you." I collapse at the final spurt, dragging her onto the bed with me, our bodies still entwined. She says it again and again until the spell fades to a whisper and finally gutters out.

A strange sensation grips me as I hold her. I will it to take shape. I carve each letter in that vacant hole in my chest. I bid them to travel up my throat. But they don't spill out. Others do.

"I will never have my fill of you." The words are halting and slow—the wrong words. "I crave you, Clara. I crave your body, your taste. Without you..." I can barely bring myself to consider it because I'm in love with her.

I'll always be in love with her.

"I...I..."

I thrust into her. Once. Twice. Three times. Saying with my body what I can't with my lips. Clara's arms twine around me, clinging to my shoulders, as she lifts her mouth to mine, saving me from my efforts. Her sex tightens around my cock, claiming me again. I empty with a roar, pouring all I am into her, giving her every last piece of me.

Hoping it will be enough.

Knowing it never will be.

· · ·

CLARA LIES IN MY ARMS, our skin slick with sweat. I press a kiss to her shoulder as her stomach grumbles.

"You need to eat," I murmur.

She twists around, sighing, as she nuzzles my neck. "We already had dinner."

"I think we might have burned through that already," I say wryly.

I hesitate before sliding out of bed. We've left it a few times. More than once, I'd convinced her to stay, naked and waiting, while I dashed down to the kitchen for water. The truth is that I want to stay here, pinning her to my life, with my cock, with my mouth, with whatever it takes.

Stepping into my jeans, well aware that security teams circle the property on the hour, I start toward the door. As I reach it, Clara shoves back the sheets and gets up. I freeze, dread sluicing through me like icy water. But she tiptoes to the closet and returns wearing nothing but one of my white button-down shirts. Her own clothes are somewhere else. The entry? Stairs? We'd dressed and undressed so many times, I've lost track.

She doesn't bother to button the shirt as she brushes past me with a smile. I don't relax until she bypasses her crumpled jeans and continues down the stairs. I follow and find her studying the leftover curry from dinner.

"I need to go shopping," I say, wishing I had more to offer her. "Or we could..."

Her head appears over the fridge door. She holds up a carton. "Do you want some?"

I can't bring myself to eat, but I nod, worried she might change her own mind if I don't. She passes me the carton of biryani while I pull two forks from the drawer.

"Do you want to heat it? There's probably a pan somewhere," I say.

"This is fine." She takes a few bites, turning to study the night sky out the window. My shirt falls neatly over her ass, covering more of her from behind. But its hem curves high, revealing the tantalizing swell of her shapely thigh and the curve of her ass.

Her back is to me, so she doesn't see me abandon the curry on the kitchen counter. I move slowly so as not to startle her and gently place my hand on her hips. Clara releases a contented sigh as I wrap my arms around her.

"What are you looking at?" I ask in a low voice.

"The night. I used to be scared of the dark when I was little. I refused to sleep without a light on," she admits, leaning the back of her head against my shoulder. "It drove my mother crazy. They went out to dinner one night and came home to every light in the house on."

"That doesn't sound unreasonable," I say, grateful for these tiny glimpses into her life.

"I was fifteen," she laughs. The sound plants itself in my chest, and suddenly I feel less hollow.

"Oh." I kiss her ear. "And now? Are you still scared of it?"

She hesitates. "Now? Now, I see it's beautiful."

I swallow at the meaning carefully hidden in her

words. She's not scared of the night or the darkness. She's a woman now. That's the simplest explanation. Or maybe...

"Beautiful, but terrifying," she adds softly. "I still wonder if I'll get lost out there."

"I'll find you," I promise her, sliding my palms to her hips. I'm on my knees before she can say anything else, gripping her hips. I nip her backside on my descent. The gesture startles her, so I kiss the spot in silent entreaty. She seems to understand because she widens her stance. My tongue dips and licks a stripe down her center. The container falls into the sink, and Clara clutches the counter, a loud moan spilling from her.

"I'll always find you," I vow before covering her sex with my mouth. I continue my assault with long, slow strokes and nips to her clit until her legs begin to shake. She unspools on my tongue, flooding my tongue with the sweet taste of her arousal. I devour her until her mutinous thighs clamp tightly around my head.

I push to my feet, finding her eyes bright, despite her shaky limbs. I grab her shirt—my shirt—and pull her to me. There's no resistance as I lift her and carry her up the stairs. We make it to the top before I can't wait a moment longer. Pressing her against the wall, I kiss her slowly, grinding against the cradle of her hips. The arms coiled around my neck tighten with each teasing circle.

"Pants," she gasps out the one-word command.

I brace her carefully and reach to unfasten the jeans I've thrown on. She shoves at them with the heel of her feet. They fall to the floor, and I step out of them with deliberation as she unwraps one hand from my neck. It finds my cock, stroking it until I take over and angle it at her entrance. I nudge inside her, but Clara pushes her hips so impatiently, I nearly lose my hold on her. Smashing her against the wall, I sheath myself in her fully. She meets every thrust, taking me deeper and harder with each one.

"It will always be like this," I murmur, burying my face against her neck. Her cunt clamps down hard like she's locking away this promise, and I spill inside her. Then I carry her to bed to make more promises.

COLD REALIZATION WAKES ME. The bed is empty. No note. Warm sheets. I strain, hoping to hear her in the bathroom, but somehow knowing I won't. A million memories flood through me but only two words.

"One night."

I'd been too stupid to hear them clearly yesterday, too blinded by the words I couldn't bring myself to say, to translate what she was really saying then:

Goodbye.

I'm out of bed in one bound, grabbing a pair of jeans I'd left on the stairwell as we made our way up from the kitchen after midnight. I push against the memory, not wanting to stain the happiness I'd felt then with the truth I face now. I'd been foolish enough to think her smiles and laughter, her breathy moans and kisses, meant more than farewell.

Had she even felt what I was trying to show her, or was she too busy saying goodbye?

The kitchen is across from the stairs, and as I move down them, I see a pad of paper resting on the counter— and her key. I nearly collapse.

One night.

Why did I think it would be enough?

Before I crash down the last few steps, I regain my footing and make it safely to the hall. Clara stands at the door, dressed with her back to me. I refuse to feel the hope that tries to spark inside me. Instead, I set my shoulders and drop the jeans still in my hand.

"This is it?" I ask.

She whirls around me, her eyes widening slightly to find me there. They rake down me. Naked. Vulnerable. An offering like the one she made yesterday. One I'd taken.

She hesitates, and I let myself believe she'd take my offer, too. Until she lifts her hand in warning. "I'm sorry."

No.

No.

No.

The word screams in my head, but I lock it up.

"Clara." Her name tastes bitter on my lips and sweet. It's possibility. It's plea. I fill my next with all the words I can't say and pray she hears them. "Please."

Her eyes close, and an eternity passes before she delivers the final blow. "I can't be your secret."

Gone. It's the only word that processes as she steps out the door and runs, just like I told her to do in the beginning. It's such a small word for the crushing weight of nothing it carries. It's different than the country somehow. There's a finality that threatens to drag me into that nothing and imprison me.

And then my eyes spot a single red rose, dropped on the stoop yesterday, still in bloom despite abandonment. An omen. A sign. I grab the jeans and pull them on as I race toward the door after her. This isn't over. It never will be. We never will be.

Because even in the darkness, I can see her. I only see her—and I always will.

GENEVA LEE is the *New York Times, USA Today,* and internationally bestselling author of over a dozen novels, including the Royals Saga which has sold two million copies worldwide. She lives in Washington state with her husband and three children, and she co-owns Away With Words Bookshop with her sister.